WILDFIRE SEA DRAGON

FIRE & RESCUE SHIFTERS: WILDFIRE BOOK 3

ZOE CHANT

AUTHOR'S NOTE

Wildfire Sea Dragon is a complete romance without cliffhangers. However, the *Wildfire* series is intended to be read in order.

Each book features a different couple, but characters reoccur throughout, and events from earlier books are referenced in later ones. There is an overarching plot that is gradually revealed over the course of the entire series.

Wildfire Sea Dragon takes place the following year after the events of *Wildfire Griffin* and *Wildfire Unicorn*. The crew has spent the winter off duty, but now it's early summer, and the start of a new fire season. The forests are tinder-dry, just awaiting a spark. And the Thunder Mountain Hotshots are once more gathering at their base in Montana, getting ready to face the dangers that lie ahead...

Or at least, most of them are.

CHAPTER 1

*J*oe Small—Heir to the Pearl Throne, Crown Prince of Atlantis, the Emperor-in-Waiting—was about to meet his one true mate.

First impressions were vital.

He wiped his sleeve across the nightclub's bathroom mirror and studied himself critically in the scratched glass.

The glitter finger-painted across his cheekbones hid the ashen shadows under his eyes. His ripped firefighter crew t-shirt displayed an indecent amount of his torso. Some enterprising woman—and he had no idea who or when—had written her phone number in sugar-pink lipstick across his exposed shoulder.

All in all, he looked exactly as a dutiful, honorable sea dragon prince shouldn't.

Perfect.

"Well, I couldn't be any more of a hot mess if I set myself on fire," he said out loud. "With any luck, she'll take one look and run screaming."

But he couldn't rely on luck. He had to be sure.

Heaving a sigh, he turned away from his disheveled, disreputable reflection. He went into one of the toilet cubicles, sliding the bolt shut behind him. The last thing he needed was for someone to barge in and catch him at this.

In the underwater city of Atlantis, the most powerful Seers spent weeks secluded in total darkness, meditating on the mystic currents of the world. On the night of the full moon, they gathered in a secret chamber grown from living coral, lit by glowing pearls. In that silent, sacred space, they poured pure seawater gathered from the deepest chasms of the ocean into a perfectly polished silver basin.

And in the rippling reflections, the greatest, most learned sea dragon Seers would strive to catch a single, fleeting glimpse of the future.

Joe lifted the lid of the toilet. He took a deep breath, closing his eyes for a moment.

He looked down into the water.

The sky glows red with wildfire. Cold chains around his wrists. A laugh rings out from the swirling smoke, cold and triumphant. Death rears above them, horned and hell-eyed, a heartbeat away. Her grey eyes look into his, alight with love, one last time. And she steps forwards, unarmored, unarmed, placing herself between him and his doom. Because she has nothing left to protect him with but her own body—

Joe wrenched himself out of the vision. For a moment all he could do was gasp like a landed fish, lungs filled with terror rather than air.

He never just *saw* the future in his visions. He *lived* it. And that particular moment, he'd lived far too many times already. He didn't need to experience it again.

It was still going to happen. Everything he'd done, all his attempts to change things...it hadn't worked.

Tonight, he was going to meet his mate.

She was going to fall in love with him.

And, sooner or later, she was going to die.

"Joe?" Someone banged on the cubicle door, making him startle. "You okay in there?"

"Fine!" He fumbled for the toilet handle. Water swirled. He wished that he could flush fate away as easily. "Just—just give me a sec."

He emerged from the cubicle to find Carole, the nightclub hostess, waiting for him. He raised an eyebrow at her as he went to wash his hands. "Isn't this the men's room?"

"I'm glad you're aware of that." She leaned to one side, pointedly checking that the cubicle he'd just left was now empty. "You better not have been entertaining a guest in there. Or doing drugs. I can't make exceptions to the club rules. Not even for you, Joe."

"I know." He gave her a genuine smile. It was wonderful to be among ordinary humans, none of whom knew that he was heir to a vast underwater empire. "You don't let me get away with anything. It's one of the reasons I like you so much."

She wrinkled her nose at him. "Sometimes I think you have serious mommy issues."

"You have no idea," he muttered. "Did you want something, or were you just checking that I wasn't having a rather unsanitary and painfully cramped orgy?"

"You left your phone at the bar again." She handed him the device. "It's been driving me mad. There's only so many times a girl can listen to the first verse of 'Shake It Off', you know."

"Sorry, bro. Forgot to put it on silent."

"That's would just mean it would be vibrating all night. If you're never going to answer, just leave it at home." Her head tilted. "Someone sure seems keen to get hold of you."

He glanced down at the screen. The most recent notifications glowed up at him accusingly.

NEW MESSAGE: Rory

Where the hell are you? Seriously, last chance or you're off the squad. I can't string Buck out any longer.

MISSED CALL: Rory

MISSED CALL: Rory

NEW MESSAGE: Blaise

You massive [eggplant emoji]. Get in touch OR ELSE [fire emoji]

NEW MESSAGE: Wystan

Please call. We just want to know you're all right.

MISSED CALL: Callum

MISSED CALL: Rory

NEW MESSAGE: Mom

You leave me no choice. I've sent out the Knights. They're coming to escort you back to the crew. For your father's sake, please don't make a scene.

[+48 other notifications]

Carole was watching his face. "It's your hotshot crew, isn't it? Aren't you meant to be heading back to Montana for the start of fire season?"

He dropped the phone into his pocket. "I'm exactly where I'm supposed to be."

"It's your funeral." Carole shrugged. "Well, if you haven't got to rush back to the day job, there's a woman at the bar who is *very* keen to meet you."

His heart thudded against his ribs. "Is she the most beautiful woman in the world?"

Carole shrugged again. "I think that's a matter of opinion. She looks your type, anyway."

Definitely not his mate, then.

But she couldn't be far away now. He could feel the future breathing down his neck. He was out of time, out of options…

How can I be even worse *within the next thirty minutes?*

Inspiration struck. "Hey, Carole. Can you do me a favor, bro?"

She gave him a deeply suspicious look. "Is it likely to end with me sweet-talking the cops, pacifying a rioting hen party with free cocktails, or hiding you in the fridge?"

"Not this time." He scrubbed at the lipstick on his shoulder, straightening himself up as best he could as he spoke. "Tell the woman at the bar I'm already taken. I'm waiting for someone."

One of Carole's perfectly shaped eyebrows rose. "Got a hot date?"

"Yes." He pulled his sunglasses out of his pocket, slipping them over his eyes. "With destiny."

CHAPTER 2

Seven had never imagined that her epic quest to become a Knight of Atlantis would involve quite so many casinos.

Other novices get charged with battling kraken in the deepest abysses of the ocean, she thought morosely as yet another annoyed bouncer shoved her none-too-gently out onto the sidewalk. *Me? I get sent to Las Vegas.*

At the moment, she would much rather have taken the lightless depths and the tentacled monsters.

Her sponsor and mentor—the Lord of the Azure Reaches, Knight of the Order of the First Water, Defender of Atlantis, and General Pain In Her Ass—was waiting for her outside, glaring at the entire surroundings as though he was expecting a giant squid to drop from a streetlight at any moment. From the deeper-than-usual scowl on Lord Azure's face, she suspected that yet another tourist group had mistaken him for a casino attraction. Lord Azure didn't know what a 'selfie' was, but it was clear he'd decided it was a slight on his honor.

"Well?" he snapped as she approached.

She automatically performed the deep bow appropriate for someone of her station addressing a sea dragon noble from one of the most ancient and honorable families. "No sign of the Prince here either, my lord."

Lord Azure fixed her with an all-too-familiar withering look. "That is the *Crown* Prince of Atlantis, Emperor-in-Waiting and Heir to the Pearl Throne to you, Seventh Novice."

Seven pressed her lips together, hiding her face with another deep bow. No matter what else, being Lord Azure's squire was doing *wonders* for her abs. "My deepest contrition and apologies, my lord. The Crown Prince of Atlantis, Emperor-in-Waiting and—"

"Yes, yes, I heard you the first time." Lord Azure cut her off with an irritated wave, neon lights reflecting from his pearl-inlaid gauntlets. "Well, that spineless jellyfish of a royal spawn has to be around here *somewhere*. The Seers were certain they'd scried him in this cursed human city."

"Perhaps we should return to the Imperial Champion, my lord?" Seven ventured. "We have been searching for hours without success. It may be time to regroup and see if any of the other teams have located the Prince's trail."

From the look Lord Azure gave her, she might as well have suggested that they order a couple of Jaegerbombs and join a blackjack table. "A true knight does not ask for *help* when on a quest, Seventh Novice. A true knight has no need. One draws upon one's inner strength and honor to defeat any foe. Not that I would expect you to understand, given your heritage."

Wonder which bit of my heritage he's referring to this *time?* she thought in bleak humor as she performed yet another penitent bow. *My animal, or the fact that I was born on land?*

Knowing Lord Azure, probably both. Not for the first time, she wondered what in the ocean had made him agree to take her on as his squire at all.

Just be grateful that he did, she commanded herself. She squashed all other emotions down into the deepest chasm of her soul, where she kept her beast. If she was ever going to be a knight, she couldn't afford to be anything *except* grateful.

She had to be perfect. Perfectly respectful, perfectly courteous, perfectly honorable, no matter how much Lord Azure set her teeth on edge. She'd fought too long and too hard to fail now.

Because if she did...she'd never have another chance to prove herself.

"We cannot rest until our quest is done," Lord Azure declaimed, squaring his armored shoulders. "We are to locate the Prince. We shall not contact the Imperial Champion except to inform him that his son is safely under our protection. So hurry up and find the royal runaway, Seventh Novice."

So much for drawing on one's own inner strength and honor to succeed single-handed, whispered the snide human part of her that she'd never quite managed to silence. She reminded herself that Lord Azure didn't *mean* to be hypocritical. As far as Lord Azure was concerned, as his squire she was simply an extension of his own self. He didn't ask for her help any more than he asked for the help of his sword or his helmet; he just used them. And her.

She just wished he'd use her for something she was good at, or at least could even attempt.

She knew it was futile, but she tried again anyway. "My lord, I am humbled by your faith in me, but I fear that in this case it may be misplaced. I am doing the best I can with the information we received from the Seers, but I'm running out of places to search."

"I personally assured the Empress and her Imperial Champion that your background and nature meant that you would be able to assist in finding the Prince, Seventh Novice." Lord Azure narrowed his eyes at her. "Will you make me a liar?"

Seven gritted her teeth. "No, my lord. I will find him, on my honor. It would just be easier if—"

"A true knight does not seek ease," Lord Azure interrupted. "If you are ever to be worthy of joining the Order of the First Water, you must learn to swim against the current, not with it."

He was lecturing *her* about not taking the easy path? She swallowed hysterical laughter, forcing her voice to stay politely neutral. "I will bear that in mind, Lord Azure."

"Do so." Lord Azure waved her onward with airy condescension.

"Now continue, Seventh Novice. Your talents may be shallow compared to the true magics of a sea dragon, but in this task they are of some small use. Your savage instincts have led us this far, have they not?"

In fact, Google StreetView had led them this far. Of course, to Lord Azure, that was just as arcane as any theoretical power her animal might have granted her. Stifling a sigh, Seven pulled out her phone, and tried once again to make the second-hand descriptions of the Seers' visions of the Prince's location match up with an actual street address.

"This way, my lord," she said, trying to sound firm and decisive, and not at all like she was picking a direction at random.

The streets were becoming more crowded as the evening darkened into night. They were some way off the main strip, thank the sea, but there were still more than enough bars and casinos around to attract tourists. Seven led Lord Azure through the thickening throng, uncomfortably aware of the eddy of amusement and curiosity swirling in their wake. Even in Vegas, a pair of people dressed in armor tended to attract stares. She wished she'd been able to persuade Lord Azure to swap his mother-of-pearl greaves for a pair of jeans.

Human thinking, she chided herself. She lifted her chin, mimicking Lord Azure's aristocratic disdain for the double-takes and raised cell-phone cameras. She tried to view the gawking tourists like a sea dragon would—mere land dwellers, to be pitied for their inability to ever understand the wonders beneath the waves.

Still, she found herself dropping one hand to the hilt of her sheathed stunsword. The smooth pearl pommel comforted her sweating palm. If the worst happened—if all those wide eyes narrowed, if the whispers turned to shouts, if the crowd surged forward with yells of *freak, freak!*—at least this time she could defend herself.

Her animal stirred, somewhere in the depths of her mind. Seven drew in a deliberate, calming breath, banishing the old memories before they could rouse her beast any further. That was the last thing she needed right now…or ever.

Go back to sleep, she told the silent, mindless killer that shared her soul. *There's nothing for you here.*

To her alarm, her animal refused to settle. She could usually banish its sleek, silent presence without trouble, but now it surged up from her subconscious like a whale breaching the surface of the ocean. The glare of neon signs was abruptly brighter, shimmering with unnamed colors beyond human perception. The dry desert air rasped against her skin, stirred by the breaths of uncountable living creatures.

So many warm bodies. So much prey…

Not now! Seven clenched her teeth together as hard as she could, but it was impossible to block out the flood of tastes. All around her, a thousand thousand trails stretched out, each with its own unique, tantalizing flavor…

And one that tasted of home.

"Seventh Novice?"

She hadn't been aware of closing her eyes, but they flew open at Lord Azure's voice. The sea dragon was frowning at her with an expression of mild annoyance, as though she was a cellphone with a flaky signal.

"The Prince." She took a shallow breath through her mouth, struggling to separate out that salt-sea whisper from the barrage of human scents. "I think…I think I can find him."

Lord Azure made a noise somewhere between a cluck of exasperation and a sharply plucked harp string, which translated as a distinctly uncomplimentary comment if you happened to understand sea dragon language.

"No, I know that's what we were trying—I mean, I can actually *sense* him, my lord!" Seven rotated on the spot, grasping for that tenuous thread. "He's close…this way!"

She plunged down a side-street without waiting for a response. Her beast seemed as eager to follow the trail as she was, pulling her onward with mindless determination. She'd never before felt so close to her animal, not even when wearing its form. An aching, maddening hunger hollowed her guts. She *needed* this prey, to catch him, taste him, claim him…

Okay, that's enough. Alarmed, Seven hauled her animal back. It fought her even harder than before, thrashing in the net of her willpower. For a heart-stopping second, she wasn't sure she could hold it.

The bright, maddening flavors in the air faded as she regained control. It was like having a weighted blanket dropped over her head. She blinked, feeling muffled and confused, struggling to make sense of the world through merely human senses.

"The Prince is here?" Lord Azure said, sounding distinctly dubious.

Blurs of color resolved back into recognizable objects. Seven found herself squinting up at a flashing neon sign depicting a winking cat rubbing up against a...chicken?

"I think it's a nightclub," she said, not entirely sure herself.

Lord Azure sniffed. "It is a hovel. But what can one expect of humans? Wait here, Seventh Novice. You are just a squire, but they cannot deny *my* right to enter."

It took Seven a second to work out the misunderstanding, by which point Lord Azure was already storming down the street. She pelted after him, dodging a giggling, stumbling hen party. "No, Lord Azure, wait! Not a club *for* knights!"

The bouncer lounging by the club's door did a double-take at the six-foot-nine fully armored figure bearing down on him. A brief moment of pained calculation flickered over his face—*am I being paid enough for this?* Apparently he was, as the man straightened.

"Hold it, Jon Snow." The bouncer barred the sea dragon's way. "Security check."

Lord Azure drew himself up to his full height, regarding the smaller man coldly. "I do not know this 'Jon Snow' of whom you speak. You have the honor of addressing—"

"Aragorn," Seven panted, grabbing Lord Azure's arm. It was impossible to squeeze it in warning through the plate mail, but fortunately the flagrant breach of etiquette appeared to have stunned him into outraged speechlessness. "From *The Lord of the Rings*. Sorry, he takes his cosplay very seriously. Hates being misidentified. Can we come in?"

With the expression of a man who was regretting all his life's decisions, the bouncer produced a metal detector. "Can you pass a security check?"

Seven looked at the metal detector. She looked at Lord Azure.

The sea dragon knight glowered at them both. "I fail to see the problem. I am extremely secure. Carry out your check, if that is your duty, small human male. And be quick about it."

With a shrug, the bouncer waved the device over Seven. It let out a few hiccups over the studded rivets of her stingray-leather armor, but was otherwise silent. For once she was grateful that as a squire she wasn't permitted to carry a real blade. Her stunsword was made from coral and pearl, so didn't register as a weapon to the metal detector.

Evidently the bouncer didn't recognize it as a weapon either, as he waved her aside without comment. The instant he turned the metal detector in Lord Azure's direction, the machine let out a shriek like a howler monkey being fed into a car wash. Seven was only surprised it didn't actually burst into flame.

"Next time, try wearing pants that don't clank, buddy." The bouncer holstered his metal detector. He jerked his chin at Seven. "You can go in as you are, but Spartacus here is going to have to strip down."

Lord Azure's broad shoulders bunched ominously. "I am a Knight of the Order of the First Water, oath-bound and honor-sworn to complete my mission or die in the attempt. The Pearl Empress herself entrusted me with this duty. Do you truly wish to stand in my way?"

The bouncer's brow furrowed. "I don't remember any Pearl Empress in *The Lord of the Rings*."

"One of the lesser-known appendices," Seven said, grabbing Lord Azure's arm again before he got them arrested, shot, or both. "My lord, may I beg your indulgence for a moment?"

Lord Azure grumbled something under his breath in sea dragon but allowed Seven to drag him away a few steps. "If I but had my blade, I would challenge that sea slug to a duel for his impudence."

"Alas, my lord, we do not have the time to retrieve your weapon from our hotel." Seven was *very* grateful that even Lord Azure had been forced to accept that it was not possible to carry an enormous golden broadsword through the streets of a human city without attracting unhealthy amounts of attention. They'd had more than one police cruiser slow to a crawl as it went past them as it was.

"Please, my lord," she said. "Let me go in alone. Your skills and expertise would be wasted in such a menial task."

Lord Azure started to make a retort, then hesitated. His gaze went from her to the nightclub and back again.

"The Imperial Champion did promise the…honor of guarding the Prince to the first warrior who found him," he said slowly.

He had indeed. It was possibly less of an incentive than the Imperial Champion had intended. Seven had a sneaking suspicion that the other knights were searching the rest of the city very, very slowly.

Lord Azure was evidently having much the same thought. "Very well. Seventh Novice, it seems fate that this quest falls to you."

"A quest?" Her heart gave a great leap. "My lord, you would consider this a formal quest? Sufficient to qualify me for knighthood at last?"

Lord Azure blew out his breath. "I cannot deny that dragging the wayward Prince away from this den of vice and back to his duty would indeed be a great feat. Perhaps one difficult to write a heroic ballad about, but a feat nonetheless." He paused, studying her. "You realize that should you accept, you will have to go with the Prince. Guard his life with your own, as he performs his duties on his fire crew. You will be far from the sea, landlocked, surrounded by dangers unknown."

Her pulse thrummed with excitement. Like the rest of Atlantis, she'd heard rumors about the perils that the Prince's firefighting crew had faced last year. Demonic creatures, foes worthy to test the strongest knight…

If she saved the Prince from something like *that*, no one would doubt her honor or abilities ever again.

She adopted a formal attitude of humble beseeching, dropping to one knee. "Please, my lord. I am not afraid. Honor me with this quest, I beg you."

Lord Azure gave her a long, considering look. Then he nodded. "Very well, Seventh Novice. If you can convince the Prince to accept you into his service, you may consider this your quest. Protect him well, and you shall be a Knight of the First Water."

Seven saluted, fist to heart. "Thank you, my lord. I shall not fail you."

Lord Azure narrowed his eyes at her. "Behave with utter decorum, Seventh Novice. Remember that no matter how he may act, the Crown Prince is of the blood royal, and our future Emperor. I am trusting you to act as my right hand. Do anything to shame me, and I shall strike you off without hesitation."

Seven was certain that Lord Azure would cut off his own *literal* right hand if he decided it had offended his honor. She hid the flutter of nerves in her stomach with another deep bow, then hastened back to the bouncer before Lord Azure could give her any more motivational pep talks.

The cover charge turned out to be eye-watering. Seven reluctantly peeled twenties from her rapidly diminishing roll of bills, all of which had come from her personal bank account. Money, like so many things, was an unknown concept to Lord Azure.

Oh well. It's not as if I ever planned to live on land again. Nonetheless, Seven couldn't suppress a pang as her hard-earned money disappeared into the bouncer's pocket. In her previous life, that would have fed her and her mother for the better part of a month.

Of course, that was mere spare change to the Crown Prince, born to inherit all the treasures of the sea. She'd always tried to ignore undersea gossip, but it was impossible to live in Atlantis without hearing about the Prince's extravagant exploits.

He must go through money almost as fast as he goes through women, Seven thought sourly as the bouncer held the door open for her. *Born with everything, knows the value of nothing.*

Stepping into the club was like getting hit by a tidal wave. Glaring, whirling lights and harsh, thudding bass overwhelmed her sensitive shifter senses, leaving her deafened and blinded.

She sucked in a gasp of air—which was a mistake. Lust and sweat and frustration and glee...the heady cocktail of hormones spiked straight to the deepest, most primitive parts of her brain. Her inner beast surged, mouth gaping wide.

For a moment, it was all Seven could do not to turn and flee straight back into the night. Only the thought of her quest kept her feet rooted in place. She scrunched her eyes closed, fighting her animal instincts while the pulsing music shook her bones like a dog.

How can the Prince stand this? Why would any *shifter come to such an awful place?*

"Welcome to Cock and Pussy!" said a professionally bright, cheerful voice.

With heroic effort, Seven forced her eyes open, and found herself staring at a pair of nipples.

They had tassels on them.

Pink ones.

Now Seven understood why the Prince frequented this particular establishment.

"You look a little lost," said the owner of the nipples. "I'm Carole, and I'll be your hostess for the evening. Would you like me to show you around?"

"Uh..." With some difficulty—*how are those stuck* on?—Seven managed to wrench her gaze upward. "I'm, uh, I'm...looking for someone."

Carole quirked an eyebrow. "Well, we pride ourselves on catering to all tastes here. What kind of 'someone' did you have in mind?"

"No! I mean I'm looking for a man. A specific man." Seven stretched one hand above her head as high as she could reach. "About six foot eight? Dark brown skin, turquoise eyes, black hair with blue highlights?"

The hostess's glossy smile cracked for a moment, revealing a flash of true interest. "He said he was waiting for someone. Is that you?"

Surely the Pearl Empress must have sent at least a few texts to her errant son before dispatching armed warriors. "Yes," Seven said, trying to sound confident. "He's expecting me."

"Huh." Carole's gaze swept over Seven's armor. "Gotta say, you're not what I was expecting. Well, well, well. Follow me, hon. I'll take you to him."

A nearby woman, who must have been eavesdropping, barred the hostess's way. She wasn't the sort of person Seven would have expected to see at a tacky strip joint. From her Manolo Blahnik shoes to the black cocktail dress clinging to her curves, everything about her discretely murmured money and class. A long, scarlet silk scarf wound around her long, elegant throat. She wore a second, matching scarf as a head wrap, pulled low over her forehead. A lush mane of midnight hair tumbled down her back.

"Excuse me, but I couldn't help overhearing," the woman said to Carole, not sounding at all apologetic. Even Lord Azure would have envied her aristocratic hauteur. Her hard, light brown eyes flicked to Seven. "*I* was here first."

"I'm sorry, ma'am," Carole said, in sweet tones that carried a distinct undercurrent of *screw you, bitch*. "I'll get to you as soon as I can, and do my best to make sure you leave satisfied. Please, enjoy another drink in the meantime. On the house."

Seven found herself dragged onward, Carole's arm firmly wound through hers. She could feel the scarf-wearing woman's stare through the back of her armor.

"Gah. There's always one creep," Carole muttered. She patted Seven's hand, releasing her again. "Sorry about that, hon. This way."

Seven followed, trying hard to ignore her surroundings. She wasn't a prude, exactly, but chastity *was* one of the Seven Knightly Virtues. These days it wasn't as strictly enforced as it had once been—even the most hidebound traditionalists like Lord Azure had grudgingly accepted the exception for knights who found their true mates—but lewd behavior was still considered deeply dishonorable.

Honor did not appear to be uppermost on anyone's mind here.

Courage, courtesy, compassion, chastity, charity, constancy, candor. Seven mentally chanted the Seven Knightly Virtues in her head as

Carole's swinging hips led her through the club. *Get the Prince, get him to Montana, and try to forget this ever happened.*

The club was busier than Seven would have expected from the entrance fee. She had to force her way through packs of hooting, inebriated men—and a surprising number of women—crowded around the base of a long, elevated glass stage. Seven kept her gaze grimly fixed on the back of Carole's head, trying very hard not to look up. Even so, she couldn't help being aware that there was a lot of… gyrating going on.

Her opinion of the Prince, which had not been high to start with, sank to new depths. Bad enough that he—from all accounts—changed partners as frequently as most people changed their underwear. It was one thing to indiscriminately oblige any woman who had a hankering to handle his crown jewels. It was quite another to pay to ogle dancers who were no doubt just counting down the minutes until they could get out of their torturous high heels and into a pair of comfy slippers.

Doesn't he have enough women throwing themselves at him? Seven thought irritably as she dodged yet another marauding pack of bros too distracted by the heavenly bodies above to pay any attention to where they were going.

Carole guided her out of the packed bar to a long corridor flanked by closed doors. Some were painted with sinuous, winking cats, while others were decorated with strutting chickens.

Not chickens. Seven bit back a groan as she got the pun at last. *Cockerels. And pussycats. Kill me now.*

"He's right through there," the hostess said, indicating one of the rooster doors. "Private room number four."

Wonderful. Not only did the Prince apparently have a taste for both strippers and terrible puns, he spent so much time here he had his own room. He probably had a loyalty card too.

Seven raised a hand to knock, then hesitated. "He's not, ah, got anyone in there at the moment, has he?"

"He's all yours, hon." The hostess lowered her voice, leaning forward. "Listen, sorry if this is sticking my nose where it isn't wanted, but I've gotten to know that hot mess of a man pretty well over the last few months. And whatever's going on between you two, you look *far* too serious for it to end well. You want my advice? Forget about him. Turn around and walk right back out the front door. Whatever you're hoping to get from him, you won't. He's not the kind of guy to pin your heart on."

"I have no intention of doing that," Seven said stiffly. "And I need to see him."

"Not my circus, not my monkeys," Carole muttered under her breath. With another shrug, the hostess turned away. "Well, I hope you find what you want, hon."

What Seven wanted, more than anything, was to be back under the ocean in the quiet, dignified streets of Atlantis. But she had her quest. Steeling herself, she knocked on the door.

"Come in," called a man's voice.

CHAPTER 3

*I*t was worse than he'd ever imagined.

Joe had thought himself prepared. He'd seen her countless times before, after all—in visions, in dreams.

But nothing compared to *seeing* her.

In the tawdry darkness of the strip club, she gleamed like a sword blade. Built in strong, straight lines; hard and elegant, compact and deadly. A single glimpse, and he was pierced to the heart.

She, on the other hand, looked like she was wishing her armor was a whole lot thicker, and possibly had an antibacterial coating.

Showtime.

He touched his sunglasses, making sure that they were secure. As long as she couldn't see his eyes, she wouldn't know that he was her mate.

He adopted a casual, careless tone. "Come in. I promise I don't bite." He let his mouth stretch in an arrogant smirk. "Not unless you want me to, that is."

Her cheeks flushed. She was unusually pale for a sea dragon, with creamy skin and long, steel-grey hair pulled back in dozens of thin braids. Either she had mixed human blood in her ancestry, or she hailed from one of the reclusive, isolated Arctic tribes. Given her painfully traditional outfit and general aura of utter dismay at her surroundings, he assumed the latter. There was no way she'd ever spent more than a handful of days away from the sea. If this wasn't the first time she'd ventured into a human city, he'd eat his turn out gear.

Good. She was sea dragon to the bone, just as he'd seen her in his visions. That would make it easier to horrify her.

He leaned back against the gold-upholstered chaise lounge, striving to be every inch the decadent playboy. "I said, come in. And close the door behind you. I think this should be a very *private* audience."

She obeyed with clear reluctance, stepping through the doorway as though expecting the crimson carpet to lunge up and grab her. Her gaze flicked over the small room, taking in everything from the zebra-print wallpaper to the velvet swags covering the high ceiling. Her armor-plated shoulders twitched as though restraining a shudder.

"Hey, don't blame me." The words slipped out, not part of his pre-planned speech. "I didn't choose the decor."

She glanced at the prominent stripper's pole and visibly winced. She turned to him, spine straightening even further. Like most Arctic sea dragons, she was short—the top of her head would barely have reached his shoulder if he'd been standing up. Yet she carried herself with such poise she seemed to fill the room.

"Crown Prince of Atlantis." To his surprise, she spoke in English rather than sea dragon. "Heir to the Pearl Throne, Emperor-in-"

"Don't do that," he said sharply.

Her blush deepened. "My sincerest apologies. I meant no disrespect." With the grace of a trained warrior, she sank to both knees in a posture of formal submission. Silver honor-charms braided into her hair flashed as she bowed her head. "Crown Prince of Atlantis, Heir to the Pearl-"

"No!" He grimaced, gesturing at her to stand back up. "Look, it's Joe, okay? Just Joe."

From her expression, he might as well have demanded that she address him as 'bro'. "I…do not think that would be appropriate, Your Highness."

He winced at the hated honorific. "Gah. Considering I'm over a foot taller than you, that just makes me feel like you're making fun of me. Try again."

She bit her lip. "My prince?"

Oh, he was. Hers, now and always, forever...

"That'll have to do." He tried to look casual, draping his arms across the back of his chair. "And what shall I call you?"

He already knew the answer, of course. But he found himself desperate for any excuse to stretch the conversation as long as possible.

Because if all went well, these few precious, shining minutes were all he'd ever have with his mate.

Her armored shoulders relaxed a little. Clearly the return to formality comforted her. "I am the Seventh Novice of the Order of the First Water, Squire to the honored Lord Azure."

"Not your sea dragon name." He waved a hand dismissively, trying not to show how his heart was hammering against his ribs. "You must have an air name, surely? A human name?"

Her posture stiffened. Somehow he'd struck a nerve, though he'd no idea how. "I am Seventh Novice, my prince. Some people call me Seven."

"Well, Seven." He treated her to his laziest, most infuriating grin. "*I shall call you Sexy.*"

If looks could kill, he would have been floating belly-up on the waves. "As it pleases you, *Your Highness.*"

Sea, he loved her.

Seven drew in a deep breath, expression smoothing out again into blank courtesy. "My prince, on behalf of your noble mother, the Pearl Empress, I have been tasked with—"

"Hold it." He raised a hand, stopping her. "Before you report, there's something you need to do first."

Alarm flashed across her grey eyes. "I am sorry, my prince. I am unaccustomed to the honor of addressing a member of the royal family. If there is some aspect of formal etiquette I have neglected, I sincerely apologize."

"No, you haven't done anything wrong." He stood up, moving to one side. He gestured at the seat he'd just vacated. "Sit down."

She eyed the chaise lounge as though it was upholstered in bear traps.

"I'm waiting." He leaned against a wall, hooking his thumbs into the waistband of his pants. "We can't continue this conversation until you sit down."

Gingerly, she lowered herself onto the chair, making the minimum possible contact with the golden velvet.

"See? That wasn't so hard, was it?" He tilted his head in the direction of the minibar. "Do you want a drink?"

"I am on duty, my prince." Seven ploughed on without a pause, as though worried what *else* he might offer her if she let him get a word in edgeways. "As I was saying, I am here to-"

"Fifty bucks," he interrupted her.

Her mouth hung ajar. "What? I mean, I'm sorry, my prince?"

"There's a minimum charge for a private room." He held out his hand. "You'll have to give me fifty dollars."

A muscle ticked in Seven's jaw. "With all due respect, *I* am not the one with access to the Imperial treasury. My prince."

"No, but you're the one who wants to talk." He raised his eyebrows at her, then realized that she wouldn't be able to see that over his sunglasses. He shrugged instead. "Fifty dollars. Take it or leave it."

Seven's mouth thinned. She pulled a thin wad of bills from her belt pouch, counting off five tens. From what he could see, it was more than half of her funds. She thrust the money at him as though wishing it was a dagger.

"Great." He took it from her. With his other hand, he palmed a discrete control panel set into the wall. "Then we can begin."

Soft, pulsating music began to play over the hidden speakers. Seven started as the lights dimmed. Her hand closed over the hilt of a short pearl-inlaid baton that hung at her side.

"What the—" She stopped, clearing her throat. "My prince, the mood lighting is unnecessary. And I do not require a soundtrack."

"No, but I do." He stepped onto the low stage. He tossed the bills into the air, grinning at her through the fluttering green rain. "And you, Sexy, just bought yourself a pole dance."

~

Oh sweet heaven, he's actually serious.

Seven's jaw dropped as the Prince grabbed hold of the pole. He swung himself round with easy, languid grace, grinning at her the whole time.

Her assumptions whirled like the fluttering bills, falling into a new, even more appalling configuration. "You *work* here?"

His free hand caressed his own torso, fingers sliding underneath one of his suspender straps. "My father gave me an ultimatum last year. Return to Atlantis and take up my royal duties at last, or…" He snapped the strap at her. "Become a firefighter. So here I am."

She *had* been vaguely perplexed by his outfit, which was hardly club wear—sturdy yellow work pants held up with wide suspenders, a tight white t-shirt clinging to his chest, bare feet.

Now she realized…it was a *costume*.

"B-but," she stuttered. "You joined a hotshot crew. You *did*. A real one."

"Yep. And you wouldn't believe the tips I get when women find out I was a real, live firefighter." He spun around the pole again. "Turns out it was worth spending a summer choking on smoke and eating mystery meat out of self-heating packets."

Was a firefighter?

Before she could ask what he meant by that, the Prince's arms flexed. His feet lifted from the ground.

Seven had never given much thought to pole dancing before, but if she had she would have assumed it was something that only appealed to men. A scantily clad woman grinding her crotch against a long, hard shaft…the symbolism was hardly subtle.

There was absolutely nothing feminine about what the Prince was doing now.

He spiraled smoothly up the pole, barely seeming to touch it. He swam through thin air, body arching in a sinuous curve, legs swinging out behind him. His white t-shirt clung to his back like a second skin, revealing every flexing muscle.

She wrenched her gaze away, fixing her eyes on the opposite wall. "My prince—"

"Hey." He snapped his fingers. "I'm up here."

He'd *taken one hand off the pole.*

Everyone knew the Prince was a soft, spoiled man-child with no honor or discipline, who did nothing except drink and indulge his base desires. And yet here he was, supporting himself on a single rigid, flexed arm, upside-down, body straight as a sword. If he hadn't been doing it right in front of her eyes, she would have said it was impossible even for a shifter.

"That's better." Only the slightest edge to his tone, a bare hint of strain, betrayed how much strength it was taking to pose like that. "If we're going to talk, you can at least look at me. What were you saying?"

"I—I—" She unstuck her tongue from the roof of her mouth. "I'm supposed to take you back to your hotshot crew. I've been assigned as your bodyguard."

"Lucky me." The Prince wrapped his ankles around the pole, dangling six feet off the ground. He stretched languidly, arcing his spine. "Though now I'm wondering who you pissed off, to get stuck with this duty. Was it my dad? Please say it was my dad."

"No! I mean, I wanted this assignment. It's an honor." His t-shirt had come untucked, falling loose to display a sliver of chiseled abs. With a heroic effort, she kept her eyes fixed on his face. "My prince, would you please come down from there?"

"Hey, you were the one who bought a dance." He ran a thumb underneath one suspender, pulling it off his shoulder. "Honor demands that I *fully* satisfy you."

Her voice shot up an octave. "What are you doing?"

He shrugged out of the other suspender. "Stripping. What did you think people pay me to do here?"

"No, don't-!"

Too late.

His hands fisted in his t-shirt. With a sharp jerk, he ripped the material in half. The dark planes of his chest gleamed, washed in shades of blue and green from the ever-shifting lights.

Her thoughts scattered like startled fish. She could only stare, mouth dry, as he rolled upright, muscles moving smoothly. His smirk had faded. His hidden eyes held hers.

For the first time, he looked utterly serious.

He braced himself on the pole with both hands, letting his body swing free again. His hips flexed in time to the throbbing music. Warmth pulsed between her own legs in answer. She found herself leaning forward, her entire being yearning towards his...

What was she *doing?* She shot to her feet, horrified by her body's treacherous response. "Stop! Please stop!"

He responded instantly, dropping from the pole so fast that she instinctively lunged forward to break his fall. Her hands smacked onto smooth, oiled skin, velvet over steel.

Heat roared through her. Her knees gave way. She'd intended to catch *him*, yet he ended up supporting her, her palms pressed against his hard torso.

He stared down at her, his mouth only inches away from hers. His sunglasses were still in place somehow. The mirrored lenses showed Seven nothing but her own pale reflection.

She tore herself free, stumbling backward off the low stage surrounding the pole. "I'm sorry! I'm sorry! I, I thought you had slipped. Fallen."

"I have." His bare chest heaved. She couldn't look away from the pulse leaping in the hollow of his throat. "I mean—uh, never mind. Thank you."

The memory of the Prince's hot skin was seared into her palms. She'd felt his heartbeat, pounding as hard as her own...

She took refuge in formality, offering him a deep bow. "I apologize sincerely for my breach of etiquette, my prince. It won't happen again."

"Well." He seemed to have regained his breath. He leaned back against the pole, his mouth stretching in that cocky grin once more. "Yeah. Pole dances are strictly hands-off. Now, if you wanted to tip me another twenty for a lap dance...?"

"No!" she yelped, trying to ignore the way her body was screaming *yes!* "Um, that is, thank you for the offer, my prince. But we should really be going."

He tipped his head to one side. "Where?"

"Montana, of course, my prince. We must leave straight away, if we are to rejoin your crew in time for fire season." A droplet of sweat was slowly rolling down the center of his chest. She tried very hard not to look at it. "Er, do you perhaps have a spare shirt?"

He shoved his hands into his pockets, which did very distracting things to the way his firefighter pants hung from his lean hips. "I'm not going to Montana."

"But...everyone is expecting you. Your father, the Imperial Champion, said that you had sworn to him that you would return to your crew."

He rolled one shoulder in a careless shrug. "You've seen my sweet set-up here. Women throw themselves *and* money at me, every night. Who'd want to abandon all this for hard labor at the ass-end of nowhere?"

"You gave your word!" She couldn't stop her voice from rising. Her chance, her one and only chance at knighthood, and it was slipping through her grasp... "Does honor mean nothing to you?"

"Oh, it does," the Prince said cheerfully. "It means that my dad can't do a single thing to stop me. He said I had to be a firefighter. He didn't specify anything more than that. So if he tries to drag me away from here, *he's* the one who'll be breaking his honor."

Outraged choked her. It was just as well, given that what she *wanted* to say to him would have landed her in serious trouble with Lord Azure.

Lord Azure. A bolt of pure horror went through her, chilling her body's ardor at last. When Lord Azure heard about this, she would be expelled from the Order so fast, small fish would be sucked into the riptide.

She wasn't just going to lose her chance at knighthood.

She was going to lose everything.

"Hey." The Prince's voice softened, as though he'd somehow detected her distress. "It's okay. I promise, no one will ever know what went on in this room. Your honor is safe with me. Just go back to your lord and tell him I'm a terrible, cowardly waste of space who refused to go with you. Everyone knows that I'm impossible. No one will blame you for not being able to drag me back to my duty."

She closed her hand around the hilt of her stunsword, clinging desperately to hope amidst the roaring in her ears. "Even, even if you aren't returning to the crew, I could still be your bodyguard."

He made a scoffing sound. "Oh, come on. The worst that can happen to me here is a hen party getting a little handsy. Even my parents will have to admit that I don't need a bodyguard."

He paused, then flashed a wicked grin at her. "Unless, of course, you'd *like* to watch me strip off every night?"

If she stayed, she'd be a laughingstock. She'd be the squire who chose to be assigned to a strip club. No one would *ever* take her seriously.

"Seven." The Prince's grin faded. He moved forward, looking oddly intent. "You don't want to be stuck here with me. Go back to Atlantis. It's for the best. I promise."

His salt-sea scent wrapped around her, rooting her to the spot. His hands closed on her shoulders. She found herself unable to move away, unable to even breathe, as he bent to press a soft, chaste kiss to her forehead.

"Everything will be fine," he whispered. He released her, pushing her toward the door. "Goodbye, Seven."

CHAPTER 4

Joe collapsed against the closed door, letting out his breath. He shoved his sunglasses to the top of his head with a shaking hand. Every muscle in his body burned, and not just from the effort of pole dancing. His dragon writhed beneath his skin, roaring to get out.

His mate. *His mate.*

When a sea dragon met his mate, he danced for her. In the cradling currents of the ocean, sinuous and strong. Coils twining, scales caressing, every movement a seduction and a promise.

He'd danced for her. Started the mating ritual. Offered her his heart.

And she would never know.

He heard the clack of high heels coming down the hallway, then a knock on his door. "Hey, Joe?" Carole called. "You free now?"

"Y-yeah." He moved aside to let her in. "What's up, bro?"

"It's that creepy woman out front. She is *really* not taking no for an —" She cut herself off as she took in the state of him. "You okay? You look like you've seen a ghost."

"Not a ghost." Joe attempted to force his face into something resembling a smile. "Just the love of my life."

Carole's eyebrows winged upward. "The woman in the World of Warcraft get-up? Got to say I wouldn't have pegged her as your type. Who was she, anyway? Ex-girlfriend?"

"Not exactly." Joe rubbed his forehead, wishing he had a glass of water so he could check the future. "Is she gone?"

"Yeah, she stormed past me looking pissed enough to boil your bunny. I don't think she'll be back." Carole cocked her head at him. "Is that a good thing or a bad thing?"

"Good," he said firmly, trying to drown out the bereft cries of his inner dragon. "It's very good. What were you saying about a creepy woman?"

"It's the patron I told you about earlier. She's asking for you by name, and I can't persuade her to go for any of the other dancers instead." Carole blew out her breath. "She looks like she's made of money, but something about her gives me the heebie-jeebies. Want me to bounce her?"

It was tempting, but Joe shook his head. "No. I could do with a distraction. Send her in."

"If you're sure." Carole cast a significant look at his groin as she left. "I'll give you a moment to calm down, though."

Underneath his firefighter pants, his banana hammock was indeed suffering a significant wardrobe malfunction. Seven had been considerably more stimulating than his usual clientele. He was thankful that she *hadn't* paid for him for a lap dance.

He adjusted himself as best he could. His t-shirt was beyond salvaging, but they never lasted longer than a single set anyway. He stripped off the last shreds, dropping them in the trash, then grabbed a fresh shirt from a hidden cupboard in the corner.

He'd barely finished resetting his costume when the door opened again, this time without warning. He hastily pulled his firefighter suspenders back up as a woman entered the room.

"Hi." He pasted his professional sexy smile onto his face. "I'm Joe. I'll be your entertainment this evening."

The woman glided forward, letting the door swing shut behind her. Without saying a word, she reached out to him, with the casual arrogance of someone who'd never seen anything they couldn't have.

A jolt went through him as her hand stroked up his bare arm. There was nothing objectively unpleasant about her touch, yet it felt...*wrong*.

Because it's not her *touch,* his dragon roared. *We belong to our mate! No one else!*

Joe jerked involuntarily. The woman tightened her grip, crimson nails digging into his skin. Light brown eyes gleamed up at him beneath her scarlet headband, predatory and triumphant.

Yesterday—hell, half an hour ago—he would have found her wildly attractive. Now it was all he could do not to scream and shove her away.

"Um," he said as she circled him like a wolf eying up an injured deer "Look, it's nothing personal, but I'm going to have to ask you to keep your hands to yourself. Club rules, I'm afraid."

She laid a finger against his lips. "Shhh." Her finger ran down to caress his chin, making him flinch. "Rules are for other people."

Uh-oh. "You realize you bought a dance, right? Nothing more."

The woman didn't step out of his personal space. "Is it true that you're a real firefighter? You used to work for a hotshot crew?"

"Uh, yeah. Thunder Mountain Hotshots."

His sense of wrongness grew. His dragon surged under his skin, demanding to take control of his body. To fight, or flee…

He *couldn't* dance for her. Not now that he'd met his mate. The thought of flirting with anyone else—even just for pretend—made him feel physically sick.

"Listen, I'm really sorry, but I can't do this. I-I'm not feeling well." He tried as politely as he could to twist free of her grip. "I'll get you a different dancer. More than one. As many as you want. On the house."

She shook her head, not letting go. "No. You're the one I need, Prince."

"Or the club can return your money—" He cut himself off as his brain caught up with his ears. "Wait. What did you call me?"

The woman laughed, cold and triumphant. "Oh, I know *exactly* who you are, Prince of Atlantis."

A laugh rings out from the shadows, cold and triumphant.

He knew that laugh. Knew *her*. From his vision, his oldest vision, his nightmare—

In that split-second of frozen horror, the woman's manicured nails bit into his arm like claws. She whirled on him, teeth bared in a feral snarl. Light flashed from something in her free hand.

She plunged the syringe into his neck, and the world dissolved into darkness.

CHAPTER 5

Seven stormed through the club, seething. She'd never before been in total agreement with Lord Azure on anything, but for once she found herself in perfect alignment with his views.

The Crown Prince was a disgrace to the Pearl Empire. A *disgrace*.

How dare he? How dare *he?*

He had no honor. Worse, he was taking advantage of his father's honor, finding the slimmest of loopholes to evade his duty. He'd *grinned*, pleased with his own cleverness. He'd admitted to being an utter coward, without a hint of shame.

And he hadn't respected *her* honor. He'd tricked her.

He didn't hold your eyes open, her conscience whispered. *He didn't make* you *watch as he stripped. He didn't force you to run your hands all over his—*

Seven clenched her jaw. A sharp, unexpected stab of pain made her wince. To her dismay, she realized her teeth had sharpened, lengthening into points.

She took a deep breath through her nose, forcing herself to banish the memory of the Prince's heartbeat pounding under her palms.

Control.

She ran her tongue over her teeth, finding them human again.

Good. A Knight of the First Water was supposed to remain calm and dignified at all times, no matter what the provocation. It wouldn't do to appear rattled in front of Lord Azure. It was going to be bad enough when she had to admit that she'd failed.

I failed.

Finally, *finally*, Lord Azure had given her an actual Quest. She'd had a shot at knighthood.

And that arrogant, smirking, *infuriating* man had ruined everything.

She tried to tell herself that there would be other chances. There *had* to be other chances. She would volunteer for any duty, no matter how perilous or boring. She would earn her blade cleaning the royal toilets, if she had to. Anything that kept her under the sea, and far away from the Crown Prince.

She never wanted to see his wicked, gorgeous grin ever again.

And then she was running, back the way she'd come. Because she abruptly knew, *knew*, that he was in danger.

His distress filled the air like blood billowing through water. Her animal surged up, pure predatory instinct swamping her conscious mind. She could no more *not* have responded to that silent scream than she could have shifted on dry land.

She barged through the club, knocking people aside without the slightest thought for courtesy now. The hostess started to intercept her, then saw her face and wisely stood aside instead. Seven charged past, ignoring the startled protests rising in her wake. Because Joe needed her, needed her *now*—

She skidded round a corner into a corridor at the back of the club. At the very end of the dimly lit hallway, she glimpsed the dark-haired woman with the red silk headband. She was supporting a tall, masculine form, heading for an emergency exit.

To all appearances, the woman was just escorting out a friend who'd had far too much to drink…but the emotions Seven could taste told her otherwise.

"Stop!" Seven shouted. "In the name of the Pearl Empress!"

The woman didn't pause. She kicked open the emergency exit,

hoisting the slumped form of the Crown Prince across her shoulders as she did so. With inhuman strength, she dragged him out into the night.

Seven charged after her, drawing her stunsword without missing a step. She burst out into an alleyway—and only countless combat drills saved her.

Her sword was moving to block before she even realized she was under attack. A snarl turned into a howl of pain as her blade smashed into a gaping maw lined with jagged fangs.

On pure reflex, Seven tightened her hand, activating the magic stored in the pearls set into the hilt of her weapon. Her blade sparked with an electric blue glow. Her assailant tumbled back, howl cutting off abruptly.

Seven was already whirling, intercepting another creature. Burning red eyes, bristling fur, dripping fangs—she still had no idea what she was fighting, but that didn't matter. All that mattered was that they were coming between her and the Crown Prince.

She was in fight time now, dancing between the seconds, every heartbeat thudding in her ears like the slow, ponderous tolling of a great bell. She wove through the attacking beasts, meeting every lunge and slash with her blade.

Her sword flared with each strike, lighting up the dark alleyway in strobing pulses. She was careful to unleash only the minimum power with each hit, not knowing how many opponents she faced. At full power, her stunsword could drop even a dragon in its tracks, but its charge was limited.

Seven targeted the beasts' throats and mouths, doing her best to make sure that each strike hit a vulnerable spot where the magic would be most effective. Even so, she was painfully aware that the creatures weren't going to stay down for long. The first one that she'd struck was already staggering back to its paws, groggily shaking its head. But Seven didn't have time to turn and protect her back. She had to protect *him*.

The woman was dragging the Prince toward a black SUV parked under a streetlight at the end of the alleyway. He seemed to be stirring, trying to fight her off, but his movements were slow and weak. His drugged distress filled Seven's senses.

She snap-kicked a snarling beast, smashed the hilt of her sword into the fangs of another—and then she was through, and running for him.

The woman glanced over her shoulder, and her eyes widened. For a second, Seven could have sworn they glowed red, unearthly flames kindling in the amber depths. In the slow stretch of combat time, she could see furious calculation flicker across the woman's face.

"To me, Knights of the First Water!" Seven shouted, in a sudden moment of inspiration. "Defend your Prince!"

"Lupa!" A grey-haired man leaned out the driver's side of the SUV, addressing the woman. His gaunt, lined face twisted in worry. "Leave him! Get to safety!"

The woman bared sharp teeth in a frustrated snarl. She shoved the Prince away from her, into Seven's path. Caught off-guard, Seven slammed into him, barely managing to avoid losing her footing.

He grabbed her shoulders, in a crushing grip that she felt even through her armor. He lurched to one side, dragging her off-balance. For a second, they were doing a kind of mad waltz, both of them trying to get in front of the other.

"No, no," the Prince was babbling in her ear as she desperately tried to keep her guard up. His voice was slurred and frantic, completely unlike his previous suave tones. "Leave me, go, *run!*"

"For sea's sake, get behind me you idiot!" Seven shoved him against the wall, flipping her stunsword to her off-hand. She smacked another beast in the skull, and *finally* she had space to take up a proper defensive position.

She set her feet, the Prince at her back. The pack hesitated, apparently recognizing that the tides of battle had shifted.

"I am the Seventh Novice of the Order of the First Water!" she shouted at the ring of burning eyes, hoping that Lord Azure would hear her. "I am honor-sworn to defend the Pearl Empire, and I shall protect the Crown Prince of Atlantis with my life! Face me if you dare!"

"Cowards," Lupa snarled at the uncertain pack. She'd retreated to the SUV, but hadn't taken shelter inside. "She isn't a dragon! Take her down before her reinforcements arrive!"

One of the circling creatures turned its muzzle, sniffing the air. It let out a bark of alarm.

"It's too late, Lupa!" The man revved the SUV's engine, his tense voice rising. "Please, we don't need him. We still have plan B. For your father's sake, come on!"

With a last hate-filled glare at Seven, Lupa leapt into back of the SUV, slamming the door behind her. The whole pack followed the vehicle in a mass of shadowy, dark-furred bodies as it roared away.

Adrenaline deserted her. Time resumed. The stunsword felt like lead in her hand. She lowered the blade, but didn't retract it, just in case the pack's apparent retreat was a feint.

She turned to the Crown Prince. He was leaning against the wall, breathing in shallow gasps. His rich brown skin had paled, taking on a sickly grey tinge.

She'd reached out to support him, but he flinched away from her touch. His recoil brought her back to her senses, reminding her of their relative stations.

Seven straightened into a salute despite her aching muscles. "My prince, my apologies for speaking out of turn, but I am concerned for your wellbeing. I know it is a breach of protocol, but please allow me to assist you."

"No. No help," the Crown Prince croaked out. His mouth curved in a thin, wavering ghost of a grin. "Be...be all right. Just need a minute."

Seven wasn't nearly as confident about that. He'd lost his sunglasses at some point. His eyes were screwed tight shut, as though even the dim light of the alleyway was too much to bear. She'd never heard any rumor that the Crown Prince had unusually sensitive eyes, so she could only assume it was an effect of whatever the would-be kidnapper had drugged him with.

"Are you having trouble with your vision, my prince?" she asked, concerned. "Did your assailant strike you? You could have a concussion."

He made a slight, abortive motion, as though he'd started to shake his head and then had to quickly desist. Seven leaped to support him as he swayed. Royalty or not, she couldn't have him collapsing at her feet. This time he accepted her help, sagging against her.

His ashen pallor was really starting to worry her. As politely as she could, she reached up to check his temperature. He made a short, sharp intake of breath as her hand brushed his cheek, and her own pulse gave a strange leap. His skin burned against her palm.

"My prince." She tightened her fingers, forcing him to turn his face down to hers. "Joe. I need you to look at me. Look at me, Joe."

His eyes opened at last. Seven had only been intending to check whether his pupils were even…but instead she found herself dropping into endless blue. The warm turquoise of tropical seas surrounded her. She floated, weightless. She could swim forever in his eyes.

And a part of her that had always been silent said: *Mine*.

"Yes," he whispered, as though he too had heard that internal voice —and then, much louder, "No!"

He shoved her away, with shocking force. The world rushed back. She caught herself against the wall, her body abruptly feeling heavy and ungainly, as if the tide had suddenly retreated to leave her beached on the shore.

The Prince backed away from her, keeping his head wrenched to one side as though he didn't dare make eye contact again. His breathing came in short, panicked gasps. Without warning, he turned on his heel and ran.

MINE!

Human reason dropped away, leaving only pure, simple purpose. He was hers, hers alone, and he was *getting away*.

Her stunsword was still in her hand. Without thought, Seven lunged.

Even with predatory instincts roaring through her blood, some conflicting urge made her pull the blow. The blunt point barely kissed the back of his neck, delivering the mildest possible charge.

He still went down like a cut tree.

The sound of the Prince collapsing to the ground hit her like a bucket of icy water. Sanity returned, far too late.

Her stunsword clattered from her hand. She stared down at the limp, motionless form of the Prince…and then up into a face that reflected her own appalled horror.

"Seventh Novice," breathed Lord Azure. "What have you done?"

CHAPTER 6

The forest was on fire.

Flames slunk through the undergrowth like hungry wolves, gobbling up old, dried pine needles and fallen branches. They licked at the tree trunks, trying to climb into the branches. Bark popped and cracked. Flurries of sparks whirled through the air, bright in the smoky darkness.

"I never thought I'd say this." Blaise flung a cut branch away from the fire line, and wiped the back of her glove across her sweaty, sooty brow. "But I really miss Joe."

But he was there, he was watching...

"Me too." Wystan never paused in hacking at the ground with his Pulaski. He turned the tool over, using the hoe-like blade to scrape down to bare mineral soil. "I didn't fully appreciate last season just how convenient it is to have one's own portable, dragon-shaped bulldozer."

If he'd been there, he would have shifted and knocked a line straight through the forest, uprooting whole trees with his claws. The squad would already have contained the fire. For a second he could see *it, in a confusing doubling of vision. His head spun like a kaleidoscope. He was there/not there, and at the same time he was somewhere else entirely...*

"Less talk," Callum grunted from behind Wystan. "More digging."

"Come on, team!" Rory called from the front of the line, over the roar of his chainsaw. Off to one side, Edith was tackling a dead tree with her own chainsaw, bringing it safely down out of reach of the approaching fire. "Buck's counting on us to contain this on our own. If we don't finish this line in time, everyone in Bluebrook could lose their homes. Step it up!"

He automatically reached for his own Pulaski, slung at the side of his pack...but it wasn't there. He didn't have his gear. He didn't have hands. *His body was somewhere else.*

*Some*when *else.*

Blaise kicked a smoldering log out of the way, rolling it into the approaching fire. "I don't like this. The wildfire shouldn't even be heading toward the town. The conditions are all wrong."

Yes, it was wrong, all wrong. He was supposed to be there. He'd knocked the future onto the wrong course. Whenever this was going to happen, he wasn't going to be there.

Fenrir was ranging alongside the rest of the squad, backfiring the undergrowth with short, sharp blasts of his fiery breath. The hellhound paused, his ears swiveling. At the same moment, Callum stiffened. He too stared into the smoke.

Rory lowered his chainsaw, letting the blade idle. "Please don't tell me the Thunderbird is coming to make our day even more interesting."

"Not that." Callum's forehead furrowed. The pegasus shifter closed his eyes, concentrating on his gift for sensing living beings. "For a second, I thought I sensed...no. They're gone."

Rory's shoulders tensed. "Do you think it could have been demons? We did see them appear out of the ground last year, in the unicorn forest."

Callum lifted his hands in a helpless gesture. "Can't tell."

"I don't think it can be demonic activity," Wystan said, brow creasing in thought. "The Thunderbird isn't here. We've never seen demons without it appearing as well. Callum may not be able to sense those creatures consistently, but it seems the Thunderbird can, and over a great distance too."

"So either our zap-happy frenemy is sleeping on the job, or this isn't demons." Blaise blew out her breath. "Wonderful. So now we've got ghosts."

He *was the ghost. A ghost from the past. None of this had happened yet.*

Fenrir let out a noise that started as a growl and ended in a quizzical whine. The thick, black fur on his neck and spine stood up, but his head cocked to one side.

Can smell something, the hellhound said telepathically. His tail moved in a slight, uncertain wag. *Is good...maybe?*

"Help! Someone, please, help me!"

The entire squad jerked, swiveling as one in the direction of the shout. Fenrir sprang forward, his huge, doglike body stretching into a run.

"Fenrir!" Rory shouted as the hellhound vanished into the smoke. "Damn it. Callum?"

"I can sense one life form near the edge of the fire." Callum's frown deepened. "Though for a second, it felt like more."

"Well, we have to check it out. Callum, take point." Rory passed his chainsaw to Blaise. He rolled his shoulders, loosening his muscles for a fast shift into griffin form. "Wystan, yellow alert."

"Already on it." The unicorn shifter had his hands outstretched, ready to use his power to create an impenetrable shield around the group.

Dread filled his mouth like ashes. He knew, knew, *that he was seeing this because it wasn't supposed to happen...*

Callum led the squad toward the edge of the fire. Heat haze rippled the air. Some trees were already smoldering, caught by advance sparks blown from the main fire.

Fenrir's deep bark echoed through the smoke. The hellhound stood stiff-legged near a sprawled form. A woman lay on the ground, propped up on her elbows, eyes locked on Fenrir's. Both the woman and the hellhound stared at each other, motionless.

"Fenrir," Rory called, his voice flexing with the sharp, irresistible command of his alpha power. "Come here."

The hellhound backed away with clear reluctance. The woman stirred as though a spell had been broken. She sat up, wincing. One of her legs was trapped under a fallen tree.

"Oh, thank God," she exclaimed. Her face was in shadow, hidden under a baseball cap pulled low over her brow. "I can't get free, please help me!"

Rory gestured to the others to stay back. He went to the woman, crouching at her side.

No, Rory, don't-!

"Stay still," Rory said to the woman. "I'll get you out of here."

He put his hands against the tree trunk. Though he strained with his full shifter strength, it didn't budge. The woman cried out in pain.

"Rory," Blaise said urgently. She was staring into the smoke, shoulders tense. "Hurry. We haven't got much time."

Rory swore, sweat standing out on his brow. "Wystan, Callum, I need help."

NO! He couldn't shout, couldn't do anything to stop them, to warn them—

The other two shifters joined him. As they bent to the fallen trunk, the woman lifted her face. Her eyes glittered, lips pulling back in a triumphant snarl.

He knew her. She'd looked just the same, before she'd plunged the syringe into his neck.

"NOW!" the woman shouted.

And then—

~

"No!" He thrashed, trying to fight free of the weight pinning him down. He had to save them, had to save his friends— "NO!"

"You are safe, you are safe," someone was saying, over and over. A deep, gentle voice, speaking a language that no human throat could replicate. "All will be well. You are safe, my son."

The low, soothing notes resonated in the secret heart of his soul. He relaxed, panicked shudders fading away. Hearing that voice, for a moment he was a child again, held in strong arms, knowing to the core of his being that he was loved.

"Dad?" he croaked, his throat raw with screaming.

"Good. You're awake at last." His father released Joe's wrists, sitting back. He raised his voice, apparently addressing the rest of the room. "Just a nightmare. You may all stand down."

Joe levered himself to his elbows, and discovered that he was fenced in by a ring of armor-clad backs. Half a dozen knights surrounded him, swords drawn and pointed outward. One of them appeared to be menacing a coffee maker.

He frowned around at them all, wondering if he was still trapped in some bizarre vision of the future. "What's going on?"

"When one yells 'look out, it's a trap!' in a room full of professional warriors, they tend to react," his father replied, rather dryly. "Lord Azure, that device is supposed to be making that noise. I assure you, it is not about to lunge for our throats. I repeat, everyone *stand down*."

The knights sheathed their blades with varying degrees of reluctance. They moved back a little, settling into parade rest. Their ornate armor looked wildly out of place in the blandly neutral hotel room.

Something nagged at him about the scene. There was something wrong, something missing...

Seven.

All the warriors around him wore ornate metal shoulder-guards and jeweled bracers, signifying that they were full knights. None of them were shorter, paler, dressed in the humble leather armor of a squire.

Good, he told himself, even as his heart sank. It was *good* that she wasn't there. She was still repulsed by him. She didn't want to be anywhere near him. That was good.

Somewhere deep in his soul, his dragon roared. He had a nagging sense that it was trying to tell him something, but its voice was too distant to understand, muffled by the lingering effects of the drug. His head felt as though someone had been using it as a piñata.

He rubbed his eyes, trying to get a grip on reality. "This isn't Bluebrook? Fire season hasn't started?"

His father gave him a somewhat perplexed look. "You have only been unconscious for half a day, my son. We are still in Las Vegas."

"I have to get to Montana." Joe swung his legs over the side of the bed, regardless of the way the room spun around his head. "I have to get back to the crew. Right now."

His father's concerned look shifted into a much more familiar expression of tightly restrained aggravation. "If you were intending all along to honor your vow and return to your fire crew, you might have saved a great many people considerable time and effort by *telling* us that."

Once, there had been a future where his father had finally been proud of him. He'd seen it. If he'd stayed with the squad instead of running away to Vegas, it would have happened.

He thrust away a pang of regret for what-could-have-been. "I wasn't going to. But now I am. I have to."

His father put out a hand, stopping him from attempting to rise. "My son, you cannot. You were attacked. You must return to Atlantis. It is no longer safe for you on land."

"It was never safe! You were the one who insisted that I take a job that literally involves running into burning forests."

"Some danger is necessary. But there is a difference between a wildfire and an assailant who seems to be targeting you personally. Much as you attempt to ignore it, you are the Crown Prince of Atlantis. You are the Heir to the Pearl Throne. The ocean cannot afford to lose you."

His father paused, and when he spoke again, his voice was softer. "*I* cannot afford to lose you."

No, no, no! Even as he wanted to scream, he couldn't help appreciating the irony of the situation. Given how much he'd protested being sent there in the first place, how in the sea's name could he now convince his father that he *wanted* to return to the hotshot crew?

Well, Dad, I get these visions of the future...

He'd never told anyone about his talent. He wasn't about to start now.

"Whatever that woman drugged me with, it wasn't enough to completely put me under," he said, skirting around the edges of a lie. "I learned her plans. She's not just after me. She's going to go after my friends as well."

His father did not look entirely convinced. "You are certain you were not just delirious?"

"Completely certain." It was impossible to mistake a true vision for anything else. He was still chilled from the cold grip of fate. "And then I slipped from her grasp. Since she couldn't nab me, I'm certain she's going to concentrate on kidnapping one of the others instead. Blaise in particular, I think." A realization hit him across the back of the head like a two-by-four. "Oh, for the love of little fishes. I am an *idiot*."

"Self-knowledge is the first step to self-improvement," his father murmured.

Joe decided to ignore that. "Her headband. And her—" he very nearly said *baseball cap*, but caught himself just in time. She hadn't worn that yet. "And her hair. Remember those demon-things I told you about, the one that the squad ran into last season? When their possess someone, there's a tell-tale sign. Horns. They seem to start growing pretty quickly after the demon moves in. That woman was being very careful to cover up her temples."

His father's blue eyes sharpened. "You believe that she was possessed."

"It all fits." He hesitated, remembering what Wystan had said in his vision. "Except that the Thunderbird's not here. Then again, we're a long way from Montana. Maybe this is outside its jurisdiction."

"If so, then we are fortunate. From what I have heard, that creature's way of dealing with demons is to set fire to a wide area. In a tightly packed human city, a single demon on the loose seems the lesser evil." His father glanced at one of the surrounding knights, all of whom were politely pretending to be deaf. "Lord Azure, is there any news on tracking my son's assailant?"

The addressed knight made a respectful bow. "As far as we can determine, the honorless worm and her canine minions are no longer in the area. We cannot, alas, offer any insights into their current whereabouts."

"They're going to Montana to hunt my crew." Frustration made his hands curl into fists. He didn't have *time* for all this. "Dad, I can't explain how, but I *know* they are. My friends are in danger, and I'm the only one who can protect them. I'm going to Montana."

"I am afraid that is not possible, Crown Prince." From his patronizing tones, Joe half-expected Lord Azure to pat him on the head and offer him a lollypop in consolation. "While your concern for your comrades is admirable, it is completely unthinkable to allow you to-"

Joe dropped into sea dragon language for the first time. *"I am the Emperor-in-Waiting, Heir to the Pearl Throne. I was not making a request."*

The snarling, imperious notes hung in the air. As one, every sea dragon knight averted their eyes in instinctive submission. Lord Azure's hand jerked in a quickly stifled salute.

"It wasn't a request," Joe repeated, in English this time. He turned his glare on his father. "The only way I'm going anywhere else is if you drag me there in chains."

His father held his eyes for a long, long moment. His own were as unfathomable as the ocean.

Then his shoulders dropped in great, heartfelt sigh. The gold honor-tokens braided into his dreadlocks chimed together softly as he shook his head.

"Were she here, your mother would take great delight at this point in reminding me of the human saying, *be careful what you wish for.*" His father sighed again. "It was my greatest desire that you should show some understanding of honor. And now that you have, I find myself sincerely wishing that you had not."

Joe spent a second trying to work out whether or not that was a back-handed compliment, then gave up. "So you aren't going to try to stop me?"

"You choose a most inopportune moment to discover the virtue of constancy…but I cannot chastise you for it. Nor will I attempt to stand in your way." The barest hint of a smile tugged at the edge of his father's stern mouth. "I know only too well how strongly stubbornness runs in the family."

"Imperial Champion!" Lord Azure sounded aghast. "You cannot—that is, the Sea Council will not approve of this."

"I have parted the sea with song and fought the Master Shark tooth to claw in single combat. I have no fear of the Sea Council." His father paused, a slight wince crossing his face. He glanced at Joe. "*You*, however, can explain this to your mother."

"Mom will understand," Joe said, hoping it was true. "She's always told me to follow my heart."

His father's expression softened a little, in the way it always did when he was thinking of his mate. "I, of all people, cannot argue with that." His tone turned stern once more. "I can, however, insist on one condition."

His heart, which had been rising, turned over. Because he'd heard those words before...or would have done, in another future.

On one condition.

That you agree to take a bodyguard.

Only in that vision, it had been early spring, not nearly the start of fire season. And they'd been at Thunder Mountain, celebrating Wystan's wedding. In that future, he'd insisted on staying with the crew all along. In that future, like now, his father had insisted that he take a bodyguard for protection. And then Seven had stepped forward, and their eyes had met for the first time...

He'd run away from the squad. He'd missed the wedding. He'd thought that he'd avoided that future.

Yet Seven had still caught up with him. And now here was his father, saying—

"That you agree to take a bodyguard," his father said.

Fate's cold, cruel laughter echoed in his ears. He opened his mouth to say no, to stop what inevitably came next—

"Lord Azure," his father continued, turning to the richly dressed knight. "It seems this duty must fall to you."

...What?

Lord Azure had the expression of a fish that had just discovered the hook hidden inside a juicy worm. "I am…unworthy of this honor, Imperial Champion."

"Yet I must insist." There was a glint in the Imperial Champion's eye that suggested he was taking some secret satisfaction in Lord Azure's obvious discomposure. "Given earlier events, you seem greatly concerned with honorable action. Now is your chance to lead by example."

Joe barely noticed the politely concealed bickering. His head had finally cleared enough to let him make sense of his animal's roars.

OUR MATE! His dragon's distress filled his ears. *WHERE IS OUR MATE?*

Finally, he remembered. Grey eyes, looking deep into his, widening in recognition…

That hadn't been part of his vision. It had actually happened. Seven knew he was her mate.

And in all the futures where she knew, she had never, ever left him.

Yet she wasn't there.

She knew he was her mate, yet she *wasn't there.*

"Wait," he interrupted, his mouth dry with sudden dread. "What's happened to Seven?"

CHAPTER 7

Sea dragons were tremendously civilized about everything. Even dealing with disgraced traitors to the Pearl Throne.

She had a five-star hotel room bigger than her entire childhood motorhome. She had air conditioning, and all the room service she could order. She even had a frankly obscene ninety-inch plasma television offering endless entertainment.

Lord Azure would much rather have thrown her in an actual dungeon. Unfortunately for him, those were in short supply in Las Vegas (except, perhaps, for the sort of dungeon that people *paid* to get thrown into, and thank the sea Lord Azure didn't know about those). He would at least have bound her hands, had the Imperial Champion not stopped him.

"That is not necessary," the Imperial Champion had said, in tones that brooked no dissent. He'd glanced at her—just for a second, and yet Seven had felt as transparent as water under that deep blue gaze. "You may hold the right to determine your squire's fate, Lord Azure, but *I* have the duty to uphold the rights of all the Pearl Empress's subjects. I insist that you treat her humanely. Regardless of your interpretation of her actions, I am convinced that she is an honorable warrior. Her word will be bond enough."

Lord Azure clearly had not shared the Imperial Champion's opinion on that. In addition to the luxurious hotel room amenities, she also had a very large, very uncomfortable sea dragon guard. At the moment he was settling for staring into the middle distance with an expression of intent concentration, as though he could remove her inconvenient existence if he ignored her hard enough.

It seemed to be her day for that.

Her animal sent her yet another wave of cold fury. She could feel it physically shoving at her. It was in a near-frenzy, blind with the desire to escape.

To go to *him*.

Seven stayed motionless, kneeling on the soft carpet, head bowed. Her nails bit into her palms.

You've already cost me everything, she told her inner monster, savagely. *At least let me keep my dignity.*

Her inner animal ignored her, of course. It nudged at her again. Try as she might to block it out, she couldn't stop the beast's senses from overlaying her own.

Even in the over-processed, air-conditioned hotel room, she could taste the trails of the living beings around her. The guard's acid-bitter suspicion; the bland porridge of human guests and staff nearby, going about their own lives oblivious to the shifters among them…and a rich, heady taste that burst in her mouth like the finest champagne.

The Crown Prince of Atlantis.

The Heir to the Pearl Throne.

Her…mate?

It was ridiculous. She couldn't think of two people who were more unsuited to each other. He was the highest of sea dragon nobility, born into unimaginable wealth and power. Even more than that, he was a lazy, arrogant playboy who cared nothing for honor, except how he could use it to manipulate people for his own ends.

They were *nothing* alike.

And yet the moment their eyes had met, she'd felt the shock of her soul resonating to his.

No. True mates were supposed to meet in, in a magic sparkle of golden stars and angels singing, from what she'd gathered. She'd never heard of someone whose first reaction to meeting their true mate was to club him over the head with a blunt object.

Or, indeed, to run away.

He'd fled. He'd taken one look at her and *fled*.

They couldn't be true mates.

She'd just been high on blood-lust, she decided. Half out of her mind from the fight, frenzied by her animal's instincts. Her kind were drawn to power, and he was—for all his clowning—the Heir to the Pearl Throne. Her beast had latched onto him out of nothing more than base hunger. That was the only reason he drew her so strongly. That was the only reason she could still taste him on her tongue, with every breath she took...

That faint, tantalizing flavor changed. She surged to her feet without thinking. Her guard jolted upright as well, one hand closing over his sword hilt.

"Stand down, prisoner," he rumbled. "No sudden movements."

"Can't you feel that?" She took a helpless step forward, drawn by the silent call of distress. His hand tightened on his sword. "Something's happened. Something's wrong."

He eyed her suspiciously. "I shall not succumb to feeble attempts at deception."

"It's not a trick!" She would have bared her teeth at him in frustration, except that would have only gotten herself skewered. "It's the Prince. He's—"

What he was, abruptly, was in the room. The Prince slammed through the door like a hurricane. The poor guard came close to joining her in disgrace, half-drawing his sword before he realized who he was threatening.

The Prince knocked the gaping man aside. He lunged for Seven, grabbing her by the shoulders. "Seven! Are you all right? I swear, if anyone so much as touched you—oh, sea, I'm so sorry. This is all my fault."

As he spoke, his fingers ran over her arms, her shoulders, her neck, as though trying to convince himself that she was really there. Any lingering doubt she had that she really *was* his mate was wiped away by the tsunami of heat that swept through her at the contact. The very concept of language vanished from her mind. She could only stare at him, mute as her animal, overwhelmed by his presence.

The Prince seemed to be having no such difficulty. Words poured out of him in a frantic torrent. "They didn't tell me—I didn't realize—I should have come to find you straight away. I'm sorry."

His fingers twisted in her unbound hair—and stopped. A deep anger lit in his eyes, but it wasn't aimed at her.

He let go of her, turning to address someone behind him. "You took her honor tokens?"

"She assaulted a member of the Imperial family!" Lord Azure blustered. The Imperial Champion loomed behind him, his expression impassive. "It is high treason to raise a weapon against the Pearl Throne."

"She hit *me*, not the entire concept of hereditary imperialistic monarchy," the Prince snapped. "Which also deserves to be smacked over the head, but I digress. You should be *grateful* she hit me. Trust me, if she hadn't, we wouldn't even be having this conversation."

"The individual formerly known as Seventh Novice—" Lord Azure started.

"She is *Seventh Novice*." The Crown Prince's voice sliced across the knight's like a sword. "Though you damn well should have knighted her on the spot for her service to the Throne, not stripped her of her rank, armor and honor. You will return them. *Now*."

Lord Azure's nose flared in outrage. "With all due respect, Crown Prince, you overstep your authority. Traditionally, not even the Pearl Throne may interfere with the private business of the Order of the First Water."

The Prince grinned. Not his lazy grin, or his flirty one, or his teasing one. This one was *weaponized*. Lord Azure actually took a step back.

"Lord Azure," the Prince drawled. "Have you ever heard *anything* about me that makes you think I give a flying fish for tradition?"

Lord Azure hesitated. His eyes cut toward the Imperial Champion as though in search of rescue.

The Imperial Champion spread his hands, palm up. His expression was as solemn as a tombstone, but a spark gleamed in his indigo eyes. "I have never been able to restrain my son, Lord Azure."

"Perhaps...perhaps I was a trifle hasty." Lord Azure sounded somewhat strangled. He cast Seven a poisonous glare. "Given the Crown Prince's further explanation of context for events, I can forgive your actions, Seventh Novice. I accept you back into my service."

He said it in the same tone of voice as *eat worms and die*...but he'd *said* it. She felt as though she might float off the ground. She was Seventh Novice again. She might be the lowliest and least member of the Order of the First Water, but she was *back in*.

And it was all thanks to the Crown Prince. He'd come to her rescue. He'd known that she was in trouble, and he'd done everything in his power to put things right.

Because he was her true mate.

A stunned awe that trembled on joy filled her soul as she accepted it at last. He *was* her true mate, and now—

Now he was turning away.

"Great. That's all sorted," the Prince said, as brisk and business-like as though up-ending her entire fate had been a minor item on his agenda for the day. He clapped his hands together. "Lord Azure, give your squire any instructions you need conveyed back to Atlantis. Dad, can I tap the Imperial treasury? I don't think I can pay for a helicopter to Montana with fan-folded dollar bills."

"Montana?" It was hardly her place to speak, given how precarious her newly restored position was, but she couldn't help it. "My prince, you are returning to your crew after all?"

He didn't even glance at her. "Yeah. Something came up. I'll...catch up with you in Atlantis after fire season, if I can."

Was he trying to *brush her off*?

If so, he wasn't going to find it that easy.

"My lord." Seven rounded on Lord Azure. "Does my Quest still stand?"

"Your quest?" Lord Azure blinked. An unpleasant smile spread across his face. "*Oh*. Yes. Yes, it most definitely does, Seventh Novice. Imperial Champion, given my squire's reinstatement, it seems that *she* shall now have the honor of protecting the Crown Prince."

"No," the Prince said flatly, before the Imperial Champion had a chance to respond. He pointed at Lord Azure. "I want him. He's a full knight. She's just a squire."

"Who has already saved your life once," the Imperial Champion murmured. He looked at Seven for a long moment, his deep blue eyes thoughtful. "We met once before, long ago. Do you recall?"

As if she could ever forget the day that had changed her life. She nodded, as tongue-tied now as she had been then.

The Imperial Champion's gaze moved from her to his son, and back again. "I think perhaps I did better than anyone could have foreseen, that day. Seventh Novice, will you give me your oath to guard my son's life, to your dying breath?"

"*No*," the Prince said again, louder. "Anyone but her."

The Imperial Champion raised his own voice, drowning out the Prince's objection. "Will you swear on your honor to stay by his side, always, no matter how he might protest?"

"I so swear." She didn't have her sword, to swear on as the ancient ritual demanded. She could only hold out her hands, palm up, as though an invisible blade lay across them. "On my honor, I will never leave him."

"Then I entrust you with my son." The Imperial Champion smiled, the expression lighting up his stern features with surprising warmth. "I hope you will not have to hit him over the head *too* often."

Seven gave him a deep bow that was more sincere than any she'd ever offered to Lord Azure. As she came up, she snuck a sideways glance at the Prince, to see how he was taking this. The way the blood had drained from his face made her jerk upright much faster than she'd originally intended.

"My prince?" She started to reach out for him, but checked herself at Lord Azure's scandalized expression. "Are you feeling unwell?"

"I really need a drink," the Prince muttered. He scrubbed a hand across his face, emerging looking drawn and ill. "Dad, can I have a word with Seven? Alone?"

The Imperial Champion nodded. "I shall make the necessary arrangements for your departure. Come, Lord Azure." He treated Seven to another of those long, enigmatic looks before turning away, motioning to the guard to follow as well. "I believe my son and his new protector have much to discuss."

Seven bowed again as they all left, as much to delay looking at the Prince as out of courtesy. The door swung shut. The room suddenly seemed way too large, and also utterly full of Prince.

He flashed her a brief, wan smile, not quite looking at her. "I wasn't kidding about that drink. Is there something?"

The hotel room had a minibar. She went over to it, glad to have something to do with her hands. "What is your desire, my prince?"

Behind her back, he made a strange, choked sound, half-laugh and half-groan. "Oh, sea. Let's not go there. Water. In a glass, please."

Her fingers felt as stiff and uncoordinated as the first time she'd tried to swing a sword. She was painfully aware of his scent. She filled a cup with ice and water from the dispenser built into the minibar fridge.

As she passed him the cup, his fingertips brushed hers, for the briefest moment. Water sloshed over her hand as they both jerked.

"Sorry," he muttered. He took the cup from her, retreating a step. "Thanks."

He took the briefest sip, then stared into the drink as if he too was grasping at any excuse to avoid eye contact. She stood awkwardly off to one side, not sure what to do. What neither of them was saying echoed from the walls.

A tiny clinking noise broke the uncomfortable silence. It took her a second to identify it as ice rattling against the side of the glass. The Prince's hand was shaking.

"My prince?" She wondered if he was still suffering the after-effects of whatever the woman had drugged him with. "Do you need to lie down?"

He didn't move, still staring down into the water. "You know that old moral dilemma, the one where all your loved ones are drowning and you can only save one of them? Who would you rescue?"

Oh no, he *was* delirious. She readied herself to catch him if he started to topple over. "I see no point in hypothetical situations designed to have no right answer. In real life, I would save them all. Or die trying."

"Yeah. Me too." He set the cup down on the bedside table, as carefully as if it was filled with nitroglycerine. "I wish to the sea we'd never met."

The words hit her harder than any blow. "But I'm your—"

The word *mate* lodged in her throat like a fish-hook. He hadn't said it yet, and she didn't want to be the first.

It was the hardest thing that she'd ever done, but she lifted her chin to face him head-on. "My prince. I know I'm, I'm not what you could ever have expected."

He interrupted her with a short bark of laughter. She faltered to a halt, wondering what she'd said that was so funny.

"Sorry. Never mind." He let out his breath, running a hand across his cropped hair. She realized that she'd never before seen a sea dragon male who wore his hair short, without any honor tokens at all. "Seven, think for a moment. You know only too well the sort of person I am. Can *you* see any future in which this works out?"

Until five minutes ago, she hadn't thought she had any future at all, let alone with him. Now the reality of the situation hit her like an icy wave.

Her mate would be the Pearl Emperor one day. Ruler of all the shifters of the sea.

Hard as it was to picture him on the Throne, it was even more impossible to picture *herself* there as well. Someone like her, the Royal Consort? Mother to the *next* Emperor or Empress? Their children—*their children!*—might not even be sea dragons. The political implications would be sea-shattering.

He was right. It would have been better if they'd never met.

She swallowed hard, forcing down the lump in her throat. "I-I understand, my prince. Nonetheless, I swore a vow to protect you. I cannot break that. I would lose my only chance at knighthood. More than that, I would lose my honor."

"And that means everything to you," he said softly.

"It's all I've ever had. All I've ever wanted." She hesitated, then plunged on, before she could lose her nerve. "Until now."

He looked at her properly at last. Once again, she fell into the turquoise mystery of his gaze. Warmth wrapped around her like tropical seas, cradling and supporting her—

He blinked, dumping her out into the cold air once more. He turned away, hiding his expression.

"Well, it doesn't look like I've got any choice," he said, his voice gruff. "So you'll come with me as my bodyguard. But you have to promise me something."

"Anything." Her palms ached with the need to touch him. She put her hands behind her back, straightening to attention. "I am yours to command, my prince."

He met her eyes again…and this time his own were cold and hard as arctic ice.

"You will *only* be my bodyguard," he said. "Ever."

CHAPTER 8

ust his bodyguard.

Seven was grateful that the thudding roar of the private helicopter made conversation impossible. The Prince had barely looked in her direction since they'd left Las Vegas. Now he slumped in the seat furthest away from her, legs stretched out, staring fixedly into a plastic bottle of water. Every line of his body shouted how little he wanted to be there.

She was looking at his body *again*.

Seven wrenched her gaze away from the swell of his biceps. She occupied herself with redoing her hair, weaving her handful of honor-tokens in one by one. Her stick-straight, baby-fine hair was entirely the wrong texture for the traditional dreadlocks of a sea dragon knight, but she could at least approximate the style with rows of tight, narrow braids. She felt more herself with their weight tugging at her scalp.

I am Seventh Novice, every tiny clink of silver against silver reminded her. *I am bodyguard to the Crown Prince of Atlantis himself. I will be a Knight of the First Water. I will have a place at last.*

Just not with her mate.

She hadn't grown up with shifters. When she'd first come to

Atlantis and heard people talking about true mates, she'd scorned the entire concept as a ridiculous fairy tale. No one could *actually* fall in love in a single moment of eye contact.

And now she knew that she'd been right.

This gaping, cavernous craving was nothing as gentle and civilized as love. It was *need*. It was *hunger*. It was a pure, primal instinct to grapple and bite and claim, sweaty skin against sweaty skin, bodies slick and surging—

Seven took a deep breath, and mentally worked her way through all twenty-seven stanzas of the rules for honorable duels.

Just his bodyguard.

The Prince stirred at last, dropping his untouched bottle of water into a pocket. Seven tried not to stare too openly at the line of his neck as he leaned forward to peer out the window.

"We're here," he shouted over the thunder of the helicopter blades.

She pressed her face to her own window, shielding her eyes against the glare of the sun. A wrinkled landscape of green and brown lay below. Rocky mountain peaks thrust toward them, flanks blanketed by thick pine forest. A few thin, winding roads cut through the wilderness.

The helicopter's shadow flickered over a small town, buildings huddled together as though for warmth. The pilot brought the machine round, following the line of a road that curved up the flank of the mountain. Tips of pines waved in the downdraft from the helicopter's blades.

Seven clung to a strap, teeth rattling as the pilot brought them down into a broad clearing. The Prince was moving even before the helicopter's skids touched the ground, unclipping his harness.

She started in alarm, scrabbling for her own seatbelt. "My prince-!"

She lurched, tossed off her feet by the unfamiliar movements of the machine. His hand closed over her arm before she could fall, holding her upright.

"Sorry," he shouted in her ear. He slid the door open, balancing effortlessly in the swaying metal deathtrap. "Force of habit. We had to do a few aerial drop-offs last season. Learned to jump out as quickly as possible. Hold on to me."

She didn't have much choice, since it was that or pitch unceremoniously headfirst out the door. She clung to his waist, trying to ignore the heat of his body against hers. She wished she was still wearing her armor.

She'd dressed to match the Prince, in jeans and a plain t-shirt. After so long wearing the all-enclosing leathers of a sea dragon squire, she felt naked in the flimsy human clothes. At least she still had her stunsword, discreetly holstered at her hip.

"Ready?" he said, gathering up their bags with his free hand and tossing them out the hatch. "On three. One. Two. Three—"

She yelped as he pulled her out the door. She braced herself, only to discover that the ground was far closer than she'd expected. A jarring impact went through her legs as her boots hit the ground. Instinctively, she absorbed the momentum, curling into a roll that would bring her gracefully back to her feet.

Or at least, it *would* have been graceful, if she hadn't still been tangled up with the Prince.

"Argh," he said from somewhere underneath her thighs, as the helicopter rose back into the sky and thudded away. "Let's hope no-one saw that."

"Too late," said a deep, amused voice.

Seven twisted her head, and found herself staring up at a broad, upside-down grin.

"Trust Joe to arrive late, in a private helicopter, and entwined with a beautiful woman," the man said. He bent to offer her a hand up. "I'm Rory MacCormick, A-squad boss. Welcome to Thunder Mountain."

More out of politeness than necessity, Seven accepted his hand. His palm was rough with calluses, though not in the pattern of a swordsman.

Rory pulled her to her feet with a smooth, easy motion. He stood a good four inches or so taller than she was, though still nowhere near Joe's height. He was broad and rugged, with tanned skin and bronze hair. His eyes were startling—rich and golden as a lion's, and just as penetrating.

He's the griffin, she realized. His family was famous in Atlantis. She'd heard poets singing the ballads about the deeds of his father Griff, who was oath-brother to the Imperial Champion. There was a whole epic saga about the many adventures they'd shared as part of the famous Alpha firefighting team in England. Recently, she'd even heard a few songs about Rory himself. Meeting him now, she could believe that they hadn't been exaggerated.

"Seventh Novice of the Order of the First Water, Squire to the honored Lord Azure," she said, turning her grip into a handshake. "People call me Seven for short."

Rory's tawny eyebrows rose slightly at this introduction. "Nice to meet you, Seven. And not to be rude, but *why* are we meeting? Joe said he was bringing someone back with him, but he was a little hazy on the details."

"Isn't it obvious?" A tall, broad-shouldered blonde woman shouldered Rory aside. She had a snub nose and freckled cheeks, and the most unabashed, infectious smile Seven had ever seen. "She's Joe's mate!"

Seven felt like she'd been punched straight in the gut. Was it *that* obvious?

"She's Joe's *what?*" Before Seven could even open her mouth, a second woman pushed past Rory. She too was dressed in a black T-shirt with THUNDER MOUNTAIN HOTSHOTS written across the chest in bold yellow letters. She adopted an exaggerated, mournful expression. "I'm so, so sorry. If you want to run for the hills, we'll hold him down to give you a head start."

"Hey!" the Prince said, struggling upright. "I'm not *that* bad."

"You are," Rory told him.

"Oh, Blaise, don't be silly," the first woman said. She fixed Seven with an earnest expression, as though she was genuinely concerned Seven might take Blaise up on her offer. "I'm sure that the two of you will be perfect for each other. You're a shifter, right? So you must have known straight away. You're so lucky, it took me ages to trust my feelings about Rory. I'm Edith. Rory's my mate. This is Blaise, and those three over there are Callum, Wystan, and Fenrir."

Seven followed Edith's pointing finger, and discovered two more men—one red-headed, the other a pale, silvery blond—standing a bit further back. The red-head had a cool, reserved expression, but the other man gave her a little wave of greeting, smiling. A huge, black-furred dog sat between them, head cocked to one side.

The pegasus, the unicorn, and the hellhound. The poet's songs had mentioned them too, and Edith. Blaise, however, was a mystery. A half-remembered line floated through Seven's head—*and at their side, the fire's shadow*—but if that had referred to Blaise, it didn't give her any clues as to her shift form.

"Fenrir can't shift, but don't worry, you'll be able to talk to each other telepathically once the pack-bond kicks in," Edith continued without pausing for breath. "Are you really named Seven? I like your hair. How did you meet Joe? Was it romantic?"

Seven was still reeling from having been literally knocked off her feet, and the barrage of questions wasn't giving her any time to regain her metaphorical balance. Without meaning to, she blurted out, "I hit him over the head."

"I *like* you," Blaise informed her.

"Congratulations." Rory clapped the Prince on the shoulder, his grin widening. "You now officially have the most embarrassing meeting-my-mate story out of all of us. And to think you said nothing could ever top me falling off a fire tower while being savaged by a rabbit."

"For the love of sweet little fishes." The Prince swatted Rory's hand away. He scowled around at his colleagues. "She's my *bodyguard*, okay? Seven's here as my bodyguard."

For all that she'd agreed it was best to keep their *other* connection hidden, hearing him say the words still twisted something deep inside her. She lifted her chin under the startled stares, not letting any of her inner hurt show in her face.

"She's your bodyguard?" Blaise sounded skeptical. "*Just* a bodyguard?"

"Why wouldn't I tell you if she was more?" The Prince shrugged. "What shifter wouldn't be desperate to show off his true mate to his best friends?"

Something about the way he phrased that caught Seven's attention. He hadn't said that he *wasn't*. And he'd said that she was here as his bodyguard—which was true—not that she wasn't his mate.

She'd sworn to uphold the Seven Knightly Virtues, which included candor—which was just a fancy word for honesty (whoever had first codified the seven Knightly Virtues had clearly been deeply fond of both alliteration and the letter 'c'). *She* couldn't tell a direct lie...but he hadn't made the same oaths. That was why he'd told her to let him do the talking.

So why didn't he just lie?

Blaise folded her arms. "Something's fishy here. Seven, what isn't Joe telling us?"

Her stomach lurched, but the Prince leapt in before she had a chance to open her mouth. "Don't you dare start badgering poor Seven. I've been back for *two minutes*. Let me catch my breath before you start the cross-interrogation. I promise, I'll tell you all about strip club and the demons and the kidnapping in my own good time, okay?"

"Demons?" Rory said.

"Kidnapping?" Callum said at the same time.

"Strip club?" said Blaise.

"My word." Wystan raised a white-blond eyebrow. "You *have* been busy."

"Yeah." The Prince's aggrieved expression faltered, revealing something more real underneath. "I...I'm sorry I missed your wedding, Wys. I really wanted to be there."

Wystan came forward to clasp his hand, his green eyes gentle. "I know you would have come if you could."

"Thanks, bronicorn." The Prince pulled him into a brief hug. "Now tell me the bad news. Exactly how pissed off with me is Candice?"

"She saved you a piece of cake," the unicorn shifter said, extricating himself. The corner of his mouth hooked up. "Admittedly, I think she's planning to throw it at your head."

"Though perhaps that wouldn't be a good idea," Rory murmured, his gaze lingering on Seven's sheathed stunsword.

"Oh, Seven's just here to protect me against foes." The Prince drew himself up, adopting an uncharacteristically regal expression. "Seven, I hereby declare that you are *not* to defend me from any beatings my friends see fit to dispense. Except Blaise."

Blaise threw a mock-punch at him, which he ducked, laughing. Seven felt a strange pang in her chest. It wasn't the horseplay—that was all clearly good-natured. Her animal lay quiet, untroubled. It wasn't its protective instincts that made her heart twist.

It was *him*.

In the club, he'd been all calculated seduction and playboy charm. With the Imperial Champion and Lord Azure, he'd been stiff and spiky, aggressively trampling over the expected etiquette. But here… here, he was different.

Among his friends, his shoulders had relaxed at last. His grin flashed like the sun breaking out from clouds, dazzling and unguarded. For all that he was clowning around now, pretending to cower in fear from Blaise's wrath, she had the oddest certainty that she was finally seeing *him*, not a role he was playing.

In contrast to everyone else's smiles, Edith was looking anxious. Her hands jerked in a nervous, fluttering gesture. "Seven, I'm sorry I assumed that you were Joe's mate. I didn't mean to offend you."

She hadn't been offended at all. Quite the opposite. Just for a moment, she'd been enfolded and included. *Welcomed*.

It had felt…nice.

"No apology is necessary." Her voice sounded stiff and awkward even to herself. "It was an understandable conclusion. I am sorry to have appeared unexpected and unannounced. I thought you were forewarned."

"Joe generally prefers to ask forgiveness rather than permission," Rory said dryly. "When he bothers to ask anything at all. Joe! Did you at least tell *Buck* about our new friend?"

Joe—she abruptly found that she couldn't keep thinking of him as *the Prince*—broke off from his mock-sparring with Blaise. "I'm not a total idiot, bro."

"Just ninety-nine point nine percent," Blaise called.

Joe good-naturedly flipped her off. "Come on, Seven. I'll take you to our glorious leader. Don't worry. He'll love you."

A flutter of nerves stirred in her stomach. She covered her apprehension by stooping to pick up her discarded backpack—and nearly cracked her head against Joe's as he bent to do the same. For a moment, they both tugged at the bag, trying to claim it from the other.

Fenrir let out a deep woof that sounded awfully like laughter.

Seven flushed, realizing how ridiculous they must look. She let go, allowing Joe to claim her backpack. She grabbed his instead, glaring at him as she hoisted it onto her shoulder.

"My prince," she hissed as quietly as she could. "It is not seemly—"

"You're really going to have to break that habit," he interrupted. "There are two other squads in the crew, all regular humans. Buck's the only person who knows that we're shifters. If someone catches you deferring to me like royalty, we're going to have a *lot* of explaining to do."

He sauntered off without waiting for a response, heading for a cluster of low buildings at the other end of the broad clearing. Seven had to trot to keep up with his long-legged stride. The others followed in their wake, but they quickly outdistanced them, even though Joe *looked* like he was just lazing along.

He's good at that, she realized.

She remembered how he'd casually he'd posed one-handed during his pole-dance, as though anyone could have done it. How, just now, he'd evaded his friends' questions with the conversational equivalent of a handful of thrown glitter. He'd danced and deflected and played the fool, and never given a hint that how hard he'd been working to avoid having to tell them a direct lie.

He was *very* good at making it look like he was putting in no effort at all.

Why?

She stretched her legs to catch up with him. It might have been her imagination, but she thought he shortened *his* stride, just a little, matching his step to hers. She was able to walk at his side without having to keep breaking into a half-jog.

A rutted dirt track cut across the clearing, leading to the buildings. The track flattened out into a parking area, home to a handful of dirty pick-up trucks and Jeeps. Three larger, bright yellow vehicles stood out from the others, like bulls in a herd of cows.

"Behold our noble steed." Joe gestured at one of the hulking transports. THUNDER MOUNTAIN HOTSHOTS was written on the side in stark black letters, with the letter *A* in a smaller font underneath. "I keep trying to persuade the others to let me jazz her up a little. I had this great design sketched out, incorporating all our shift forms, but Buck confiscated my spray cans before I could start painting. Something about being a hotshot crew, not a 'motherloving metal band.' No appreciation for art, that man."

Seven pictured the enormous vehicle covered in lurid illustrations of sea dragons and griffins. "He sounds like a person of excellent judgement and good taste."

Joe laughed. "I think you'll like him. From what I saw, he's better than your Lord Azure, at least."

Privately, Seven thought that was a very low bar to clear. Wild krakens couldn't have made her admit it, though.

Joe gave the crew vehicle a last fond pat before ambling on. "That big building over there is the mess hall. The others will tell you shameless and terrible lies about my cooking. If you feel moved to challenge them to a duel for such foul slurs on my honor, feel free."

He swung his arm, pointing out another rough-hewn wooden building. "And over there is the torture chamber. Sorry, gym. We do two weight-training sessions a day—the first alongside the rest of the crew in the morning. That one's just for show. The second session is when we *actually* sweat. Rory makes us come back after all the humans have finished for the day. The sadist."

As he talked, Seven studied his face more than the buildings. For all his deprecating words, there was fondness in his eyes as he gazed around the dusty, unprepossessing compound.

"You like it here," she said, startled. "Don't you?"

"What, this place?" Joe made a theatrical shudder. "I used to spend my summers lounging on golden beaches while beautiful seal-maidens peeled shrimp for me. Why in the sea would I prefer to be *here*?"

Which wasn't a denial, Seven noted. She was learning to pay attention to what he *wasn't* saying.

"Sometimes the place where we belong isn't the most comfortable one. Or where other people assume we belong." If anyone knew *that*, it was her. "You're at home here, no matter how you attempt to hide it. You're glad to be back. Why were you so determined to stay at the strip club, before the attack?"

He turned away sharply, hiding his face…but he couldn't hide the leap of his pulse. She could taste his sudden spike of fear, sharp on her tongue, calling to her deepest instincts.

"Ah, there's the man himself," Joe said brightly. He sounded like he hadn't a care in the world. "Come on, Seven. Time to meet the big boss."

What in the sea is he hiding?

There was no opportunity to probe deeper. Joe was waving exuberantly at a man who'd just emerged from one of the buildings. The man did not seem to be nearly as glad to see him. A deep scowl creased his face as he strode over.

The man addressed Joe in a curt, gravelly voice. "You're late."

"That's a matter of opinion," Joe replied, without the slightest hint of shame. "The way I see things, I'm right on time. Nothing's on fire yet, is it?"

"It constantly amazes me that your pants don't spontaneously combust every time you open your mouth." The man switched his attention to Seven, raking her with a glare worthy of a sea dragon drill sergeant. From his weathered skin and greying hair, he had to be in his late forties, but his body was as hard and muscled as any of the younger crew members. "This her?"

Joe stepped to one side, flourishing one hand at Seven. Although the gesture was typically flamboyant, his voice dropped into formal cadences, turning serious. "It is my honor to introduce Seventh Novice of the Order of the First Water, Squire to Lord Azure, Oath-Sworn Guardian of the Sea's Heart."

Seven started at the new additions to her name. She hadn't thought of it before, but she supposed her new status as the Prince's bodyguard *did* require a change. A sea dragon's name reflected their status and deeds, precisely indicating the honor that they had won and the respect that they were due.

But still: *Guardian of the Sea's Heart?*

It wasn't a title she'd ever heard before. Then again, *she* hadn't grown up in the Imperial Palace, tutored from birth in sea dragon history and etiquette. She could only assume it was some traditional honor given to the royal family's personal guards.

The man shot Joe an incredulous look. "Are you motherloving kidding me?"

"Hey, you should hear *my* sea dragon name." Joe reverted to his usual flippant tone, grin flashing. "If you're ever feeling insomniac, I can recite it for you. I promise, you'll be sleeping like a baby before I'm halfway through."

"Motherloving shifters." The man turned back to Seven, shaking his head. "By the time I got through your tongue-twister out in the field, we'd all be burned to a crisp. You got a nickname?"

"Seven." His scent crackled on her tongue, like the electric tang of an approaching storm. Prompted by an impulse she couldn't quite name, she offered him the deep bow she'd given the Imperial Champion. "Sir."

The man huffed. "Well, you got better manners than this overgrown idiot. Not that that's hard. I'm Buck Frazer. Superintendent of this sorry lot, for my sins. Now, you may be here as his bodyguard, but that doesn't mean I'm not going to put a Pulaski in your hands and expect you to work like a dog cutting line alongside the rest of the crew. You got a problem with that?"

"No." She squared her shoulders, meeting his glare without flinching. "It will be my honor, sir."

Buck made a not entirely displeased grunt. "Buck'll do. Chief, if you insist on getting fancy. I warn you, I'm going out on a limb for you here, Seven. I'm having to do some very creative paperwork to cover your presence on the crew. And I will *not* have you endangering anyone, you hear? Over the next week, you're going to get a crash course in wildland firefighting. And I don't care how badly I need another dragon. If you don't pass with flying colors, you're out."

She'd been nodding along, but at the word *dragon* she froze. She looked at Joe, waiting for him to correct the Chief's mistake.

"Hey, don't look like that." Joe smiled at her, his turquoise eyes warm. "You got into the Order of the First Water. I promise, this will be a piece of cake in comparison. *I* was able to pass fire training, after all."

"But I'm..." He knew, surely he *had* to know? She swallowed hard. "Prince—Chief—I'm not a sea dragon."

Joe stared at her. *"What?"*

"What," Buck repeated, in far flatter tones.

She hated to even *think* the word. But now she had no choice but to say it.

She took a deep breath, steeling herself. "I am a shark."

CHAPTER 9

"A shark. A motherloving *shark* shifter." Buck glared at Joe from behind his paperwork-strewn desk. He'd dragged Joe into his office for a private meeting, leaving Seven standing guard outside the closed door. "Do you know how many miles inland we are? What in the seven bells were you *thinking?*"

"I didn't know." Joe couldn't believe it himself.

Although he'd known her name from his visions, he'd always been careful to avoid learning anything about the Seventh Novice of the Order of the First Water. Following her life—her victories, her struggles—would only have made it harder to stay away.

Even so, he'd thought he'd known everything about her. He'd seen the way she fought, whirling and dancing through the elegant forms of a sea dragon duelist. He'd seen the traditional honor-tokens gleaming in her hair.

But he'd never seen her shift. He'd never even heard her speak in sea dragon language. Not in any dream, any vision.

It had never occurred to him to wonder why.

"How could you *not know?*" Buck demanded, echoing his own thoughts. "Don't you freaks sniff each other's armpits or something? I thought you could recognize each other."

"Some shifters can, but not sea dragons." He shook his head, still mentally kicking himself. "I just assumed that she was one of us. For sea's sake, she's a member of the Order of the First Water! There's never been a knight who wasn't a sea dragon."

Even through his whirling bewilderment, he couldn't help feeling a spark of awe and pride. Somehow, his mate had forced the idiotic, hidebound knights to accept a *shark* into their ranks.

He'd known she was extraordinary. He just hadn't appreciated *how* extraordinary.

Buck scowled at him as though the entire situation was his fault—which, to be fair, it was. "I suppose it's too late to send her back for a refund."

"Believe me, I wish I could persuade her to stay under the sea where she'd be safe. But she's oath-bound to stick to my side. The Pearl Empress herself could order her back to Atlantis, and it wouldn't do any good. Seven would rather die than be dishonored."

*Cold chains around his wrists...*he pushed down the fragment of future memory. There was still time to find a way to make it not happen. There *had* to be.

"A *shark*," Buck muttered, in tones of deep disgust. "I thought I was hiring something useful. What's she going to do, flop the demons to death?"

"Hey!" His dragon bristled at the insult to their mate. "She's already saved me from a whole pack of them single-handed."

Buck folded his arms across his chest. "If those things really were demons."

"I'm certain that they were. I think most of them were possessing wolves. I was too drugged up to notice much, but Seven said they definitely had glowing red eyes."

"So does one of your colleagues."

"Okay, fine," Joe snapped. "Maybe it's not the demons. I mean, I only personally killed one of them last year, no reason they might hold a grudge. I'm just a *giant freaking dragon*, heir to all the power of the ocean; it's not like any demon would give its metaphorical left nut to possess me. No, clearly I've somehow randomly pissed off a hellhound pack that we had no idea existed."

"Never underestimate your ability to piss people off." Buck sighed, rubbing his forehead. "But point taken. So you think the demons are coming after the squad in revenge for last year?"

"I think it's more than that."

He'd been thinking about it all through the long helicopter ride back to Montana. Parts of his reoccurring vision—the one that had haunted his dreams since childhood—were finally starting to make sense

And he did *not* like the picture that was emerging.

"The woman who attacked me could have just bitten me on the spot," he said, picking his words with care. "We saw last year that a demon can take someone over pretty instantly, if it can get its teeth into them. But she didn't. She was trying to drag me away and take me somewhere else. I think she wanted me for something special."

Buck's eyebrows drew down. "Like what?"

Cold chains around his wrists. Death rears above them, horned and hell-eyed...

He said, "Like a sacrifice."

~

"A sacrifice?" Blaise said skeptically. "Like in a 'O Great Beast, Devourer of Worlds, accept this our humble offering' kind of way? I don't know, Joe. Have you been reading those cheesy fantasy novels again?"

In the light of the flickering campfire, Rory, Edith, Wystan and Callum were looking equally unconvinced. Even Fenrir had a distinctly doubtful tilt to his ears. Seven was the only person who seemed to be reserving judgement. She stood at parade rest at the edge of the circle of firelight, a little way apart from the rest of the crew, her face studiously neutral.

He hadn't had a chance to talk to her since she'd dropped the bombshell about her animal. What with physical training, equipment checks, and mandatory fire safety refresher sessions, there hadn't been an opportunity to sneak a private moment with either her or the rest of A squad all day.

Now it was late evening. The vast Montana sky had darkened to a deep violet blue, glorious with stars. They were sitting around the communal fire pit outside the mess hall. The last yawning humans from B and C squads had wandered off in search of their beds, finally leaving the shifters free to talk.

Joe was about ready to fall over from exhaustion himself, but warning his friends was more important than sleep. Not that he ever needed any *extra* incentive to avoid his bunk as long as possible. He added another splash of Tabasco to his ink-black coffee.

"I know it sounds nuts, but think about it." He took a gulp, grateful for the familiar mule-kick of the caffeine/chilli combo. "That woman was dragging me off *somewhere*. There has to be a reason for that."

"True. And it does sound like she was possessed," Rory said. He spread his hands. "But you have to admit, it's a bit of a stretch to leap from there to deciding she wanted to bend you over a pentagram."

Joe clenched his jaw in frustration. He'd been afraid of this. It was hard to build a convincing case when you couldn't reveal half your evidence.

It was even harder when you'd carefully cultivated a reputation for being hare-brained and ridiculous.

"Is it so weird to think someone has to be summoning the demons?" He looked around at his friends' faces, searching in vain for any spark of agreement. "I mean, there has to be some kind of reason why they show up where and when they do."

"I had the impression that it must be a natural phenomenon," Wystan said. The unicorn shifter was sitting on a log with his elbows resting on his knees, fingers steepled in thought. "Nobody could have called the ones that appeared in the unicorn forest, after all. It was surrounded by an unbreakable barrier. Moth might have been forced to bargain with the demons when they started to emerge, but I'm certain that neither she nor any of the other unicorns would ever have summoned the creatures in the first place."

"We saw them popping out of the ground all by themselves." Edith, who was leaning against Rory, gestured in demonstration. "Like mushrooms."

"Evil mushrooms," said Blaise, poking at the dying fire with a stick.

"But even mushrooms don't come from nowhere," Joe argued. "They don't grow without the right sort of conditions. The seeds need fertilizer and water, right?"

Edith's forehead wrinkled. "Mushrooms come from spores."

Joe fought an urge to bury his head in his hands and scream. "Can we please forget the fungi? All I'm trying to say is that maybe demons need the right sort of conditions too. Specifically, something to eat. Some*one* to eat."

"Joe may be onto something there, actually." Wystan rested his chin on his hands, looking pensive. "I spent some time over the winter analyzing the data Buck has gathered over the past ten years on the Thunderbird's appearances. If we assume that it only starts fires where it senses demonic activity, then the demons *do* only emerge when there are people nearby. All the wildfires were in remote areas, but in almost all cases there were campers or hikers present who reported seeing lightning coming out of a clear sky."

"Like when the Thunderbird started a fire near me?" Edith asked.

"Exactly. All the witnesses were human. The Thunderbird is invisible to ordinary people, just like we mythic shifters are in our other forms." Wystan frowned a little. "Which makes it distinctly odd that *Buck* can see it, but I digress. In any event, it does seem that the demons are drawn out by the presence of potential prey."

"Like Edith." Rory's eyes were feral in the dark, reflecting the light from the campfire. "Remember the first demon that we encountered? Edith's old fire watch tower was the only building for miles, and the demon appeared right next to it."

"I'm glad that it did," Edith said to her mate. She snuggled closer against him. "Otherwise we wouldn't have met. I was lucky that you were in the area."

"It wasn't luck." Rory's arm tightened around her. "It was fate."

It *hadn't* been luck…and fate had had a helping hand. Joe had seen the squad battling a forest fire outside Edith's fire watch tower, two months before it had actually happened. He'd been drinking a beer at the time. His reaction to the unexpected vision had resulted in him having to explain to a biker gang that he hadn't *meant* to hurl an entire Budweiser into their very large and very unamused leader's face (thanks to the ensuing brawl, Joe was still banned from that bar).

As with most of his visions, he hadn't seen enough context to know exactly what was going to happen—the demon itself had been as much as a surprise to him as to anyone else. But he'd known, bone-deep, that the squad *had* to be there.

He was still secretly pleased with how well he'd managed it. It had taken him hours of searching through photos online to identify the right location, and even longer to work out how to arrange for the squad to be passing by at exactly the right time.

Not that any of them would ever know that.

"Ugh." Blaise rolled her eyes theatrically at Rory and Edith, though a slight, affectionate smile softened her mouth. "Get a room, you two. Okay, let's say Joe's right and the demons need people to eat when they hatch out. Why do they bother lurking around the ass-end of Montana for random campers? Even downtown Billings would be an all-you-can-possess buffet in comparison."

"Noise," Callum said.

They all looked at him. "Care to elaborate on that, Cal?" Rory asked.

Callum shifted position a little, uncomfortable as ever with being the center of attention. The firelight caught in his red-gold hair, making it look as bright as the flame itself. "Cities are noisy. Not just literally. Hard to be around people."

Shadowhorse speaks true, Fenrir put in, his deep telepathic voice growling in all their minds. *Too many two-legs drives out most creatures. Would be stranger if snake-things* could *nest in your dens.*

Seven started, her head pivoting toward the hellhound. "I can hear you."

Of course. Fenrir scratched unconcernedly behind one ear with a back paw, his yellow harness jingling. *Is pack now, Deep Bitch.*

"He was literally raised by wolves," Joe said hastily, as Seven's expression froze. "As far as he's concerned, *bitch* is a term of highest respect. Sorry."

"He calls me Stone Bitch," Edith said, with more than a little pride. "Because I'm tough and strong and non-autistic people have difficulty reading my face. Fenrir gives the best nicknames."

"As someone stuck with *Birdcat*, I kind of disagree," Rory murmured. "Though he does tend to have good reason for his choices. Why 'Deep', Fenrir?"

The hellhound flicked one ear in a canine shrug. *She is. Goes down a long way, underneath the surface. More than first appears.* Fenrir's muzzle turned, and Joe found himself the subject of the hellhound's unnerving orange-copper stare. *Very like Seasnake.*

That was a little too close to home. Joe clapped his hands together, breaking the uncomfortable moment.

"Returning to the topic of demons," he said, flashing a slightly strained grin round at everyone. "We agree that any one of us would be a hot snack to a hungry hatchling, right?"

"Sure." Blaise shrugged. "But I still don't see what that has to do with your would-be kidnapper."

"What if some demons are more powerful than others? What if they need something more than an ordinary animal or human to possess? What if there's a, a," he tried to find words that would convey the terror of the shadowy, towering *evil* he'd seen in his vision, "a kind of alpha demon, that *can't* emerge unless it's got a special victim laid out and waiting for it? What if that woman tried to kidnap me in order to serve me up as the dish of the day?"

"It's...possible, I suppose." Wystan's expression said he didn't think it was likely. "In that case, do you think she'll try to grab you again?"

"I'm certain of it." His original vision of Lupa ambushing the squad at Bluebrook couldn't come true now...but he'd still gotten enough brief flashes to know that she was still planning to lay some kind of trap there. "And I can't explain why, but I have a hunch that she's going to set a fire to do it. She knows we're a hotshot crew. I'm sure she'll try to draw us out to somewhere remote, where she and her demons can attack us."

"Well, if she does, she'll regret it." Blaise stretched, her words slurring into a yawn. "Don't look so worried, Joe. No demon will get through us. We've got your back."

"It's not me I'm worried about!" He looked round at them all, *willing* them to take this seriously. "I'm not the only one at risk here. You're all in danger."

"We've faced danger before, Joe," Rory said, in the infuriatingly warm, understanding tone he used when he thought you were being irrational, and was trying to reassure you anyway. "We can handle demons. Or whatever else this woman throws at us." He stood up. "As long as we're all well-rested and prepared. Come on, team. Time for bed."

"We're *not* prepared," Joe said wretchedly, as everyone else got up too. "You don't understand. This is bigger than anything we've ever faced before."

Rory patted him on the shoulder. "Get some sleep, Joe. You've had a long day. Things will seem better in the morning."

"Where are you sleeping?" Blaise asked Seven. "There's a spare room in my cabin, if you want to share with me."

Seven straightened to attention. "No. I must stay close by the Prince."

Oh no. What with everything else occupying his mind, he'd overlooked the problem of sleeping arrangements.

He had a sinking feeling any attempt to dissuade her was as doomed as the Titanic, but he tried anyway. "There isn't space in my cabin, Seven. There are only two rooms, and Callum already has dibs on the other one. Don't worry. He's a pegasus shifter, he'll sense if anyone approaches."

Except Callum won't, he thought with a twinge of unease. In his vision, Callum hadn't sensed the ambush that the woman had laid for the squad...

He shook his head, pushing the moment of doubt aside. That

future couldn't happen now. He was back with the squad. Even if they weren't taking the threat seriously enough, *he* would.

He'd keep them safe.

"Go with Blaise," he said to Seven. "It's a small base. You'll be close enough if anything happens."

Seven shot him an icy look. She turned to Callum. "I apologize for the inconvenience, but may I take the second room in the Prince's cabin?"

Callum nodded. He handed her something.

"Er, thank you." Seven looked down at the small plastic packet, then back up at the pegasus shifter. "What is this?"

"Earplugs," Callum said. "You'll need them."

CHAPTER 10

Seven soon discovered that Callum hadn't been kidding about needing the earplugs.

It wasn't that the Prince snored.

He *screamed*.

Seven hadn't been asleep, though she hadn't really been awake either. Like many types of shark, Great Whites had to keep swimming to breathe, so they *couldn't* sleep like most other animals. Instead, they slowed to a resting state, the body moving on autopilot while the mind was unconscious.

Being able to emulate that trancelike blankness was one of the few useful traits from her inner animal. She'd been sitting upright with her eyes open and her brain switched off, her stunsword across her knees, when Joe's cry yanked her to her feet.

She was bursting into his room before her human mind had fully wrestled control back from her animal. Her stunsword flicked out, crackling with blue energy—but there was no one to fight.

Joe twisted alone on his bed, tangled up in a white sheet, shoulders tense and shaking. Sweat gleamed on his mahogany skin.

"*No!*" The word was a chord of utter agony. The musical notes of sea dragon speech ripped from his throat in a symphony of despair. "Seven, *no!* Run!"

Seven drew in her breath, but tasted nothing except his salt-sea scent. No foreign presence, no threats. Her shark surged through her blood, near-frenzied by the Prince's distress.

"My prince." She sheathed her stunsword, thrusting her inner animal back down at the same time. "You're having a nightmare."

"Leave me," he pleaded, still speaking his native language. His eyes flickered under tightly shut lids. "Seven, no, leave me, save yourself —*Seven!*"

"Joe." Hesitantly, she put a hand on his hot, slick shoulder. "Wake up, Joe."

His eyes opened at last. They looked up at her from the depths of hell.

"Seven?" He twisted, surging upright. His hands came up, trying to push her away. "Seven, no, run-!"

"Joe!" She grabbed his wrists. She pinned him to the bed, afraid that he might hurt himself in his confusion. "It's just a dream. Wake up!"

His eyes focused properly on hers at last. She was so close to him, she could feel his short, panicked breath against her own lips.

"Seven?" he whispered, in English this time. His voice cracked and broke on her name. "You're here? You're safe?"

"I'm fine. I'm right here." She loosened her grip, relieved that he was finally awake. "Everything's fine. You were just having a nightmare."

His dreams still haunted his eyes. He touched her face, tracing the line of her cheek. She could feel his fingers shaking. She was shaking too, trembling with the effort of controlling the desire roaring through her body.

"I saw you die." His fingers ran through her hair, tangling in her braids. "I always see you die. Oh, sea. I thought you were dead. *Seven*."

His hand tightened on the back of her neck. He pulled her down to his hungry, desperate mouth.

Everything else vanished. He kissed her like he needed to devour her, like he needed to verify with every sense that she was really there.

It was like the first time she'd ever stepped into the ocean. Her lips, her body, her entire soul opened to him, coming home to a place she'd never been before: *Yes. Yes, this is what I was missing.*

He made a low, feral sound into her mouth, back arcing. His strong arms enfolded her like the waves, pulling her against him. She straddled him, only a few thin layers of cloth separating his body from hers. She could feel the hard planes of his chest, the tight buds of his nipples, the ridges of his clenched abs. Every part of him taut and perfect and *hers*.

He was glorious. He was maddening. Every touch of skin against skin was a revelation. She needed more.

"More," she breathed, kissing him back, pressing herself against him, drunk on his scent. "More."

His tongue swept through her mouth, teasing and caressing. She tasted the sudden tang of blood.

She jerked back, covering her mouth with both hands. "I'm sorry!"

He looked dazed, eyes dark with desire. He touched his lip, then blinked at the crimson drop on his fingertip as though wondering where it had come from.

"Stop." His voice was hoarse, rough. "We have to stop."

She scrabbled back, keeping one hand firmly clamped over her mouth. She would have retreated all the way off the bed and out of the room—and ideally, out of the country and into the lightless depths of the sea—but he caught her wrist.

"Hey." He sat upright, sliding his legs out from underneath her. "It's okay. You didn't do anything wrong."

She shook her head, still hiding her treacherous teeth, utterly mortified. "I *bit* you."

"And I liked it." He pulled more of the sheet onto his lap, grimacing. "Trust me, *you* don't need to be embarrassed about an involuntary physical reaction. I think we'd both better take a moment to…calm down."

That was difficult, given that he was still mostly naked. Frustrated heat throbbed between her legs. Her teeth shifted further, sharpening into double rows of razor points.

She jerked her eyes away from him, clenching her jaw. She tried to think of boring, human things. Vacuuming. Buying milk. Filling in tax returns.

It didn't help.

"Seven." Gently but irresistibly, he drew her hands down. He brushed his thumb across her tight-pressed lips. "They're nothing to be ashamed of."

She looked away, ducking her head. "They're ugly. Bestial."

"No, they aren't. They're part of you, like your animal. Why do you hide them?" A crease appeared between his eyebrows. "Actually, *how* do you hide them? I've never met a shark shifter who could completely pass for human."

"I'm not like other—" The hated word stuck in her throat. "I'm not like them."

"No." He leaned back against the wall, regarding her intently. "No, you really aren't. Seven, why didn't you tell me?"

"I thought you knew."

"Of course I didn't know! What, you thought I just didn't *care* that I was condemning you to spend months trapped in human form, unable to shift?" He raked a hand through his hair, looking around wildly as if he could make an ocean appear through sheer willpower. "I gotta talk to Buck. To my parents. We gotta work out some way of getting you to the sea every few weeks, otherwise you're going to go stark raving nuts."

"I don't need to shift that often. I'll be fine." She'd gone years without shifting, after all. She could manage a summer. "And if you didn't know I was a shark, why did you say we couldn't have a future together?"

"Because you're honorable and noble and perfect and everything I'm not!" He stared at her. "You seriously thought I was talking about *politics*?"

"Of course I did! You're the Emperor-in-Waiting! Our people are hereditary enemies, with millennia of bad blood between us. This would rock Atlantis to its very foundations. All the sea fear my kind. And for good reason."

"No," he said firmly. "That's blind prejudice. My godfather is the Master Shark, and he's the wisest, gentlest man I've ever met. Sharks don't deserve their bad reputation."

"Deserved or not, we do have a reputation. No sea dragon would accept a shark becoming a Princess of Atlantis. It would be an utter disaster for the whole Pearl Empire."

"I can't think of anything *better* for the Pearl Empire. We'd finally have a chance of healing this stupid rivalry between sharks and sea dragons." He caught his breath, pure delight spreading across his face. "Sea, just imagine our children. A future Pearl Emperor or Empress could *be* a shark."

He said it as though it wasn't a curse. As though he couldn't think of anything more marvelous than being a brutal, savage animal rather than an elegant, magical sea dragon.

His utter astonishment earlier, his clear enthusiasm now—neither of them could be feigned.

He really hadn't known. He really didn't *care.*

The reason he didn't want her—it wasn't because she was a shark. Which meant…

It could only be that he didn't want *her.*

CHAPTER 11

*H*e'd said something wrong, though he had no idea what.
One moment, Seven's eyes were wide and unguarded, her full lips slightly parted, no longer hiding those cute pointed teeth. The next moment, she'd retreated behind her armor again. Her expression froze into that familiar, blankly polite mask.

"I see," she said. She rose, giving him a stiff, formal bow. "My apologies for interrupting your rest, Your Highness. I shall not disturb you further."

"Seven. *Seven.*" He scrambled out of bed, nearly forgetting to grab the sheet in his haste to intercept her. "Hey. Stop. What's wrong? What did I say?"

She stopped in the doorway, her back to him. He could see her drawing herself up to her full height, shoulders setting.

"You said nothing, my prince." She didn't turn around. "And if you do not mind, I would prefer to keep it that way. Some things I do not need to hear spoken out loud. May I be dismissed, please?"

He should let her go. Whatever he'd done, however she'd misunderstood him, it was bad enough to drive her away. She'd put up a wall between them, shielding her heart.

That was good. That was *necessary*. He had to let her go. For her own good.

But she was hurting.

He'd hurt her.

"Seven." He put a hand on her shoulder. She stiffened. "I'm sorry. Please talk to me. I don't understand why you're so upset."

She pulled away from him, turning around at last. Moonlight caught in her pale grey eyes, bright with unshed tears.

"You don't?" Her tone was scathing, but her lower lip trembled. "You don't want me. You are my *mate*. And I am such a monster that even you don't want me."

He stared at her. She was pale and furious and shaking, and so beautiful that she took his breath away.

And she thought he didn't *want* her?

"What," he managed to croak out at last.

She closed her eyes for a moment, breathing in through her nose. Her mouth firmed into a hard, tight line.

"It doesn't matter," she said quietly. "I understand. I am not..." Her hand fluttered, gesturing from her muscled shoulders to her narrow hips. "Not desirable."

"Sweet little fishes, are you serious?" He was genuinely tempted to drop the sheet and showing her the effect she was having on him at that exact second. "Seven, you do realize that I'm having a hard time talking right now because very little of my blood is making it to my brain, right? You are the most gorgeous woman I have ever seen. And trust me, that is not a short list."

She folded her arms across her small breasts. He remembered the feel of them crushed against his chest, her tight nipples pressing through her shirt, and had to adjust his grip on the sheet again.

"Is that how you sweet-talk so many women into bed?" she spat. "Lie to them?"

"No. I never lie."

She started to shape an angry retort—and stopped, a peculiar expression crossing her face. She looked at him as though she'd only just seen him.

"No," she said softly. "You don't, do you? Not even when it would be easier. Why is that?"

She *saw* him.

A strange thrill, terror and exaltation, pierced his heart. She was the first person to ever notice that for all his vocal scorn for sea dragon customs, he had his own private code of honor. The first person to ever look past the surface. She *saw him*.

"Well, you know." He affected a flippant shrug. "Candor is a virtue."

"And you are not a knight," she countered. "And you are doing it again."

"Doing what?"

She jabbed him in the center of the chest with one finger. His whole body rang like a bell in response, desire thudding through him.

"Doing *that*," she said. "Telling a different truth to avoid the one that you don't want to speak. Dancing away with a smile and a joke. But I am a hunter. I am your mate. You cannot evade me."

"I don't want to," he whispered.

"And you don't lie." Her grey eyes pierced through his soul. She saw him, oh, she *saw* him. "So. You knew I was your mate before I did. You did your utmost to prevent me from realizing it. When I found out anyway, you fled. You have tried again and again to push me away. But you *do* desire me. You say it isn't the fact that I am a shark that holds you back. So what is it?"

His mouth was dry. "You—you shouldn't want *me*. I'm all wrong for you. The whole sea knows how terrible I am. I can't even count how many women I've slept with—"

"All true." She tossed back her braids, her whole body tensing as though she was about to challenge him to a formal duel. "And all irrelevant. Because I *do* want you, Joe of the Thunder Mountain Hotshots, Crown Prince of Atlantis, Emperor-in-Waiting, Heir to the Pearl Throne. And now you must decide how important your honor truly is to you. Because I am asking directly, right now: What stops you from claiming me as your mate?"

He looked around wildly. "I need a drink."

She caught his wrist. Her slim fingers were cool against his fevered skin. *Cold iron round his wrists...* "No. No more evasions. *Now*, Joe."

There was no reflecting pool. Nothing he could use to check the future. Everything hung in the balance, and he was blind in the dark.

He could lie to her. He could break his honor at last. Truly be what everyone thought he was. No one would ever know.

Except him.

"Because I can see the future," he said. "And if we mate, you will die."

CHAPTER 12

It was so far removed from anything that she'd been braced for him to say, that for a moment Seven could only gape at him.

He's lying, was her first proper thought. *He's lying at last.*

Except that he wasn't.

Sharks were sensitive to distress. They could taste the thousand different flavors of it, pick out the faintest trail and follow it across miles of open ocean. There was a difference between the blank terror of a lost seal pup and the fearful bravado of an injured bull walrus; the weary grief of a whale too sick to swim and the thrashing confusion of a sea turtle trapped in plastic.

She knew the sour-sweat guilt of someone afraid of being caught in a lie. She knew the steel-sharp scent of someone bravely facing their greatest fear at last, refusing to turn tail and flee.

A shark knew its prey.

Joe was frightened. More than that. He was *terrified*. She could taste the hammer-beat of his heart, the leap of his blood, the sweat running down his back.

But he wasn't lying.

He looked away, hitching his sheet a little higher around his waist. "Can I find some pants? I feel that this conversation requires pants."

"Yes," Seven said faintly. And then, as he turned around to reveal the powerful curves of his back, she added, "Also a shirt?"

"Good idea." He gestured at one of the battered armchairs in the small common room that lay between their two bedrooms. "Take a seat. I'll be right back."

She followed him anyway, just in case he was actually planning to leap out a window. He flashed her a pained grin over his shoulder, as though he'd read her train of thought.

"No more running away." He ducked to pick up a discarded pair of jeans from a pile of clothes on the floor. "I promise. But feel free to keep watching if you want."

He let go of the sheet. Seven shut her eyes just in time.

"So, uh." she said, trying to distract her imagination from the sounds of rustling cloth. "You. Ah. You say you can see the future."

"Yep." His voice was muffled, as though coming from the depths of a t-shirt. "You probably have questions."

Seven had *all* the questions. Starting with: *Are you clinically insane?*

She was still trying to work out a more tactful way to phrase that when he spoke again. "I'm not crazy, if that's what you're wondering. Though I guess opinions vary on that one. I concede that I'm probably a bit crazier than average. But I'm not delusional. I really do see the future. It's safe to look now."

Seven cracked open an eye, and found the Prince was once more decently clothed. Which still meant that he was wildly, ridiculously attractive, but at least it wasn't a heroic struggle to keep her eyes above the level of his chin.

He cast a glance at the bed, cleared his throat, and gestured toward the door. She allowed him to steer her back into the common room.

Joe sank down into one chair, leaning forward with his elbows on his knees. She took the chair opposite. She felt as though she was conducting a job interview. Or possibly a psychiatric exam.

He let out his breath. "Well, this is awkward. I guess I'd better start at the beginning. How much do you know about the Seers?"

"Very little." The knights tended to have little contact with the various branches of the sea dragon mystic arts. There was the rare knight who had talent in both sword and magic—Joe's father, the Imperial Champion, was one of them—but Seven was far too low in rank to interact with such august personages. "I do know that they can use pools of water to view remote places."

"Far-seeing. That's the easiest form of scrying." The corner of his mouth hooked up. "It also happens to be one that I can't do, ironically enough. I spent a year with them, you see. The Master-Seers were in utter despair by the end. Told my parents I had no talent at all."

"But…you just said that you can see the future."

"Yeah." He spread his hands. "I don't know how. I just *do*. It started when I was about fourteen or so. At first, I thought it was just nightmares. I'd wake up screaming…" He trailed off, swallowing. "Well, you've seen that for yourself. But then I started seeing the visions when I was awake. Reflected in puddles, pools, baths, anywhere there was water. It got to the point where I was scared to even pick up a drink. That's when I asked to go to the Seers."

At fourteen, she'd started training as a knight. She wondered if he'd been entering the quiet, darkened halls of the Seers at the same time as she'd been picking up a sword for the first time.

"Did you tell them what you were experiencing?" she asked.

He shook his head. "You're the first person I've ever told. Not even my mom knows what I can do."

The *Pearl Empress* didn't know? "Why didn't you tell anyone?"

"At first, because I was scared I was going mad." He let out a hollow laugh. "And then, because I was scared I wasn't. I soon discovered from the Seers just how rare my so-called talent is. Normally it takes decades of dedicated study and practice for a Master-Seer to even *glimpse* the future. There are only a couple currently living who can do it at all. They're treated like saints. The other Seers practically kiss the ground under their feet."

She frowned, not following. "Why would that be a reason *not* to tell people?"

"Because I'm already the sea-damned Crown Prince!" His voice roughened, turning savage and bitter. "My entire life, I've been treated as a walking embodiment of the Pearl Throne. I have to be twice as large as life just to force people to see a person rather than a title. If sea shifters found out about my talent? No one would ever care about anything else. No one would ever see who I am rather than what I can do. No one would ever see *me*."

She thought of how hard she'd had to work to persuade the knights to accept her. How she'd always had to be twice as good as any other candidate, just to avoid being judged by her animal.

"I understand," she said softly.

"Yeah." He met her eyes. "I thought you might."

She longed to hold him, shielding him from the world with her own body. Her palms ached to stroke away the quiet, weary grief in his face. She wanted to reassure him with her touch that she saw *him*, not what he represented. That she would always, always see him.

He looked away first. "Anyway. The Seers couldn't help me. They only know how to train people to be *more* sensitive to visions. It never even occurred to them that I was there to learn how to make them stop."

"You can't control them at all?"

"Not really. I mean, I got a little better. These days, I mostly only see them when I'm asleep, or deliberately scrying in water. Occasionally one still leaps out at me unexpectedly, though. Those tend to be the really important ones."

"So it's…like watching a movie? In the surface of the water?"

"Not even a little bit." His hands clenched together, so hard that his knuckles whitened. "I don't just see things. I *live* them. As if I'm there. And I can't choose what fate decides to show me. Sometimes it's something that needs to happen. Sometimes it's a warning, something that needs to *not* happen." He made a slight, pained sound. "Sometimes it's damned hard to tell the difference."

He'd been screaming her name… "You said you first started seeing visions in your sleep. You were having one tonight, weren't you?"

He said nothing for a long moment, staring down at his hands. Every muscle in his arms was rigid as iron.

"If something's really important, I see it over and over again," he said at last. "There's one vision that keeps coming back. Every night. It was the first one I ever had."

"About me?" she whispered.

He nodded, stiffly, barely moving his head. "That stuff I was saying to the others earlier, about there being some kind of alpha demon? I wasn't speculating. I've *seen* it. I've seen it since I was fourteen. It's just taken me until now to work out what I was seeing."

Her initial disbelief had utterly evaporated. She knew, down to the marrow of her bones, that he was telling the truth. She could *feel* his agony, as if an invisible thread connected their hearts.

She swallowed, her mouth dry. "Tell me. Tell me about the vision, Joe. Please."

"I'm in chains." His voice was barely audible. "A woman laughs, cold and triumphant. I'm…in a forest, I think. It's hard to tell, because it's night and the sky is full of smoke. I see a great evil rising above us. I see you step forward to shield me."

"And I…" She made herself say it. "I die?"

He looked up at last. His eyes blazed with turquoise fire, fierce and feral.

"It's not going to happen." Sea dragon harmonics shivered around the human words, singing utter determination. "In my vision, we're mated. As long as we don't mate, it *can't* happen."

She stood up, abruptly, unable to sit still any longer. She could only pace a couple of steps in the small room. She was a shark in a tank, the walls pressing in on her.

"That's why you've been trying so hard to push me away," she said, turning on her heel to face him again. "Because you thought it was the only way to keep me safe."

He'd leaned back in his chair, tucking his long legs out of the way to give her more room. "It *is* the only way to keep you safe."

"I don't accept that," she snapped. Her hand sought the hilt of her stunsword, as though she could beat destiny into submission. "You said that these reoccurring visions are warnings. This one is a warning about *you*. You're the one who's important, not me."

"Not to me."

She shook her head. "*I am not the Heir to the Pearl Throne.* If my death keeps you safe—"

"It *doesn't*." He surged to his feet, fists clenching. "And even if it did, I would *not let it happen.* Seven, don't even think about it. I will never let you sacrifice yourself for me. *Never.*"

"I am your oath-sworn bodyguard. It is my duty and my honor." She held up a hand as he started to retort. "But it seems that is irrelevant. If you perish in this vision as well, then the warning is clear. You can't be here. We have to go back to Atlantis immediately."

"You think I haven't thought of that?" Joe shot back. "Seven, I've seen what happens if I'm not here. My friends die. *All of them.* And the demon still rises."

"Then we must find a way to stop it."

"I'm *trying*. I'm not Netflix. I can't select the future that I want to see and watch how it all unfolds. I just get glimpses. Fate hands me a puzzle piece or two, and expects me to work out the entire damn picture!"

"Then let me help you decipher it." She let go of her stunsword, taking one of his hands instead. "You do not have to bear this burden alone, Joe. Not anymore. Let me help."

His shoulders unknotted a little. He let out his breath, rubbing at the bridge of his nose with his free hand.

"Bluebrook," he said. "That's the only other thing I've seen. The squad is going to get called out to a fire near a town named Bluebrook. I looked it up, it's pretty close to here. There's an ambush. It's the woman who attacked me at the club. If I'm not with the squad at Bluebrook, then she takes Blaise as her sacrifice instead." His expression went bleak. "And everyone else dies."

What was it like, to have to watch your loved ones perish—not just once but over and over again? Her heart ached for him. After all the things he'd seen, how could he still put on a smile, acting as if he hadn't a care for the world?

"And what happens if you—we—*are* there?" she asked.

"I don't know," he said softly. "I haven't seen that. All I know is that I have to be there."

"Then I will be there too." She gripped his hand, raising their joined fists like warriors swearing an oath-bond. "*We* will not let this happen, Joe. I swear on my honor. Let our enemy set her ambush at this Bluebrook. We are forewarned. We shall lay a trap for her, and catch her in her own snare. She cannot raise this alpha demon if she is in chains herself. Once she is captured, you will be safe."

Something new was dawning across his face. An expression that she realized she'd never seen there before.

Hope.

His hand clenched tight around her own, strong fingers engulfing hers. "And then we can mate."

CHAPTER 13

They could mate. They could *mate*.

Joe couldn't stop grinning. He felt like bursting into song, but unfortunately swinging his crewmates into an impromptu dance number would have been overly odd even for him. He had to settle for whistling cheerfully, with the result that he'd already received sixteen sincere threats of death and/or dismemberment from various colleagues, and it wasn't even nine o'clock in the morning yet.

He didn't care. It was all he could do not to hug every last one of them. He wanted to point Seven out to the whole world, crowing like a rooster: *There, that's my mate, right there! And she wants me!* She wants me!

At the moment, she was at the other end of the storage room, listening with utter attention as Edith explained the difference between MacCleod and Pulaski cutting tools. Seven stood poised and straight, as elegant in her loose-fitting firefighter gear as she had been in her armor.

He just couldn't keep his eyes off her. His *mate*. And there were no secrets between them now.

He wished he could kick his past self. How had he been so asinine as to try to *run* from her? All this time trying to avoid fate, when he should have trusted her strength. If he'd been brave enough to be honest with her from the start, maybe they would already have been mated...

No. He gave himself a mental shake. Even if he had told her years ago, it still wouldn't have been safe to mate yet. The demon-woman was still at large. As long as she was free, Seven was at risk. The only way to be certain that his nightmare vision couldn't come true was to *not* claim her.

After Bluebrook, Joe reminded himself for the thousandth time. Bluebrook was the key to everything, his chance to end the threat for once and for all. He had to wait to claim his mate until after their enemy was safely neutralized.

No! his dragon roared. His animal seethed with impatience, coiling in his soul. *Now, win her now! Shake the sea with songs in her honor! Fill her lair with the rarest of treasures! Offer her the most delicious of delicacies!*

"Earth to Joe." Blaise snapped her fingers by his ear. "What are you doing?"

"Wrestling an overpowering urge to hunt down a tuna," he muttered.

"What?"

"Never mind." He wrenched his gaze away from Seven, turning around. "Did you need something?"

"Yeah, for you to have been ready five minutes ago." Blaise was already fully kitted out in Nomex jacket and pants, her Pulaski slung across her shoulder. "Buck's going to chew our asses out if we're late for line-cutting practice. Are you actually going to put that jacket on, or just commune with its spirit?"

He fumbled with his gear, pulling up his suspenders. "Sorry. Be with you in a sec. Got distracted."

"Uh huh." Blaise leaned to one side, pointedly looking past him. "By your 'just a bodyguard.'"

"Don't know what you mean." He put on his most innocent expression. "She *is* my bodyguard."

Seven hadn't been keen, but he'd convinced her that it was safest to continue to hide their true relationship from the crew. He knew his squadmates too well. If they got a hint of what was really going on, his friends would be trying to bang them together like a precocious kid with a pair of Barbie dolls.

Explaining why he couldn't claim his mate—couldn't claim his mate *yet*—would have required a lot more explanations than Joe was willing to give. Much as he loved his friends, he couldn't risk telling them the truth about his talent. With that many people knowing, sooner or later it would get back to the sea, and the Sea Council, and his parents.

And that would be goodbye to his freedom. It was one thing to let a silly, somewhat embarrassing Crown Prince make himself scarce on land. A silly, somewhat embarrassing Crown Prince who could see the future? That would be an entirely different matter.

He'd be lucky if they didn't *staple* him to the Pearl Throne.

"Uh-huh." Blaise's tone said she wasn't buying his denial for a hot second. "You seem to be spending an awful lot of time staring at your bodyguard's backside."

It was all he could do not to let his attention drift back in that direction now. "Well, you know me. Always an admirer of the female form."

"I'd report you to Buck for workplace harassment." Blaise rolled her eyes. "Except I'd have to turn *her* in as well."

His dragon preened. He couldn't help his grin widening. "Is she checking out my butt?"

"She is checking out your butt *right now*." Blaise smacked him on the arm. "Stop flexing."

"Sorry. Reflex." He shrugged into his jacket. "Anyway, since when is my love life any of your business?"

"Believe me, I wish it wasn't." Blaise wrinkled her nose. "But if you're going to drag your drama to work, then it becomes *all* our business. I know you, Joe. You've never had a relationship that lasted longer than forty-eight hours."

This was, he felt, a little unfair. "Hey, there was that three-day jazz festival, remember? The all-girl trombone group?"

Blaise looked like she was seriously considering setting fire to his hair. "Exactly my point. You don't do serious, Joe. And that poor woman doesn't look like she even knows what casual *is*. I don't want her to get hurt."

"Me neither. Which is exactly why I'm not sleeping with her."

Callum, who was putting on his own gear nearby, looked up sharply. "But—"

The pegasus shifter fell silent again, mouth clamping shut. Blaise pounced on him like a hawk anyway.

"Aha! I knew it. You are so busted, Joe." Blaise advanced on Callum, boxing him into a corner. "Spill it, Cal. You sensed them sneaking into the same bedroom last night, didn't you?"

Callum looked down, round, and up at the ceiling. No escape was forthcoming. He caught Joe's eye, mouth twisting in an apologetic grimace. "Sorry. Can't turn it off."

Sometimes Joe suspected Callum had drawn an even shorter straw than himself when it came to special powers. At least he didn't have his visions *constantly*.

It had to be distracting, always having the exact position and type of every life form in a five-mile radius intruding on your consciousness. Joe was pretty sure that was why Cal didn't talk much.

Normally, the pegasus shifter was as tight-lipped about what he sensed as he was about everything. But all of them had difficulty keeping secrets from Blaise. Even when she was at her sweetest, you couldn't help but be uncomfortably aware of the power that she *could* bring to bear on you. It was like having a nosy little sister with a pet assault tank.

"It's okay, Cal." Joe turned back to Blaise. "For the record, Seven just came in to check I was okay. I was having a nightmare."

"He does have nightmares," Callum confirmed. He looked hopefully at Blaise. "Can I go?"

Blaise pursed her lips, but allowed the pegasus shifter to escape. "So you're claiming nothing happened?"

"That's what I said."

"And can you swear to me that nothing is *going* to happen?"

"Ah, now, who can tell the future?" He struggled to keep his tone light, bantering. "Look, I promise I won't do anything that could hurt the squad, okay?"

Blaise narrowed her eyes at him. "And Seven?"

"I will never hurt her." Despite his best efforts, his dragon's snarl echoed the words like distant thunder. "I *couldn't* hurt her."

Blaise stared at him. "Are you *sure* she's just your bodyguard?"

Rory saved him, inadvertently. The griffin shifter leaned through the doorway, his raised voice ringing from the rafters of the storeroom. "Come on, guys, we were due at the field five minutes ago! What's the holdup?"

"Coming!" Edith yelled back. She passed a Pulaski to Seven. "Sorry, I could talk about this stuff all day."

"And I would gladly listen," Seven said, sounding genuinely interested. "I did not realize there was so much strategy and tactics involved in firefighting. It strikes me as remarkably similar to the arts of war."

"I'd really like to hear about that, but it'll have to wait until later." Edith hefted her pack onto her back. "Joe, can you grab a water cooler? We're going to need to refill our canteens, working in this heat."

He turned to the storeroom shelves, reaching up for one of the large plastic drums. "Sure. No problem."

He pulled the bottle forward, sliding it off the shelf. As he did so, a shaft of sunlight pierced through the transparent plastic, illuminating the water within.

Cold chains around his wrists—

Cool fingers closed on his forearm, pulling him out of the vision. He looked down into Seven's questioning eyes.

"My prince," Seven murmured. "Do you need help with that?"

He forced his lungs to work again. "No. Everything's fine. Don't worry. Everything's going to be fine."

CHAPTER 14

"Rory," Seven said hesitantly at dinner one evening. "May I ask for your opinion on something? Your honest opinion?"

The griffin shifter glanced up from buttering a bread roll. "Sure. Go ahead."

"Does Joe…" Seven searched for the right words. "Does he generally have good ideas?"

Rory's knife paused in mid-air. "We *are* talking about the man who's currently attempting to balance a bottle of hot sauce on his nose, right?"

Across the mess hall, Joe was indeed doing exactly that, egged on by a crowd of firefighters from B and C squads. It seemed to be some kind of bet.

"Pay up, Joe," Tanner, the boss of B squad, called. Edith and Blaise were nearby, laughing along with the rest. "You'll never do it."

"No, wait." Joe crouched low, tipping his head back as far as he could. "I got this, bro. Just watch."

Seven winced at the thump of the bottle bouncing off Joe's forehead yet again.

"I don't mean about things like that," she said to Rory. "Not when he's playing around. Out on the line, in serious situations—does he come up with sensible plans?"

"Sensible?" Rory stared at her. "*Joe?*"

At Rory's side, Wystan cleared his throat. Seven distinctly saw him elbow the griffin shifter.

"Er." Rory crammed a bite of bread into his mouth, clearly in order to give himself time to think. He swallowed. "That is, I wouldn't say that planning is his greatest strength. But he has many other virtues! He's always, uh, great at building team morale."

"An under-rated skill," Wystan said brightly. "Even when things are hard, we can always count on Joe to raise a smile."

"Exactly. And he's strong." Rory flung a somewhat desperate-looking glance at Callum, who was sitting a little way off, silently working his way through a plate of stew. The pegasus shifter twitched as though he'd been poked with a pin. "And determined."

"Loyal," Callum volunteered. It was the first word Seven had heard him speak since the previous morning.

"Right." Rory looked grateful for the input. "We can always depend on Joe to have our backs, no matter what. Even if sometimes we want to shove a sock down his throat."

Wystan elbowed Rory again.

Seven could almost *see* the telepathic messages flying through the air. "Are you three colluding to try to come up with compliments about Joe?"

"What? No," Rory said, extremely unconvincingly. "Definitely not. Just being honest, like you asked."

A slight flush stained Wystan's sharp cheekbones. "It's occurred to us that perhaps, over the course of the past week, you might have come to some mistaken conclusions about him. Based on our…affectionate banter."

"Yesterday you told him that he should grow headfirst in the ground like a turnip," Seven felt compelled to point out.

Wystan coughed. "Yes. Well. In my defense, he'd been singing 'Baby Shark' under his breath for fifty-eight solid minutes. Even a saint would have been driven to strong language."

"You have to bear in mind, we've known each other all our lives," Rory said. He gestured between the three men. "Brothers always tease each other mercilessly, right? It just shows that we love each other."

Callum set down his glass, hard enough to make water slosh onto the table. He stood up, his eyes even colder than usual. "Not always."

He stalked away, abandoning his half-eaten food. Seven stared after him, then turned back to the others.

"Did I offend him somehow?" she asked.

"No, that was me." Rory grimaced, rubbing his forehead. "I wasn't thinking. I forget that not everyone gets on with his brothers as well as I do with my own twin. But that's Cal's story to tell if he wants to, not mine. Anyway, what we mean is, don't take the way we rib Joe seriously. He's honestly a great guy. Anyone should be proud to be his ma—uh."

"Friend," Wystan jumped in, not quite quickly enough. "His friend."

Seven looked at them. They both abruptly became intently interested in their meal trays, avoiding her eyes.

She dropped her head into her palms. "Has *everyone* worked it out?"

"Er. Yes," Wystan said apologetically. "It became somewhat obvious around day two of training. Sorry."

"We've been trying not to say anything because you both seemed to want to keep it a secret." Rory leaned his elbows on the table, lowering his voice—not that it was necessary, given that Joe's antics had everyone else's full attention. "But whatever is going on between you two, the rest of us are starting to get worried."

"Forgive the impertinence, but we couldn't hold our tongues any longer," Wystan said. "Seven, no matter how aggravated we get with him sometimes, he *is* a good man. He may seem your complete opposite, but I have no doubt that fate matched you two up for a reason."

Across the room, Blaise flipped the hot sauce bottle into the air. Fenrir caught it neatly on his nose, balancing on his hind legs. The hellhound's copper eyes rolled to look at Joe, gleaming with satisfaction.

"Woof," Fenrir said, to general cheers.

"Face it, Joe," Blaise said, grinning. "You've lost. Kiss your bacon this week goodbye."

"I'm not giving up yet." Joe plucked the hot sauce bottle from Fenrir's nose. "Let me have one more try."

Rory's voice was a deep, gentle rumble. "He would make you happy, Seven."

"I know," she said softly. Longing caught in her throat, sharp as a fishhook. "And I want to make him happy too. But it's not that simple."

He looked like he didn't have a care in the world. He clowned around for his friends…and not one of them knew why he screamed every night.

Five nights in a row now, she'd wakened to the sound of his agonized voice, shouting her name in sea dragon language. She'd listened, fists clenched, staring into the dark while he screamed. As helpless to save him from his vision as he was helpless to save her *in* his vision.

He was still seeing her die. Every night. Again and again.

She forced herself to look away from Joe, turning back to Rory and Wystan. "Joe and I do want to be together. But we have no choice but to wait."

"That may not be wise," Wystan said. "I don't wish to alarm you, but it isn't natural for a shifter to take things slowly when they meet their mate. In fact, it can be both psychologically and physically unhealthy. The mating instinct sets off a powerful cascade of hormones."

Oh, she was only too aware of *that*. "I appreciate your concern. And I assure you, we have a plan."

Rory and Wystan looked at each other.

"A…Joe plan?" Rory said, cautiously.

She fidgeted with her fork. "Yes. Which was why I was asking… but never mind. I have faith that he knows what he's doing. And in any event, it's not my place to question the Crown Prince of Atlantis."

"Maybe, but it is *definitely* your place to yell at your mate when he's being dumb." Rory quirked an eyebrow. "If you need some tips on that, I'm sure Edith would be happy to help. Ask her sometime."

"Or Candice." Wystan's expression went soft and fond. "She is *marvelous* at yelling."

Having met Wystan's strong-willed mate a few days ago, Seven could believe it. "I will…bear that in mind."

"Seriously, do." Rory blew out his breath. "Look, Seven. We just don't want to see you two making the same mistakes that we did. I hope Joe's plan doesn't involve waiting around for a demonic attack to force the two of you together. I can tell you, it's considerably less romantic than it sounds."

Seven had just taken a bite of stew. She choked. "Have you been talking to Joe?"

From the puzzled glances the two men exchanged, they hadn't. "We've tried," Rory said. "But whatever's going on, he *really* doesn't want to talk about it."

"For a man of many words, he's remarkably good at saying nothing," Wystan agreed. "Seven, please, will you tell us what's troubling you? We only want to help."

It was tempting. More than tempting. Over the past week of training, she'd come to fully appreciate the tight-knit strength of the squad. They weren't just colleagues, or even friends. They were *family*.

And they were inviting her to step into that circle. She longed for that, almost as much as she longed for her mate.

She looked down at her congealing stew. "I am sorry. You have all been so kind to me, and I truly wish that I could repay that with honesty. But it is not my secret to tell. If Joe will not speak of it, I cannot either."

Rory sighed. "Okay. Well, we'll keep working on him. But if you change your mind and want to talk, just let us know."

"HA!" Across the room, Joe straightened, eyes crossed and arms out-flung triumphantly. The hot sauce bottle balanced, cap down, on the end of his nose. "Behold, my bros! I retain my bacon!"

"What in dog's name is going on here?" Buck cut through the crowd, scowling. He shoved Joe's shoulder, sending the bottle clattering to the ground. "Are you a hotshot or a motherloving performing seal? All of you, get your butts on benches. I've got an announcement."

The group broke up, hotshots all scattering to their seats. Joe plunked himself down next to Seven, still beaming from ear to ear. He winked at her, and stole Callum's slice of peach pie as the pegasus shifter also returned to his place.

Buck jumped up onto a bench at the front of the room. "All right, you lot, listen up. Play time's over. We've got our first callout of the season."

A chill went down Seven's spine as general whoops and cheers filled the air. She glanced sidelong at Joe. The smile had slid off his face. Under the table, his hand found hers, gripping tight.

"It's a nice local one, too," Buck continued. "Well, relatively speaking. It's in-state at least, though only barely. A forest fire's been called in up north, right at the border. Kootenai National Forest."

Seven started. Her eyes met Joe's. They showed the same mingled relief and disappointment that she felt.

Not Bluebrook. Not yet.

"It's lovely middle-of-nowhere wilderness, so I hope everyone's got their hiking boots oiled and ready." Buck paused, his gaze lingering on the shifters of A-squad. "Initial reports say it looks like it was started by a freak lightning strike."

Now it was everyone else's turn to exchange meaningful glances. Blaise mouthed the word *Thunderbird?* at Buck. The Superintendent lifted one shoulder in the slightest of shrugs.

Buck's tone turned brisk again. "Now, there's a local team already handling initial attack, so we don't have to drop everything and scramble. But we've got orders to go in to support, so we're rolling out first thing in the morning, four am sharp. Yes, *four*," he raised his voice as a chorus of groans went up. "And you'd better pray I don't catch any of you napping. So go get some sleep while you can. You're going to need it."

Seven let out her breath as people started to get up. Much as she was anxious to get the coming confrontation at Bluebrook over and done with, it was a relief that it wasn't going to be her first callout ever.

"A practice wildfire," she murmured to Joe. "That's good, isn't it?"

He didn't reply. He was still gripping her hand, hard. She realized he'd frozen in position, staring into her glass of water.

Her blood turned to ice. She didn't know whether or not to break him out of the vision. His eyes moved sightlessly, following something that only he could see. She could taste his rising distress.

"Joe?" she whispered.

He blinked at last. He looked up at her, his pupils black holes in his grim face.

"We can't go," he said hoarsely. "Our squad. They mustn't go. We have to find a way to keep them here."

CHAPTER 15

"You could just tell them," Seven said from behind him.

Joe automatically shook his head, though she couldn't see the gesture. He kept his flashlight trained on the trickle of engine coolant draining from the radiator. "Buck wouldn't believe me. He'd think it was some kind of joke, or just me trying to get out of hard work. As far as he's concerned, I'm a lazy idiot. To be fair, he's not wrong."

"You are neither of those things."

"Says the woman who had to literally hit me over the head to stop me from running away from the best thing that ever happened to me. And trust me, I would much rather be sipping cocktails on a beach somewhere with you right now than under this truck." The steady flow of coolant had slowed to a drip. "I think we're nearly there. Just a few more minutes. We still good?"

"No sign that we've been noticed." A slight hint of strain in Seven's voice betrayed her anxiety. "All the lights are still dark in the cabins. But Joe, you should tell the truth to our friends. They'll believe you, even if Buck won't."

"Which would just put them between the devil and the deep blue sea. I can't ask the squad to go up against Buck just on my word."

Seven's tone sharpened. "That is not the real reason, and you know it."

He really couldn't hide anything from her. "Seven, I can't risk it. Rory, Blaise, and Wystan are all really close to their families. Rory's dad is literally a walking lie detector, and he's best friends with *my* dad. It would only be a matter of time before everyone in Atlantis found out."

"And would that be so bad?"

"Well, for a start, I doubt the Sea Council would be keen on a precious Prince-Seer spending his summers running into forest fires."

"Perhaps not. But the Pearl Empress has the final word. You're the Crown Prince, Joe. You're her *son*. Nothing could make you more precious to her. Yet here you are, putting your life at risk. Do you truly think your talent would change that? Make her lock you up in the Imperial treasure vault?"

The slow drip of the coolant echoed in the silence.

"No," he admitted at last.

Seven's voice softened. "Joe. I know you don't want your talent to be the only part of you that people see. But right now people *aren't* seeing you, the real you. Just the glitter and sparkle of the surface."

"I *am* glittery and sparkly."

She nudged him in the side with the toe of her boot. "Yes. But that is not *all* you are. I wish you wouldn't hide that."

"I don't have to hide it from you. That's enough for me." Joe slid out from underneath the crew transport. "There, that should do it. This baby won't be going anywhere for a while now."

Seven drew in a breath through her mouth, tasting the air. "The entire area is covered our scent. And Fenrir's nose is as sensitive as mine. Like it or not, our friends will realize that we were responsible for this."

"No, they won't." He bent to pull out the drip tray he'd used to catch the coolant, dabbling his gloved fingers in the oily green liquid. He waved his hand at Seven "How does this stuff smell to you?"

Seven wrinkled her nose. "Terrible."

"Perfect." Joe flicked coolant around the vehicle, making sure to liberally douse the area where he'd been lying. "Is that enough to cover our tracks?"

Seven tested the air again, and nodded, grudgingly. She held out the empty bottle that they'd brought so he could pour the remaining coolant into it. "I still think you should tell them the truth."

"I know." He screwed the cap on. "Come on, let's get out of here before our luck runs out."

They headed back toward their cabin, Seven automatically falling into step a little behind him. In Atlantis, he'd always hated being followed about by the ever-present royal guard, but it was different with Seven. Her quiet, watchful presence at his back was comforting.

They snuck through the silent base like guilty teenagers after curfew. Once they were safely back in their cabin, Joe went to dispose of the coolant.

Seven hovered in the bathroom doorway as he poured the oily liquid down the toilet. "Is that safe?"

"According to the local waste disposal authority, yep." Joe flushed the toilet. "I checked. I didn't want to just leave the bottle lying around. Can't risk someone finding it tomorrow and using it to get the truck running again too quickly."

Seven sighed. "I just hope this buys us enough time."

He looked down into the swirling water.

Wystan, his hands outstretched, a sparkling shield springing up to cover the base. Rory, rising into the air, beak open wide in a scream of challenge. And his own hands shifting into talons, scales wrapping his skin, a single thought filling his mind: Thank the sea we were here.

The vision popped like a soap bubble. He shook himself, the remembered relief and rage fading.

"It's okay now," he said. "We've done enough."

Seven blinked at him. "Did you just see the future in a *toilet?*"

"I told you I can get visions anywhere." He went to wash his hands in the sink. "Anyway, I think we've made it come true. It felt…thin, before, like a dream right before you wake up. It's more real now. It's hard to explain. You should get some rest. It's going to be a busy day tomorrow."

"Apparently." Seven hesitated. He could see her reflection in the mirror, watching him. "Joe, you need to sleep too. Is there anything that…helps?"

"Stops my nightmares, you mean?" He couldn't help a huff of ironic laughter. "Oh yeah. There's one thing. And much as I'd love to do it with you, that's really not an option."

Seven's mouth dropped open. "You mean—*sex?*"

A bolt of nerves twisted his stomach. They hadn't talked about the elephant in the room—or rather, his past—before. He'd had the impression that Seven had been trying not to think about it. He'd much rather not think about it himself…but he had to be honest with her.

"There's a reason for my reputation." He turned around, forcing himself to face Seven. "I had to sleep with women to be able to sleep at all."

Her grey eyes went wide and startled. "*That's* why you slept around? To stop you from dreaming?"

"Yeah. It wasn't even really the sex. It's just that most women won't let you spend the night snuggling without orgasms first."

Her eyebrows did a complicated dance, conveying a cocktail of astonishment, disbelief, and exasperation. "You do realize that it would have been considerably easier to recruit a few understanding, casual long-term partners to meet your needs, do you not?"

"Uh, well." His hands felt large and awkward. He shoved them into his pockets. "Stopping my visions wasn't the *only* reason I…did what I did. I was also doing my best to trash my reputation."

"Well, you certainly succeeded there. I won't tell you what the knights have to say about you." Seven shook her head, slowly. "*Why*, Joe? Are you truly so desperate to avoid your destiny? Were you hoping that the Sea Council might eventually declare you unfit for the Pearl Throne?"

"Well, that would be a nice bonus, but it wasn't the Sea Council's opinion that I cared about." He looked down, not quite able to meet her eyes. "It was yours."

She stared at him.

He hunched his shoulders. "I behaved awfully because I wanted you to despise me. I'd seen in my visions how honorable and noble you are. I was doing everything in my power to avoid meeting you, but…I wanted to make sure that if I failed, you wouldn't want me."

Her eyes narrowed. Her feet moved, ever so slightly, into a combat stance. He had a sudden new appreciation for just how terrifying she would be to face in a fight.

"Let me make sure I understand this correctly," she said, in a level voice. "You deliberately went for the most bone-headed and inconvenient way of getting enough sleep, purely in order to offend me?"

"Yeah." He swallowed, hard. "I'm really sorry, Seven. Even though I thought we could never be together, I shouldn't have betrayed you. I should have been stronger—"

"Stop," she interrupted. She pointed toward his bedroom. "Wait there."

The butterflies in his stomach grew to monster-movie proportions as she turned on her heel, stalking away. "Seven. Seven, please, don't walk out on me. Let's talk about this."

"I said, wait there. I'll be back." She slipped out of the cabin, leaving him staring at the closing door.

She couldn't have been gone more than five minutes, but it felt like five hours. It was all he could do not to throw himself at her like a golden retriever when she re-appeared at the door. Her arms were full of yellow fabric.

"Here." She handed him his firefighter jacket and pants. "Put these on."

"Uhhh…why?"

She put her hands on her hips. She was already fully kitted out in her own gear. "You said it wasn't so much the sex as the intimacy afterward, correct?"

"I guess so." His face heated. He couldn't believe he was discussing this with his mate. "I, um, learned that just having sex and then going back to my own bed didn't stop me from dreaming, anyway."

"Good." She nodded at the uniform in his hands. "Then we are going to snuggle. With protection."

It was his turn to stare at her, slack-jawed.

She folded her arms. One foot tapped dangerously. "Put your gear on, Joe."

He did so. It took him two attempts to get the zips fastened, his fingers were so numb. His heartbeat thundered in his ears.

"This is a terrible idea," he managed to get out, as Seven led him into the darkened bedroom.

"This equipment is designed to protect people from forest fires." She pulled him down to the bed, curling up against his back. Her arm slipped around his waist. "I think it can withstand the heat of two shifters."

Joe wasn't so sure. Even through two layers of Nomex, he was acutely aware of every line of her body. The faint warmth of her breath against the back of his neck throbbed in his groin.

"I suddenly have a new understanding of why women paid so much money to see me dance in this stuff," he muttered. "I think I'm developing a fetish."

Her arm tightened around him. She pressed her lips against his nape in a soft kiss.

"Sleep well, Joe," she whispered in his ear.

And, somewhat to his surprise, he did.

CHAPTER 16

Seven had thought she'd seen the full range of Buck's volcanic temper. He'd never made the slight attempt to hold back his ire, after all. Whether it was a sloppy fire line or a badly sharpened tool, he would express himself freely, creatively, and at length.

Now she realized that she'd never seen him actually *angry*.

His face was hard as stone. His hands were clasped behind his back. His voice was perfectly level.

"Sabotage?" he asked.

Her shark sank silently into the depths of her soul, still and quiet as though a greater predator was passing overhead. Next to her, Joe shifted his weight, just enough so that his arm bumped against her shoulder.

It's all right, the brief contact said. *I'm here. Everything's going to be fine.*

"It's not impossible," Blaise said from the depths of the engine. "But why would someone go to all that trouble just to temporarily inconvenience us?"

"There's no sign that anyone broke in last night, Chief," Rory said.

"Fenrir's scouted around, but the only scents around base are ours. And Callum would have woken up if someone was sneaking around."

Buck turned to the pegasus shifter. "You didn't sense anything?"

Seven's heart jumped into her mouth, but Callum just shook his head. "No intruders."

Buck stared hard at Callum for a long moment. Cal gazed calmly back, expression as blank as always.

"Hmm." Buck turned back to Blaise, and Seven started breathing again. "You say you can fix this?"

"The cap just got knocked loose." Blaise emerged from under the hood. She wiped the back of her hand across her forehead, leaving a greasy smear. "All the engine coolant drained out, but that's easily replaced. It'll take a while, though. I don't have any in stock. I'll have to go into town and wait for the garage to open. And once I've refilled the coolant, I'll need to run the engine for a bit to make sure all the air bubbles are out."

A muscle ticked in Buck's jaw. "How soon can you get A-squad on the road?"

Blaise shrugged. "Maybe around midday?"

"We won't be too far behind you, Chief," Rory said. "Look, the other squad vehicles are already loaded up and ready to go. We'll lose even more time if we try to swap everything round now. You take the rest of the crew, and we'll catch up as soon as we can."

Buck subjected Rory to the same long, penetrating look that he'd used on Callum. Then he turned his head to consider the rest of the squad. Seven braced every muscle, trying not to flinch as his gaze swept over her.

"Fine," Buck said at last. "Keep me updated. Tanner, Jessica! We're moving out!"

The B and C squad leaders scrambled into their waiting crew transports. With a final curt nod, Buck swung himself into his own Jeep. The three vehicles roared away, kicking up plumes of dust.

We did it. Seven took a deep breath, despite the choking fumes. *We got away with it—*

"So." The dust settled, revealing Rory's broad form, now squarely planted in front of Joe. She'd never seen the griffin shifter's golden eyes so cold and hard. "You two going to tell us what's really going on?"

~

"I can't," Joe said, for what felt like the hundredth time. "Bros, I really wish I could. But I *can't* tell you."

"So, what, you just playfully and randomly sabotaged our truck?" Blaise shoved him with both hands. She was so angry, he could feel the searing heat of her palms even through his protective jacket. "This isn't a joke, Joe!"

"You owe the courtesy of an explanation, at least." The icy politeness in Wystan's voice could have frozen the sea. "We know you did it."

"I sensed you." Callum stood next to the unicorn shifter, arms folded, equally cold. "Last night. Just never thought you might be doing something that I should stop."

"We lied to Buck for you," Rory snarled, his hands clenched into fists. "And now you don't even have the decency to tell us what's going on?"

"S-Stop!" Edith's hands clamped over her ears, her face twisting in distress. "Please!"

The guilt he felt at lying to the squad was nothing compared to the shame that washed through him. All the angry, overlapping voices must have been pure torture to Edith's autistic senses.

The entire squad instantly quieted as well, backing off. Rory enfolded his mate in a tight hug, shooting Joe a vicious glare over the top of her head.

"I'm sorry, Edith," Rory said, his voice softer but no less dangerous. "Maybe you'd better go wait somewhere else while we settle this."

"No." Edith was still pale and shaking, but she pushed herself free from Rory's embrace. "I w-want to know too. Joe. Please. We're your friends."

The hopeful faith in her face hurt even more than the others' anger. "I can't explain," he said yet again, miserably. "I wish I could. All I can do is ask you to trust me."

Rory shook his head. "I'm sorry, Joe, but that's not good enough. One last chance. Tell us, or I'll *make* you tell us."

He'd been dreading this. Joe clenched his jaw, bracing himself for the whip-strike of Rory's alpha voice.

"Rory, no!" Edith grabbed Rory's arm. "You can't. You promised."

The griffin shifter gently disentangled himself from his mate. "I don't want to use my power on our friends, but they're not leaving me any choice."

"Bring it, bro," Joe said, with a bravado he didn't entirely feel. He called on his dragon's strength, imagining his mind armored in its scales. He had to resist Rory's attempts to compel the truth out of him, he *had* to—

Rory's eyes narrowed. He stared hard at Joe for a long second… and then turned to Seven. The griffin shifter took a deep breath, his voice dropping into the bone-rattling growl of the alpha voice. "Seven—"

Protective fury drowned shame. Joe surged forward, putting himself between the griffin shifter and Seven. His fingers crooked, nails ready to sharpen into claws. *"Leave my mate alone."*

ENOUGH! Fenrir let out a sharp bark, echoed his mental roar. The hellhound shoved between Joe and Rory, his body swelling into his true hulking, bear-sized form. *Stone Bitch is right. No more snapping and snarling. We are pack!*

Rory's golden eyes bored into Joe's. "I thought we were."

We are pack, Fenrir repeated stubbornly. *When one hunter howls to turn to follow a trail, pack turns, no matter if no one else has scented the prey. Pack trusts pack, otherwise nothing but hungry bellies and crying cubs. Seasnake has not led us wrong before. Heed his howl now.*

"Please," Seven said. She came forward, drawing her stunsword out from beneath her jacket. Rory tensed, but she just knelt down in front of him, on both knees, head bowed. "You can trust Joe. I will give you my oath on that."

Alone out of all of them, he knew what she was doing. His heart contracted in his chest. "Seven. Don't."

"I won't claim to understand all the intricacies of sea dragon culture, but I've visited Atlantis enough times to know how much honor means to knights." Rory released Edith, hunkering down so he was eye-level with Seven. "I believe that you wouldn't make that sort of offer lightly. Will you swear that you and Joe have a good reason not to tell us what's really going on? And promise that your secret won't hurt anyone?"

"Yes." Seven offered Rory her sheathed sword, across her palms. "I swear on my honor that Joe is working for the good of all, no matter how strange his actions may seem. I swear that no one will come to harm. I swear that I trust him, and that you can trust him too. By my blade and my blood I swear it."

A formal oath-binding wasn't just empty words. Joe's skin prickled with the rush of power that swept over them all like an invisible wave.

He could tell that the others could sense it too. Callum and Wystan both started, looking round. Blaise hugged herself as if she was suddenly cold. The fur rose down Fenrir's spine.

Rory gazed at Seven for a moment, brow furrowing. Then he looked up at Joe. "You'd better be worthy of this lady."

"I'm not," Joe said, honestly. "But I'll do my very best. I really am sorry, Rory. If I could explain what was going on, I would."

"I believe you." Rory touched his arm, in a brief gesture of forgiveness that Joe knew he didn't deserve. The griffin shifter's voice turned brisk and businesslike. "So, do you need me to call Buck and come up with more excuses?"

There wasn't any water nearby that he could use to check the future. He closed his eyes for a moment, concentrating on remembering what he'd seen earlier. They'd been in the car park, the sun still rising in the east, barely past the tops of the trees...

"It's okay. I only needed to delay us for a little while." Joe shrugged apologetically at Blaise. "Sorry, you really will need to go into town. I flushed the coolant down the toilet."

Blaise shot him a glare that said that she wasn't going to forgive him in a hurry for any of this. "Fine. But you're going to be scrubbing out *my* toilet for the rest of the season. I'll head off now."

"Wait," Rory said as Blaise headed for the door. "That Lupa woman is still out there. The one that attacked Joe, that he thought might be possessed. Joe, is all this something to do with her?"

He nodded. "I can't say for certain, but I've got a hunch it is."

"Then none of us should be on our own, just in case." Rory turned back to Blaise. "Take Fenrir and Wystan with you."

Wystan, his hands upraised, his shield springing into life...

"Not Wystan," Joe blurted out. "Cal should go. Wystan has to stay here."

Wystan's eyebrows rose. "And why would that be?"

Because that is how Seasnake saw it, Fenrir said, matter-of-factly. *Come, Shadowhorse. We must hunt.*

And the hellhound trotted off, leaving Joe staring after his waving tail.

~

Joe puzzled over Fenrir's statement for the next hour. It would have been longer, except that he abruptly had a more pressing concern.

Because, just as the sun cleared the tops of the pines, the Thunderbird crashed into the car park.

CHAPTER 17

Seven sensed it first.

For lack of anything better to do, she'd been running through sword-drills in the empty car park, while Joe paced endlessly around the perimeter. She would have liked to talk to him privately—especially about Fenrir's peculiar statement—but there wasn't an opportunity. Rory hadn't let the two of them out of his sight all morning.

The squad boss was over by the useless truck, along with Wystan and Edith, unpacking and inventorying the squad's supplies one-by-one. It was busywork, and they all knew it, but nobody said anything. Tension filled the air like a thunderstorm.

So much so, in fact, that it took her a minute to notice the *actual* thunderstorm approaching.

It wasn't until her shark tugged at her attention that she realized the sour, electric tang in her mouth was more than just her own anxiety. She looked up.

Though the sky immediately overhead was still clear and sunny, dark storm clouds gathered on the horizon. Even as she watched, they thickened, boiling and churning. It was like time-lapse photography… except that it was happening right in front of her eyes.

"Joe." She automatically took up a defensive position in front of him, stunsword drawn and ready. "Look."

He did so, and swore in sea dragon. "So *that's* what we're waiting for. *Rory!*"

Rory's head snapped up. He took one glance at the sky and blurred into griffin form. He crouched on his feline back legs, golden wings spreading.

"No, wait!" Joe yelled. He charged for the griffin shifter, catching a handful of feathers. "Let it come to us."

Rory's tufted ears flattened against his head. He let out a hiss, his front talons digging at the ground.

"Please, bro." Joe put his hands on either side of the griffin's huge golden beak, turning it to face him. "Trust me."

Rory hissed again, but his wings dropped, no longer poised to launch into the air. He jerked his head out of Joe's grasp, turning to look at Edith.

"Like *hell* I will," Edith said indignantly, in response to whatever private telepathic message her mate had sent her. She snatched up a chainsaw, holding it poised with her hand ready to yank the chain. "I'm not leaving you to face danger alone."

"If we are in any danger." Wystan's eyes were fixed on the sky. He had his hands outstretched, but hadn't yet flung up a shield. "Which we may not be. Joe's right. Let's see what the Thunderbird wants."

Seven stared at the rapidly approaching cloud bank. Deep within, lit by flashes of internal lightning, she glimpsed a darker shape.

"That's the Thunderbird?" she asked.

"Yes," Wystan replied. "It's a powerful and unpredictable being, but it has been our ally in the past. I believe it will not harm us now."

The wind was picking up. She turned her face into it, breathing deep. Tasting.

Rage and pain and fear. The focused, knife-sharp fear of a creature fleeing for its life...

"Maybe," she said. "But it's not alone."

She could hear them now. A distant, feral, high-pitched yelping.

Edith frowned, hearing it too. "Is that—wild geese?"

Joe swore again. "Wystan, get ready! Shields up the instant it hits the ground, understand?"

Wystan opened his mouth, but there was no time for further questions. Hail abruptly lashed all their faces. Rory flung his wings around them all, shielding them from the stinging ice.

Through Rory's feathers, Seven glimpsed the Thunderbird falling out of the sky. Lightning crackled around it, illuminating the vast shape in sharp flashes. For a horrific second, she was certain it was going to smash into the base like a meteorite.

At the last moment, the Thunderbird spread its wings. The dark pinions spanned the entire width of the car park. They were all knocked off their feet by the downdraft as it fought to control its descent.

"NOW, WYSTAN!" Joe roared.

Wystan's shield sparkled into life, covering the entire base. It wasn't a second too soon. Seven heard a howl of pain as something thumped into the shimmering barrier.

A howl of pain that she recognized.

"It's the pack!" she shouted. Through the distortion of Wystan's shield, she could just make out their dark, canine forms and burning red eyes. "These are the creatures I fought off before!"

"You might have mentioned that they could *fly!*" Edith yelled back.

"They didn't, before!"

The creatures circled Wystan's barrier, searching for a way in. They ran on thin air as easily as on the ground. It was like being at the center of a nightmarish tornado made of bristling fur and bared teeth.

"I can't hold this much longer." Wystan's voice was tight with strain. His arms shook as he struggled to maintain his shield against the onslaught. "Rory! You have to fly Edith and Seven out of here!"

Seven whirled, fully prepared to smack the griffin shifter with her stunsword if he tried to snatch her up. "I'm not leaving my mate."

"We can't fight this many demons!" Wystan's arms shook as he struggled to maintain his shield. "They could possess any one of us with a single bite. We have to—"

"They don't have horns," Edith interrupted. Her sharp eyes darted from place to place, tracking each beast. "Look at them, none of them have horns! They aren't possessed!"

Edith was right. Seven looked at the hulking, canine shapes, and *knew*.

After all, she'd seen one close up, only that morning.

"They're hellhounds," she breathed.

"Oh, for the love of sweet little fishes." Joe slapped his forehead, looking simultaneously relieved and aggrieved. "Buck was right. He is going to be *insufferable*. Well, at least we'll be alive for him to be smug at…stand back, bros. I got this."

He shimmered, expanding. Seven had to leap back as he shifted into dragon form. He reared up, horns brushing the top of Wystan's shield. His tail swept round to protect them all in a barrier of gleaming turquoise scales, each one shining like a star sapphire.

His enormous jaws opened, exposing razor-sharp teeth. He roared.

And, despite everything, Seven felt her mouth twitch in a smile.

Because he'd shouted, in sea dragon language: *Come at me, bros!*

The yelping snarls of the hellhound pack faltered. One by one, they descended to the ground, massing in a tight, uncertain knot. They milled around too much for Seven to get an exact count, but she didn't think there could be more than a dozen of them.

An enormous creature pushed to the front of the pack, snapping at the others. It dwarfed them all, a pale iceberg among the sea of the smaller black forms.

It wasn't a hellhound.

A shock went through her at the sight. Its body was lean and wolf-like, with shaggy white fur…but the creature's head was a living skull, crowned with a stag's branching antlers. Eyes like frozen stars burned in the empty sockets.

Behind her, Wystan swore, sharp and profane. It was the first time she'd ever heard the usually mild-mannered unicorn shifter curse.

"A wendigo," Wystan breathed. She could taste his horror and disbelief, bitter on her tongue. "They have a wendigo. Joe, *be careful*."

The wendigo wasn't all the pack had. A proud, straight-backed figure perched on the white beast's hulking shoulders. Her long red scarf streamed out behind her like a war-banner.

Seven's hand tightened on her stunsword. Even through the swirling distortion of Wystan's shield, she knew that elegant, arrogant profile.

It was Lupa. The woman from the club. The one who'd tried to kidnap Joe.

For a long moment, the woman just stared up at the sea dragon. Although she still wore her red silk scarf, her hair was unbound, no longer held back with a headband. There was some kind of mark or tattoo on her forehead, but Seven couldn't tell what it was at this distance.

The wendigo bared massive, bear-like teeth. Despite the hot summer sun, its breath steamed in the air as though it was the depths of winter. Frost glittered on its thick fur. Even through Wystan's shield, Seven could feel the bone-numbing cold of its breath as it roared.

Joe roared right back, spreading his iridescent turquoise ruff like a cobra about to strike. For all the wendigo's eerie power, he was far larger than it. He raised one foreleg, displaying talons like scythes. Seven knew that the instant Wystan's shield failed, he'd be on the hellhound pack like a wrecking ball.

Lupa knew that too. Frustration was written all over her face. She tipped her head back, letting out another of those unearthly howls. Her steed sprang into air, massive paws somehow finding purchase on nothing. The entire pack followed, streaming into the air.

Rory shrank back into human form as the pack's yelping calls faded into the distance. He touched Edith's cheek, cupping her face. "Are you okay?"

"It's not me you should be worried about," Edith replied, though Seven could see her hands shaking on her chainsaw. "Wystan?"

"I'm fine." Wystan's shield faded away as he dropped his hands at last. He swayed, then sat down, rather abruptly. "Or rather, I *will* be fine. Nothing a nice cup of tea won't cure, anyway. I'm more concerned about our large feathered friend over there."

The Thunderbird was a vast, panting pile. When she'd seen it in the heart of the storm, its plumage had been lit up in electric-white geometric patterns, but now the markings had faded to a dim glow. It had managed to fold one wing, but the other splayed out like a broken fan. Bright red blood trickled down the storm-grey feathers.

"It's hurt," Edith said. "That's why it came to us. It needs help."

Rory held her back as she tried to move toward the creature. "It needs professional help. Wystan, is Candice at the ranch?"

"Yes, and I've already contacted her telepathically." Wystan smiled. "She should be here any—"

A bright flash of white light flared at his side. It faded to reveal a stocky woman with short blonde hair and a brisk, no-nonsense expression. Old burn scars marked one side of her face, disappearing under the collar of her checked flannel shirt. She carried a large first aid kit in one hand and a tranquillizer rifle in the other.

She was also flanked by a pair of unicorns.

The smaller one, who was barely more than a foal, pranced to Wystan's side. She nudged at him with her velvety muzzle, snorting. Seven was no expert in equine body language, but even she could tell that the unicorn was concerned.

"It's all right, Flash." Wystan patted the young unicorn's soft flank. "I'm just tired. Thank you for bringing Candice and your mother here so fast."

Candice and the other unicorn were already approaching the stricken Thunderbird. The huge creature stirred weakly, turning its head. Its eyes were the electric white of lightning, without pupil or iris. They fixed on Candice and the unicorn in an unreadable, alien stare.

Joe was still in dragon form. A deep, warning growl rumbled in his throat. Seven could tell that he was poised and ready to defend Candice if the Thunderbird so much as twitched.

"It's all right, buddy." Candice spoke directly to the Thunderbird, her voice soft and gentle. She edged toward the creature, holding out her hand, her body language loose and unthreatening. "We're here to help you. Don't be scared. We just want to help."

The Thunderbird's eyelids lowered, hiding that burning, captive storm. It opened its injured wing a little wider, holding it away from its body.

"That's it." Candice ducked under the enormous pinions without a trace of hesitation. "Let's see where you're hurt. Sunrise?"

The unicorn mare joined Candice, though she seemed to be keeping a wary eye on the Thunderbird's massive talons. Candice ran her hands through the arm-length feathers covering the Thunderbird's body, parting them to expose savage bite-marks.

Sunrise's horn lit with a pale golden glow. The unicorn dipped her head, lightly touching the tip of her horn to the nearest wound.

"I know it feels weird." Candice stroked the Thunderbird as a tremor ran through its massive form. "Just stay still so Sunrise can heal you. There's a brave guy."

"How do you know it's a male?" Edith asked.

"To be honest, I don't. Short of sticking my arm up its cloaca, there's no way to tell. And I'm not going to test its forbearance *that* far." Candice patted the Thunderbird absently. "Sorry if I'm misgendering you."

The Thunderbird made a pained, rumbling wheeze that somehow sounded amused. Its head drooped down again, the huge beak resting along the ground.

"Any idea how long it'll take to get our friend here back on his feet?" Rory asked.

Candice shook her head, still busy examining the Thunderbird's injuries. "No idea yet. The big guy is banged up pretty badly. I'm sure that Sunrise will be able to heal him, but I don't think she'll be able to do it all at once. There are limits to how much she can do before she has to rest and recover her strength."

"I was afraid you'd say that." Rory's mouth tightened as he gazed at the Thunderbird. "Flash, can you teleport something this big?"

The young unicorn perked up. She straightened, tossing her mane proudly...and then hesitated. She eyed the vast bulk of the Thunderbird. Her ears slowly drooped.

"Don't worry, Flash." Wystan stroked the crestfallen unicorn. "It takes courage to admit when you can't do something. We'll manage."

Rory sighed. "Well, we'll just have to hope that the rest of the crew doesn't return too soon. I'm going to go call Buck and let him know what's going on. As much as I can, anyway."

"Wait." Edith caught her mate's sleeve, but her face turned up toward Joe. "This is why you broke our car, isn't it? Somehow, you knew that the Thunderbird would need our help."

Ridiculous though it was to try to shield an entire *dragon*, Seven stepped between Joe and the others. "I gave you all my oath that he had reasons for his actions. You promised to trust him in return. Now you have proof that he is indeed acting honorably. I beg you, do not question him further. He has told you as much as he can."

Joe dipped his horned head. Seven thought that it was a nod of agreement—but it kept dipping, his vast bulk shimmering and shrinking. In seconds, he was back in human form. His expression was set and serious, all the light-hearted laughter gone.

"No," he said. "I haven't."

CHAPTER 18

"I'm sorry, I'm still stuck right at the beginning." Blaise stared at him. "You can seriously *see the future?*"

Once again, they were sitting round the fire pit in front of the mess hall. He'd waited until Blaise and the others had returned from their errand before finally confessing everything. It had taken...a while.

Now the sun was sliding down the sky, gilding everything with warm golden light. The Thunderbird was a dark, hunched shape at the edge of the car park, head hidden under one massive wing. Sunrise had healed its wounds enough to stabilize it, but it wasn't going to be in any shape to fly for a while. The unicorn mare was sleeping now as well, her head resting in Candice's lap, Flash snuggled up against her side.

Joe felt about ready for a nap himself. Explaining his visions had been exhausting...and curiously freeing. Even though he couldn't bring himself to look any of his friends in the eye, it felt like something had unknotted inside him.

"Yeah," he mumbled. "Sorry."

"What for?" Edith asked.

"For not telling you all earlier."

Didn't have to. Alone out of all the of the group, Fenrir looked completely unsurprised. He sprawled on his belly, gnawing complacently at a large bone that he'd brought back from his trip into town with Blaise. *Already knew.*

"Yeah, and that's something we need to talk about, bro." Joe remembered Fenrir's enigmatic comment earlier. "When did you find out?"

Fenrir flicked his ears. *Always known.*

"Well, you might have shared that with the rest of us," Rory said to the hellhound.

Did, Birdcat. Fenrir rolled his copper eyes. *Told you he was Seasnake.*

Blaise frowned. "How does your nickname for Joe relate to his talent? Not all sea dragons can do what he can do."

Not sea-like-water. Fenrir sounded faintly exasperated, as though all this should have been obvious. *See-like-eyes. Seesnake. Because he does.*

"And apparently I'm not the only one." Joe stared at the hellhound. "You gave me that nickname when we first met, before you knew anything about me at all. So how in the name of sweet little fishes did you work out my talent?"

Two legs. Fenrir went back to chewing on his bone, turning his muzzle to get a good grip on it with his back teeth. *Always asking silly questions. Can smell, Seesnake. Like any wolf. No trick to it.*

What is he? Joe thought, not for the first time. From the expressions on everyone else's faces, the rest of the squad was wondering the same thing. Fenrir was no ordinary hellhound, and it wasn't just his huge size and inability to shift.

Rory shook his head. "Fenrir, sometime we really have to track down where you came from before that wolf pack found you. Don't suppose you can help with that, Joe? Can you look into the past as well as the future?"

"Sorry, bro. It's one way only. And it's not under my control. I just see what fate wants me to see."

"And, Fenrir aside, none of us had the faintest idea," Wystan said.

"Joe, we're your oldest friends. Why on earth didn't you tell us any of this before?"

The puzzled hurt in Wystan's green eyes made his throat tighten. "Because...because I was scared."

"That we wouldn't believe you?" Blaise stretched out one leg to kick him, gently, in the shin. "Idiot."

"Not that. I was scared—I *am* scared—that if I told even one person, eventually everyone else would find out too. My parents. The Sea Council. I was scared that they'd all start looking to me for guidance." His voice cracked. "Leadership."

"You are the Crown Prince of Atlantis," Seven said from beside him. He could feel her grey eyes studying his face, even though he didn't dare look at her. "You will be the Pearl Emperor. It has always been your destiny to be our leader, regardless of your talent."

He swallowed hard, and told the truth at last. "I don't want to be the Pearl Emperor."

Silence spread out from his words.

Then Blaise kicked him again, harder this time. "Well, *duh*. If it helps, none of the rest of us want you to be either."

"Gee. That sure makes me feel better." Joe nudged her back. "Thanks so much for the vote of confidence."

She made a face at him. "Not because you'd be *bad* at it, doofus. Because we'd miss you. It wouldn't be nearly so much fun without you to yell at."

"Atlantis's loss is our gain." Wystan leaned forward, his green eyes softening. "We'll keep your secret, Joe."

The others joined in with general murmurs of agreement...all except one. At his side, Seven had gone utterly still. He made himself meet her gaze at last.

Did you mean that? her eyes asked.

And all he could do was reply, silently: *Yes*.

"Well." Rory clapped his hands together, recapturing everyone's attention. "Let's recap. Joe can see the future, and what he's seen is that the mother of all demons is going to pop up sometime soon. With the assistance of this Lupa woman, who seems to be working for the demons, even if she isn't possessed herself."

Joe dragged himself out of Seven's eyes and back to the business at hand. "I'm still not sure about that. I mean, not that she's working for the demons—she definitely is—but I still think Lupa might be possessed."

"She didn't have horns," Edith said. She indicated her forehead. "Just some kind of squiggle here."

"But her eyes flashed red when I confronted her the first time she tried to kidnap the Prince," Seven said. "From what I've heard of your encounters with possessed creatures last year, that could indicate that a demon resides within her, could it not?"

"Possibly," Wystan said slowly. "But I would like to propose a different theory. I think it's more likely Lupa's a hellhound. She was *with* hellhounds, after all."

"They can't have been hellhounds. They were flying." Edith asked. She dropped a hand to Fenrir's thick ruff, winding her fingers through his fur. "You can't fly, can you?"

Fenrir crunched thoughtfully on his bone. *Don't know. Never tried.*

"At this point, I wouldn't put anything past you," Rory muttered.

"I'm afraid that is likely to be beyond even your talents, Fenrir. At least without help. But there *are* hellhounds who can fly." Wystan glanced round the circle. "Some of you have met my aunt Hope and her wife Betty, if you recall?"

"As if anyone could forget their Christmas parties," Blaise said with a nostalgic sigh. "I know they're hellhounds, but I didn't think *they* could fly either."

"They can't, most of the time. But they're part of the Wild Hunt. It's a special kind of super-pack, composed of various types of mythical dog shifters, dedicated to hunting down supernatural criminals and bringing them to justice. When the pack is together, they collectively manifest special powers that they don't otherwise possess as individuals. One of them is the ability to run through the air in pursuit of their prey, even though none of them are shifters that are able to fly normally."

Edith's eyes were wide. "How do they do that?"

"I don't entirely know. The Wild Hunt is something of a secret society. Aunt Hope can't talk about it much." Wystan spread one hand, palm up. "But I've gathered it's something to do with the pack leader. It takes a very particular type of alpha power to be able to gather the Wild Hunt and make the pack more than the sum of individual shifters."

"And you think Lupa is an alpha like that?" Rory asked.

"Yes. One strong enough to form her own Wild Hunt. If she is, she might even be strong enough to compel other canine-type creatures to obey her. The shifters with her—even the wendigo—may not have been acting of their own volition."

"Just as well you weren't there," Candice said to Fenrir. "She might have been able to turn you to her side."

Fenrir showed all his teeth. *Tear out her throat first.*

But you don't, Joe thought, a cold shiver of unease running down his back. In his original vision—the one where he hadn't been with the squad—Fenrir had hesitated when he'd locked eyes with the mysterious woman. As if she *had* hypnotized him...

"Well, whatever she is, the most important thing is that she's our enemy," Rory said. "Lupa and her pack nearly took down the Thunderbird today. And according to Joe's visions, she's hell-bent on snatching one of us to serve up as some giant demon's first meal."

"Just me or Blaise," Joe put in. "If she can't get me, she goes after Blaise. That's what my visions have shown me."

"Me?" Blaise scowled, looking more irritated than worried at being singled out by an evil hellhound super-alpha. "Why me?"

"Power," Callum said, succinctly.

"Cal's right," Wystan agreed. "You and Joe are innately special, thanks to your respective parentages, in a way that the rest of us aren't."

Candice elbowed him. "Says the unicorn?"

Wystan smiled at his mate. "I'm not being self-deprecating. My kind may be rare, but I'm not a walking embodiment of elemental forces. I suspect this alpha demon would find me to be a distinctly unsatisfying snack."

"So we need to protect both Joe and Blaise. And possibly Fenrir, if Wystan's theory about Lupa is correct." Rory leaned back on his log, bracing himself on his hands. He stared up at the sky as though a plan might materialize there. "Joe, you said you saw—"

"Wait," Callum interrupted. The pegasus shifter was abruptly on his feet, so fast that he hardly seemed to move. "Someone's coming."

Everyone else tensed as well, but Callum held up a hand. He stared into the distance, eyes unseeing, as though he was listening to something. His taut shoulders relaxed a fraction.

"It's all right," he said, sitting down again. "It's just Buck."

Rory swore. "Is he bringing the rest of the crew back?"

"No. He's alone."

"That's a relief. I didn't want to test whether the Thunderbird can still make itself invisible even when it's hurt." Rory paused, forehead furrowing. "Funny. When I called Buck, he didn't *say* he was going to turn around and head back to us."

"Well, he is." Callum shrugged. "At speed. He'll be here in a few minutes."

Joe indulged in a groan, letting himself slump theatrically. "Great. So I have to go through all this *again*? If I'd known he was coming back so soon, I would have waited for him."

Wystan cocked his head to one side, looking curious. "*Would* you have known, if you'd scried the future?"

"Probably not. I only see stuff that's really important." He raised a finger as a speculative expression began to dawn across Blaise's face. "And before you ask, no, lottery numbers aren't included in that. Neither are the results of horse races. Believe me, I've tried."

Blaise pouted. "Pity."

"If we're all quite done exploring the potential monetary applications of Joe's gift," Rory said dryly. "Perhaps we could return to the small matter of the murderous demon-worshipping hellhound pack. Joe, you said that you had a vision of them attacking us on a callout near Bluebrook. Can you tell if that's still going to happen?"

"I can try." Joe patted his pockets, but came up empty. "Anyone got some water?"

"Yes." Callum tossed him a canteen. "Here."

Joe poured a splash of water into his cupped hand—and paused. He was uncomfortably aware of the ring of avid stares boring into him.

He squashed a sudden flutter of performance anxiety. "Well, here goes nothing."

He looked down into the water.

And what he saw had nothing to do with Bluebrook, or Lupa, or demons.

"Oh no," he breathed. "Someone, *stop him!*"

CHAPTER 19

"Stop who?" Seven asked—but she was talking to Joe's back.

He charged in the direction of the Thunderbird, flinging his handful of water aside. Seven ran after him, drawing her stunsword between one step and the next. The rest of the squad followed in a disorganized pack, shouting half-formed questions.

The roar of an engine cut through the babble. Up ahead, Buck's car shot into the car park. He was driving so fast, Seven expected to see the hellhound pack hot on his tail—but the road behind stayed empty.

The Thunderbird's head snapped up as the Jeep roared toward it. The vast bird tried to push itself to its feet, but its talons slipped out beneath it. Its geometric markings lit up, sparks of electricity crackling between the feathers.

The Jeep slewed to a halt, the driver's door flinging open before the vehicle had even fully stopped moving. Buck burst out, right in front of the Thunderbird.

"*No!*" Joe yelled.

His long legs outpaced them all. He flung himself between Buck and the Thunderbird, just as the Superintendent raised a gun.

Seven froze, along with everyone else. The muzzle of Buck's gun pressed against Joe's chest. Every part of her screamed to defend her mate, but she'd never be able to knock either of them out of the way in time.

"Chief," Joe was saying, his voice very calm. "Chief, no. You can't."

Buck's eyes and weapon stayed locked on the Thunderbird. "Get out of my way, Joe. Wystan, keep your hands down. Rory, if you so much as take a deep breath, I swear on my sister's grave I will pull this trigger."

Rory, who had indeed been drawing in his breath—presumably to use his alpha power to command Buck to stand down—let it out again unused. Wystan's fingers twitched helplessly at his sides. Even if he *did* fling up a shield, he'd only be able to protect the Thunderbird. There wasn't the slightest gap between Joe and Buck's weapon.

Step back, Seven willed Joe. If only she was a sea dragon, or fully mated to him, they would have been able to speak mind-to-mind—but he couldn't hear her silent plea.

Behind Joe, the Thunderbird had frozen as well, staring down at Buck with lightning-filled eyes. Joe kept his body pressed hard against Buck's gun, stopping him from re-aiming.

"We need the Thunderbird, Chief. I know you hate him because he starts forest fires, but we *need* him," Joe said. "He's fighting the demons, just like us. He's on our side."

"It's a motherfucking murderer!" Buck shouted. His finger was tight on the trigger. "It killed—it killed..."

"Who?" Joe said gently, when Buck didn't finish the sentence. "Who did you lose?"

"My sister. My brother-in-law." Buck's voice shook, but his hand stayed rock-steady. "My nephew."

Joe exhaled as though he'd been punched. "I'm sorry. I'm so sorry, Buck. But whatever happened, I'm sure the Thunderbird didn't—"

A soft rumble like distant thunder interrupted his words. The Thunderbird's massive head bent. Never taking its eyes from Buck, it nudged Joe aside with its beak. Wystan instantly started to raise his hands to summon his shield, but the Thunderbird's eyes flashed like lightning, stopping him.

Slowly, gently, it laid its great head on the ground in front of Buck.

The markings on its feathers had faded completely, to the barren color of ashes. It tipped its head back, exposing the soft, vulnerable pulse of its throat.

"He was a kid." Buck's voice was the barest whisper. "Just a kid."

The Thunderbird made no response.

"There can be no justification for what you did." The point of Buck's gun started to waver, just a fraction. "I don't care what you were fighting, or what was at stake. You should never have started that fire. No one should ever die like that."

The Thunderbird closed its eyes. It held very still.

Very slowly, Joe reached out. Buck's arm fell limp to his side as Joe cautiously took the gun out of his hand.

"Nobody can change the past, Chief." Holding the gun out to one side as if it was covered in maggots, Joe draped his other arm across Buck's shoulders. The Superintendent didn't resist as Joe steered him away from the motionless Thunderbird. "Only the future. And that's what we need to talk about."

∼

Buck took it all much more calmly than Joe had expected.

Then again, he wasn't sure how much the Superintendent was actually taking in. Buck had the fixed, glassy look of a man who would have been drinking steadily, had there been anything to drink.

Joe knew that look only too well. He'd seen it in the mirror, more times than he cared to recall.

And I only have to watch people I love potentially die in the future. Buck's actually lived *it.*

But he hadn't pulled the trigger.

Buck had chased the Thunderbird across the state for over ten years. But when he'd finally had his enemy helpless at his feet, he hadn't pulled the trigger.

Now he sat, blank-eyed and motionless, as the squad collectively tried to explain everything from Joe's talent to the hellhound attack. They'd moved inside, to one of the long tables in the mess hall. It was stiflingly hot and airless—Buck always growled about 'motherloving state penny-pinchers' whenever any crew member wistfully raised the possibility of air conditioning—but nobody had even suggested staying outside. They all wanted to keep Buck as far away from the Thunderbird as possible.

Candice and the unicorns were still with the creature, continuing to tend to its wounds. Callum and Fenrir had volunteered to patrol the perimeter of the base, just in case the hellhound pack returned. Joe didn't think that they would—he'd checked the future, and seen nothing except the usual *cold chains around his wrists*—but better to be safe than sorry.

"So," Buck said at last, when they'd all finally run out of words. His flat voice gave no indication what he might be thinking. "Hellhounds. Working with demons."

"Apparently," Rory said. He was watching the Superintendent carefully, with the air of a bomb-disposal expert eying a ticking suitcase. "Which is why we might need the Thunderbird."

"We know it can sense demons," Joe added. "And they're afraid of it, enough to send out some kind of hellhound hit squad. The demons are planning something big. We can't afford to lose anything that might help us stop them."

Buck's eyes flicked to him. "You've...seen this?"

"Some of it, yeah," Joe said. "Enough to know that we have to protect the Thunderbird. I'm really sorry, Chief. I can't imagine how hard this is for you."

Buck moved for the first time in an hour, stiffly. Seven, who was discretely standing guard behind the Superintendent with one hand on her stunsword, tensed.

The glare that Buck flashed her showed that he knew full well why she was hovering at his back. "Relax. Your boyfriend over there still has my gun." He rubbed both hands across his face, hiding his expression for a moment, then dropped them again. "You can give me that back now, Joe. What with all this motherloving weirdness on the loose, I want to be packing."

"Uh." The weapon was an uncomfortable weight in Joe's pocket.

He'd worked out how to take the magazine out, but he'd still rather have had a live rattlesnake down his pants. "Maybe I'd better hang onto it a little longer, okay?"

"When even Joe is questioning whether something is a good idea, you know it isn't." Blaise swapped the cold coffee at Buck's elbow for a fresh cup. "Here. Drink this. You must have been driving like a dem—uh, for a long time today. You'll feel better with some caffeine inside you."

Buck made another inarticulate growl. "Motherloving shifters. Nothing but a pain in my ass."

Despite his words, he didn't refuse the drink. He wrapped his large, scarred hands around the mug, staring down at the black liquid as though *he* was reading the future.

"Stop staring at me like that, all of you," he said after a minute. "Y'all look like you think I'm about to swallow your favorite puppy. Or burst into tears."

"Are you?" Edith asked apprehensively.

"Nope. Your damn dog is too big to fit on my grill." Buck took a sip of his coffee. "And I ran out of tears a long time ago."

They all exchanged glances.

"Do you…want to talk about it?" Wystan asked. His tone of voice indicated that he strongly preferred the answer to be 'no.'

"No," Buck said from behind his mug. He sighed, setting it down again. "But I suppose you all need to know. If only to give you second thoughts about following that motherloving monster around like little lost chicks."

"We know it's unpredictable," Rory said. "And that it doesn't hesitate to go through anything standing in its way. But I have to admit, I didn't think it would kill in cold blood. I'm sorry to have to ask you about this, Chief, but anything you can tell us about its behavior in the past might help us now."

Buck didn't say anything for a moment, turning the coffee mug round in his palms.

"It was a long time ago," he said at last. "Thirteen years or so. August. I'd just got back from deployment."

Seven's expression sharpened, as though a puzzle piece had just clicked into place. "You were military?"

"Marines," Buck said shortly. "Like I said, it was a long time ago. The Thunder Mountain Hotshots weren't even a twinkle in my eye back then. Wasn't nothing but trees, where you all have your butts planted right now. Only people living on the mountain were my sister and her family." He glanced at Wystan. "Where your wife's animal sanctuary is."

The blood drained from Wystan's face. "I thought it was just an old, ruined ranch. If I'd know what personal significance it had, I wouldn't have dreamed of asking to purchase it from you. I'm so sorry, Chief."

"Don't be. Wilma would have kicked my butt for letting the land go unused for so long." His weathered face softened a little. "She loved her horses."

"Wilma was your sister?" Edith said.

"Yeah. My big sister." Buck scowled, brushing a hand briefly across his eyes. "She took over the ranch after our parents passed. I spent as much time there as I could, which wasn't much. But I was back, when it happened. I saw it."

"The Thunderbird?" Blaise asked, when Buck didn't go on.

He nodded, jerkily, once. "Sheer luck it didn't get me too. Though whether that was good or bad luck depends on your point of view. I'd gone into Antler to have some beers, raise a little hell. Didn't notice my phone going off. She called and called, and I didn't pick up…"

He paused again, clearing his throat. "Anyway. I didn't see the missed calls and voicemail until later, when I was dialing 911. But there I was in at the bar, and I suddenly got this sixth sense that something was wrong. I decided to head back home early. Go spend some time with my nephew. He was at that age where kids started acting up. Wilma thought I might be a good influence on him, heaven only knows why."

Buck's gravelly voice roughened even further. "It was a beautiful night. Not a cloud in the sky. And as I rounded the final corner and saw the ranch up ahead, the whole world went white."

"For a second, I thought it was an IED." Buck stared straight ahead, into the past. "Wasted I don't know how long having a screaming flashback, while lightning hammered down all around. When I finally came to, my car was on its side, and I was flat on my front in the drainage ditch clutching a stick like a damn AK-47. And the ranch was on fire."

Nobody said anything. Timidly, Blaise reached out to touch Buck's hand. He didn't look round, but his fingers gripped hers.

"I saw it. Through the flames and the smoke." Buck jerked his chin in the direction of the door, and the unseen Thunderbird. "Looking down at what it had done with those evil white eyes."

Wystan frowned. "Pardon the interruption, but are you certain there are no shifters in your family tree? Regular humans aren't able to see the Thunderbird."

"Well, we can when it's hovering over the ashes of everything we've ever loved like a motherfu—like a motherloving vulture," Buck snapped. He abruptly let out a harsh, dry laugh, rubbing his forehead. "Listen to me. Thirteen years, and I'm still watching my tongue in case my nephew is listening. Wilma trained me too well. Anyway, there's no freak show stuff in my background. For a while, I didn't even believe what I'd seen. Thought I must have been hallucinating."

"What made you decide it was real?" Rory asked.

"When I saw it again. Couple of years later." Buck glanced down, and pulled his hand out from Blaise's with an embarrassed twitch. "I was a mess for a while. Left the Marines. Joined up with a wildfire crew, thinking at least I could save other people from burning to death. Then, while we were out battling a forest fire, I saw the monster sail overhead. Big as life and twice as ugly. That was when I realized what I actually needed to fight. To stop."

"Chief." Rory's voice was deep and soft, his golden eyes filled with compassion. "You know what the Thunderbird hunts."

"I know now," Buck said heavily. "And...Wilma's last voicemail, she was talking about something big prowling around the ranch. Some kind of wild animal. That was why she wanted me to come back. She sounded scared. She was my big sister, she was the brave one...but whatever she saw, it scared even her."

"It sounds very much like a demon," Wystan said. "Chief, I know this doesn't help, but...maybe when the Thunderbird started that fire, it was already too late for your family."

"Maybe." Buck stared down at his hands. "Maybe they were already gone, and the fire just took their bodies. I hope so. God help me, I hope so."

He looked up abruptly. His eyes were bright with unshed tears, and fierce as a hawk's.

"And if demons did kill my family," he growled. "I will burn every last one of them in return. *Every. Last. One.* So you'd better tell us how we can do that, Joe."

CHAPTER 20

"*J*oe." Seven touched his hunched shoulder, feeling his rigid muscles under her palm. "You have to stop. You can't keep putting yourself through this."

For a moment, he didn't respond, still lost in his vision. Then he blinked. He looked up from the basin of water at last. The corners of his mouth twitched upward in a faint shadow of his usual grin.

"I'm okay." He knuckled his bloodshot eyes. "I can keep going. Maybe I'll see something new this time."

She pulled the basin away as he started to hunch over it again. "You have not seen anything new the last hundred times. You have to rest."

Even in her arms, he'd barely slept last night. He'd been up well before dawn. She'd woken to find him cross-legged on the floor of the bedroom, hunkered over a shallow bowl of water. She hadn't even been able to drag him away for breakfast.

"You have to rest," she repeated, yet again. Her own eyelids felt heavy with exhaustion, and she'd only been watching *him*, not an endless replay of a snatch of the future. "What good will you be at Bluebrook, if you wear yourself out now?"

"I won't do any good at all if I don't discover what's coming." He tried to tug the basin back in his direction. "Everyone's counting on me, Seven. Everyone."

She held onto the basin firmly. Water sloshed over the edge. "And you will not let us down. You *haven't* let us down. You've foreseen enough that we are forewarned."

"I haven't seen enough!" His voice rose. "What am I going to tell everyone? 'Yep, still going to be a fire at Bluebrook, but all I can see of it is a glimpse of our enemy and then everything goes grey and fuzzy and I wake up in chains?' Somehow, she's able to knock me out. Somehow she's able to neutralize us all. Even though we know she's coming, even though the whole squad is prepared, even though we've got Wystan and his shield. I have to work out how. I have to work out how to stop her."

She yanked the basin away entirely, holding it out of his reach. "If you were meant to learn anything more about what is to come, you would have seen it by now."

"I'm probably not looking in the right way." He buried his face in his hands, shoulders dropping in weariness. "Sea, I hate this. Everyone's relying on me. And I'm just stumbling in the dark. I should have listened to the Master-Seers better."

She considered his slumped, despairing posture.

Then she tipped the basin over his head.

He spluttered, water running down his face. "*Seven!* What was that for?"

"For talking even more utter nonsense than usual." She folded her arms across her chest. "You told me that the Seers do this with a silver basin and purest seawater. *You* have a plastic bowl and a bottle of Evian. And even so, you've seen more than any of them could ever dream. You've *done enough*, Joe. Now stop beating yourself up about not being able to achieve the impossible."

The basin hung lop-sided on his head like a very unstylish hat. Slowly, he started to smile—a real smile this time, that made her heart flutter in answer.

"I am being kind of a drama queen here, aren't I," he admitted.

"Just a bit." She rapped her knuckles lightly on the basin, making it tip over his eyes. "Now come and have some breakfast, or I'll have to hit you over the head with my stunsword. Again."

"Ah, but behold!" He pushed the basin back, grinning at her from under the rim. "I am armored against…your…tricks…"

He trailed off, eyes widening. Then he surged to his feet, letting out an ear-splitting whoop.

"Er," said Seven, as he grabbed her hands. "What?"

"That's it! Armor! Seven, you're a genius." He swung her round in a circle, cackling like a rooster in a henhouse. "I could kiss you."

"What," she started to say again—and then lost the power of speech entirely, because he did.

His tongue plunged between her lips, fierce and triumphant. She sank into the kiss, her body molding against his. Without conscious thought, she brought her hands up, locking them around the back of his strong neck.

He pulled back at last, with a last teasing nip that made her breath catch. He pressed his forehead against hers.

"Not long now." His turquoise eyes glowed like sunlight through tropical water, alight with barely leashed desire. "Sea, I can't wait until we can claim each other. Come on! We have to go find the others."

She found herself tugged in his wake like the tail of a kite as he plunged out the door. "Why?"

"Because I figured it out." He grinned at her over his shoulder. He was still wearing the basin, perched on his head at a jaunty angle. "It's you, Seven. You're the key. It's you!"

"The key to *what?*"

"Everything." He dragged her onward, not giving her a chance to question him further. "Chief! *Chief!*"

Joe's yell was unnecessary. Buck had already emerged from his office, striding in their direction. He took in Joe's headwear, and his grim expression turned pained. Seven distinctly heard him mutter to himself, "I am *not* going to ask."

"Chief." Joe pushed the basin back from his eyes again. "I think I know how the hellhounds will try to take us out. And more importantly, I know how to stop them."

"Good," Buck said grimly. He held up a radio. "Because guess where we just got called out to."

CHAPTER 21

"Are you sure that this will work?" Rory asked Joe.

Joe shrugged. "No. But Wystan thinks it will."

Wystan was pacing around the edge of the base in unicorn form, stopping now and then to touch the point of his horn to the ground. A dozen *actual* unicorns followed him at a respectful distance. They were all adult stallions from Sunrise's herd, but Wystan dwarfed them like a racehorse among ponies.

Rory blew out his breath, watching Wystan's slow progression. "I'd just feel a lot better about this if you'd *seen* it work, Joe."

"I haven't seen it *not* work," Joe said, with a touch of irritation. "I told you, I don't see everything, bro. And until yesterday, you didn't even know I could see anything at all. Yet somehow you managed to make decisions without my blessing."

Whatever Rory might have said in response was forestalled by Wystan cantering up to them. With a shimmer of rainbow-edged light, he shifted into human form.

"It's done." Wystan looked tired, but satisfied. "The barrier is complete."

Rory stared at the base, which appeared unchanged. "I was... expecting it to glow, or something."

"That would be a bit of a giveaway, wouldn't it?" Wystan lifted his eyebrows, a small, smug smile playing around his lips. "Go ahead and try walking forward, Rory."

Rory gave him a dubious glance, but did so. He'd only taken three steps when a crackling silver shield sprang into existence, right in front of his nose. The griffin shifter leapt back with a startled curse.

Joe grinned as nickers of equine laughter drifted from the watching unicorns. "I'd say it works. Is it permanent, Wys? Like the shields around the unicorns' old mountain, or your own ancestral lands back in England?"

"No. Those wards were reinforced over many years. But one should last at least a few days without any further input from me, according to Petrichor's lore." Wystan gestured at a large stallion with a silver horn and grey eyes. "He's the herd's equivalent of a historian. Even though he doesn't have shield powers himself, he knew enough theory to teach me to create protective wards. We've been experimenting around the ranch over the past few months, before fire season started. I didn't want to leave Candice unprotected."

Rory poked at the barrier with a gloved finger, and jerked his hand back as silver sparks snapped at him. "And you're sure it'll hold if the hellhounds attack again? Their last assault seemed to drain you pretty quickly."

"That's because I was having to actively shield everyone. This is different." Wystan tilted his head, as though searching for the right words to explain it. "Think of it as building a wall out of bricks. In a pinch, I can pile them up and hold them in place with brute strength, but they'll fall apart the instant I let go. But if I have enough time, I can mortar them together to make a much stronger barrier. One which stays up even when I'm not here."

"Sounds good." Rory stepped back, and the barrier faded into invisibility again. "Although I do have to point out that you seem to have locked *us* out as well."

"That's just because I haven't given you the metaphorical key yet. Hold on."

Wystan shifted into unicorn form. He touched his horn to Rory, and a brief shimmer of light outlined the griffin shifter's stocky body. He did the same to Joe, which was a bit disconcerting. Unicorn magic *looked* pretty, but it *felt* like having a billion spiders briefly run across your skin.

Wystan shifted back again. "There. I've already given access to the others. Including the Thunderbird, but please don't tell Buck that."

"Don't tell me what?" Buck growled, emerging from the storeroom next to them.

Wystan jumped, going an interesting shade of red. "Er. Nothing, Chief."

Buck scowled indiscriminately at the unicorn shifter, the unicorn herd, and the general vicinity. "You done sprinkling glitter, or peeing on the corners of the buildings, or whatever it was you needed to do for your little magic trick?"

"Yes. The wards are all set up. And the stallions from the unicorn herd are briefed and prepared. They're ready to fight if needed."

Petrichor snorted. He nudged Wystan with the point of his horn.

"Yes, I was getting to that," Wystan told the stallion. He turned back to Buck, his blush reaching his ears. "Er. I did have to promise them two salt licks and a bag of peppermints each in return for their service."

Petrichor neighed in agreement. A few of the other stallions licked their lips.

"Wonderful. So now I have to hide 'payments to guard unicorns' in the crew's financial accounts." Buck sighed heavily. "I hate my life."

Edith emerged from the storeroom, followed by the rest of the squad. Seven came last, looking pale and worried. He tried to catch her eye, but she looked down, fiddling with the scabbard slung from her belt.

"All good, Chief," Edith said to Buck. "Everyone's ready to go."

"Everyone except me," Blaise groused. Alone in the group, she was still dressed in jeans and a t-shirt rather than full turn out gear. She cast Buck a hopeful look. "But if you've changed your mind, I could get myself kitted out in thirty seconds."

Buck nodded at Joe. "His call, not mine. I'm no happier about it than you."

The weight of responsibility was heavier than his fully loaded backpack. "Sorry, bro. You and Fenrir gotta sit this one out. This alpha hellhound chick has a special interest in both of you. We can't give her a choice of targets."

"You two can make yourselves useful babysitting *that*." Buck jerked his thumb over his shoulder at the Thunderbird, which was lurking some way off, half-hidden behind the mess hall. "I'm still not real thrilled about letting it stay while we're out."

The massive bird withdrew a little further into the shadows, as though aware it was being discussed. Its unblinking white stare stayed fixed on Buck.

"Unfortunately, we don't have a choice about that, Chief," Wystan said. "Candice thinks it'll take another couple of days for it to be fully healed. She and Sunrise are working as fast as they can, but between the hellhound pack and the crash landing, the Thunderbird sustained an awful lot of damage. Perhaps you could assist them, Blaise."

Blaise eyed the Thunderbird with distinct unenthusiasm. "I'm a firefighter, not a nurse. And that thing gives me the heebie-jeebies. It keeps staring at me like I'm a snack."

"Maybe it's hungry," Edith offered.

"Well, we're fresh out of demons," Buck growled. "It better not *need* to eat. If it takes a crap in my base, I'm rubbing its beak in it."

Will tell Stormheart that, Man-Alpha. Fenrir's mental voice was solemn, but his tail wagged with amusement. He leaned against Blaise's leg, making her stagger. *We will guard the den while pack hunts.*

"I wish you'd stay behind too," Rory said to Edith. "Just this once."

Edith's hands fluttered, but her jaw was firm. "Hellhounds or no hellhounds, there's still a fire to contain. We're already understrength. The squad is going to need me. Don't worry, Rory. I'm prepared."

"Us regular folks who can't turn into furry critters can still pack a few tricks up our sleeves," Buck said, drawing aside his jacket to reveal the gun holstered at his hip. "Let's hope it'll be enough. *Is* this going to work, Joe?"

Joe flung up his hands. "Why does everyone keep asking me that?"

"Uh, I don't know." Blaise rolled her eyes. "Maybe because you can see the future?"

"I'm not a Magic 8 Ball! *Prospects hazy, try again later,* okay? Everyone stop shaking me in the hope of getting a different answer!"

They were all staring at him, even the unicorns. With effort, he got a grip on himself again. Smiling felt like bench-pressing an elephant, but he did it anyway.

"Sorry," he muttered. "Little tense, here."

"Well, that's reassuring." Buck shook his greying head. He stomped off in the direction of the crew transport. "Come on, you lot. Let's get this freak show on the road."

Joe hung back for a second, letting the others stream past him. He fell into step with Seven, right at the back of the group.

"Hey," he said, lowering his voice. "This *will* work. And it'll earn you your knighthood at last, you know. Not even Lord Asshole will be able to argue otherwise. After today, you'll have everything you ever wanted."

Her face was drawn and pale under her helmet. "But you haven't had a vision confirming that we'll succeed."

"I don't have to." He squeezed her shoulder, feeling the hard edge of her armor under the padding of her jacket. "I have you."

CHAPTER 22

The worst part of any battle, Lord Azure had told Seven once, pompously, *is the wait beforehand.*

Nine hours ago, Seven would have agreed with him. Now, however, she had changed her mind.

Digging miles of fire line through thorny undergrowth, on a baking summer's day, with a wildfire breathing down her neck, in full armor. *That* was definitely the worst part.

"Seven." Wystan touched her shoulder, interrupting her as she hacked at a stubborn root. "Stop and drink something. We can't have you passing out from heat exhaustion."

"I'm fine," she said, though she was drenched from head to toe in sweat. She cut through the plant at last, scraping it aside to leave nothing but bare soil. "Look after yourself rather than worrying about me. How are you managing?"

Wystan grimaced, tugging at the neck of his outer jacket. His torso was bulked out like the Michelin Man by the double layer of turn out gear he was wearing. "I believe that we have invented a new and unique form of torture."

"Less talk," Callum grunted from behind them. Sweat dripped

down his forehead, but his Pulaski swung with tireless, mechanical precision. "More digging."

Out in front of them, Joe paused, turning his head. He had a tree clamped between his massive jaws, soil dribbling down from the roots. The ruff of iridescent spines on the back of his neck rippled, the sea dragon equivalent of flashing a grin.

"Something funny?" she murmured.

He was a good twenty feet away from the rest of the squad, but sea dragons could hear a whisper of song from across half an ocean. He tossed the uprooted tree to one side with a casual flick of his powerful neck, freeing his mouth.

"Trust Callum to be consistent," he said, in the low, rumbling notes of sea dragon speech. *"He said that before, in my first vision of this day. Right before the ambush. Tell Buck to be ready."*

Buck glowered up at Joe's towering form. "Is he saying something, or just burping?"

"Joe wants to know how much further you need him to break ground," Seven said, raising her voice a little. "He's getting tired."

It was a code phrase. Hellhounds had the ability to make themselves invisible and intangible—Fenrir had called it *going sideways*, though he hadn't been able to explain why—which meant that the pack could be shadowing them even now, listening to every word. Not even Callum's pegasus senses would be able to detect them.

The mythic shifters on the squad could communicate with each other telepathically, but both Buck and Seven herself were excluded from that private channel. Only shifters of the same general type could speak mind to mind...unless they were mated.

Soon, Seven thought, hoping that it was true. *I'll be able to speak to him that way soon.*

Buck nodded, a twist of his mouth showing that he'd understood the secret message. "Tools up!" he called to the rest of the squad.

They all stopped cutting line, gathering into a loose huddle. They were *supposed* to act like they were just taking a normal break, but Rory and Wystan kept craning their necks like owls at the slightest sound, and Edith was practically vibrating in place. Even Callum looked twitchy.

Then again, Seven could hardly criticize her comrades' acting abilities. Her own nerves were stretched tight. Her shark lurked just below her skin, poised to leap out.

And a lot of good that would do. Seven pushed her useless animal back down. The last thing she needed was for its mindless instincts to take control and ruin everything.

Patience, she told her restless beast. *Soon.*

Buck stalked a few steps away from the squad. Despite his gear, he moved as silently as a panther, heavy boots making no sound on the leaf litter. He shaded his eyes, staring in the direction of the approaching wildfire. Thick smoke curled through the tree trunks, and Seven could hear a hungry crackle, but at the moment no flames were visible.

Buck grunted, sounding both pleased and perplexed. "Well, there's one bit of good news. We've done enough to cut off the advance. Unless weather conditions change drastically and the fire blows up, Bluebrook is safe."

"That's...convenient," Wystan said, his forehead furrowing.

And strangely considerate, Seven thought, but didn't dare say. From the looks on everyone else's faces, she wasn't the only one wondering why their enemy had given them enough time to contain the fire. The hellhounds had obviously started the blaze in order to lure the squad out from the safety of the base. It seemed odd for demon-worshipping arsonists to care whether or not their trap actually destroyed innocent lives.

Probably just wanted to let us exhaust ourselves, Seven decided. She certainly wasn't as fresh as she had been when they'd first arrived. She rolled her shoulders, trying to shake out the cramps in her arms. Despite the smoke, she deepened her breathing, the better to be ready for combat—

And realized that the bitterness she could taste was more than just smoke.

"*Ambush!*" she yelled, just as Callum's head snapped up.

Something whined past her ears like a hornet. Wystan, who'd started to fling up his shield, abruptly clapped a hand to the side of his neck. Seven felt something strike her own left arm as the unicorn shifter collapsed. A feathered tranquillizer dart stuck out from her bicep. The needle-sharp point had penetrated her firefighter jacket, but been thwarted by the armor she wore underneath.

He was right, Joe was right! Seven cursed the crack shot that had managed to hit Wystan in the undefended gap between his collar and helmet. Assuming the evil-looking green liquid filling the dart was the same drug that the hellhound alpha had used on Joe at the club, Wystan would be out of action for the fight. She could only hope that the rest of the team had been luckier.

Play dead. Play dead!

Her every instinct screamed to turn and fight, but Seven forced herself to go limp. All around, the rest of the squad were falling to the ground as well. It was impossible to tell whether they were shamming like her, or had genuinely been struck with the tranquillizer darts like Wystan.

Through half-closed eyes, she glimpsed Joe rearing up, bared claws spreading in fury—but sea dragons, adapted to the ocean depths, were not as well armored as their land-dwelling brethren. A dart sank deep into the soft, vulnerable gills behind the hinge of his jaw. Joe's outline blurred and shrank, his furious roar dwindling into a human cry of pain.

NO, Seven shouted at her inner animal as her shark surged forward. She wrestled it back, every muscle in her body clenched and shaking with the effort of staying still. *Not yet! NOT YET!*

"Got them all," said an unfamiliar male voice, sounding distinctly satisfied. "Told you so, Lupa. Like shooting fish in a barrel."

"Don't get cocky, Gerulf," answered a woman. Seven tensed despite herself. She knew *that* voice. "Wulfric, Lycus, secure the Prince. The rest of you, make sure of the others."

Scents made a three-dimensional map in her mind. She could taste the hellhound pack closing in—some on two legs, some on four. Their churning emotions lay on her tongue like a complex cocktail. Most of them were reluctant, sweating with fear, but with an even greater underlying terror forcing them onward.

A few of the pack were more dangerous. *They* reeked of rot; fetid, gloating pleasure at the prospect of hurting someone helpless to fight back. Seven fixed them in her mind, and waited.

Not yet...not yet...

She felt rather than saw a shadow fall over her. A sulphurous breath whispered across her cheek.

NOW!

She exploded upward, flicking out her stunsword as she swung. The glowing blade cracked across the hellhound's muzzle. She didn't pause to watch it fall—she was already spinning, striking, felling the man bending over Wystan with a knife in his hand.

"Now!" she shouted. "NOW!"

A gunshot rang through the yelping barks and shouts of the hellhound pack. Buck was on his feet now too, snapping off precise, professional shots. Seven hoped that he was aiming to incapacitate rather than kill, as they'd agreed. After what she'd sensed of the pack's emotions, she was certain that Wystan was right—the majority of Lupa's pack *were* innocents, forced into obedience by her alpha power. She was glad her own weapon was non-lethal.

Callum guarded the Superintendent's flank, swinging a Pulaski like a sword. A dart dangled from one of his sleeves, the chamber still full of sickly green fluid. The doubled layers of firefighter jackets had worked to protect *him*, at least.

Rory seemed to be okay too. He was snarling as loudly as his chainsaw, his eyes blazing golden, guarding Wystan's motionless form. Edith was down on her knees behind him. For a second, Seven thought she was cowering in terror—and then Edith popped up, firing a flare gun over Rory's shoulder directly into a group of hellhounds charging at Buck. The beasts scattered, howling in pain and confusion, pawing at blinded eyes. Edith coolly dropped behind Rory again to reload.

Seven didn't have any more time to worry about the rest of the squad. A pair of hellhounds lunged, trying to pin her between them.

She pirouetted, bending backward almost to the ground, sliding under their flaming jaws. Her stunsword sent one yelping away, and a shot from Buck made the other fade into invisibility with a howl of pain.

"Hold them off!" Lupa shouted. Seven glimpsed the hellhound alpha running away, still in human form. "Get the Prince!"

Two burly men had Joe by the arms, and were trying to sling his limp form over the back of the wendigo, who was crouching with its belly to the ground. Seven tried to charge toward them, but was met by a wall of teeth.

"Callum! Rory!" she shouted.

The two shifters surged forward, trying to fight their way toward Joe—but a blast of hellfire forced them both back. Most of the pack were on four feet now, armed with fire as well as teeth and claws. Apart from Lupa and the men wrestling Joe, only two others were still in human form. They were both sighting down dartguns, back-pedaling from the melee. If either Rory or Callum shifted, the men would be able to dart them.

Rory had realized the problem too. "Seven, Buck!" he yelled. "Take them out!"

No matter how fast she feinted and struck, she couldn't break through. The hellhounds kept flickering out of existence just long enough to evade her sword, then reappearing to lunge at her.

Buck snapped off another shot that sent a hellhound howling away on three legs—then staggered, his next bullet going wild. A feathered dart stuck out from the center of his chest. Across the clearing, a man lowered his dartgun, looking expectant...and then, as Buck failed to collapse, perplexed.

"Not a shifter, motherlover," the Chief growled, and shot the dartgun out of the man's hand. The man screamed and blurred into hellhound form, disappearing into thin air.

That left only one attacker still armed with a dartgun. The man dove into cover behind a tree, taking cover from Buck's weapon.

"The instant one of you fuckers shifts, I'll have you!" the man yelled from his hiding-place. "Your gear won't protect you if you shift!"

Her shark surged forward. Seven tasted the man's terror, sharp and sweet, and the sweat-stink of bravado—

"He's lying!" She knew it was true, with a shark's clear, cold certainty. "He's out of darts!"

With a triumphant roar that turned into the shriek of a stooping hawk, Rory shifted into griffin form. Callum was only a heartbeat behind, his pegasus's flame-red wings knocking his two attackers flying.

The hellhounds facing Seven abruptly found themselves occupied with far more pressing concerns. Seven lunged between their bristling black bodies as they turned. It was a gamble—she couldn't charge and defend her back at the same time—but no burning jaws nipped at her heels. The pack had clearly decided that she was less of a threat than the rest of the squad.

She ran flat-out, smoke burning in her chest. The two men who'd been manhandling Joe surged to intercept her, shifting as they pounced. Past their flaming jaws, she caught a glimpse of Lupa leaping onto the back of the wendigo. Joe's limp form lay face-down across the huge beast's shoulders, arms and legs dangling.

"Go! *Go!*" Lupa shouted.

Her steed leaped into the air.

Time froze in ice-hard clarity. The pair of hellhounds leaping for her throat hung in the air. If she'd been a dragon, she could have shifted and knocked them aside like flies—but she wasn't.

In the slow beat of combat time, she knew—*knew*—that she was going to be too late.

With the strength of desperation, Seven leaped. She used one hellhound as a springboard, her boots kicking it out of the air as her stunsword connected with the other one's head. Her other hand reached out—

And closed on Joe's ankle.

Lupa screamed with fury, snatching at Joe, but Seven had gravity on her side now. She dropped her stunsword, grabbing onto Joe with both hands, pulling him off the wendigo's back.

Seven twisted as they fell. Her back hit the ground, but her jacket and armor absorbed the worst of the impact. She curled to break Joe's fall, his weight driving all the breath out of her.

Her chest was on fire. She had to get up, had to protect her mate, had to *fight*—but her body wouldn't obey her. She could only clutch at Joe as Lupa wheeled the wendigo around in a tight turn.

Lupa's eyes stared down at her, blazing with red fire. The mark on her forehead burned too. She was close enough to see it clearly now— a geometric, stylized snake with gaping jaws and curving horns, glowing with an eerie, hellish light.

Hooves shook the ground. Callum's gleaming copper wings spread protectively over her, shielding her from the hellhound alpha. The pegasus reared, front hooves ready to strike.

Lupa's bitter, frustrated howl echoed from the trees. Through Callum's gleaming feathers, Seven glimpsed the rest of the hellhound pack streaming into the sky, following their alpha. Their dark bodies blurred. In seconds, there was nothing left but swirling smoke.

Rory landed next to her, paws shifting into boots. He crouched to support her, helping her to sit up. "Are you hurt?"

She shook her head, still too winded for speech. She gestured urgently at the sky.

Callum shook his head, shifting as he did so. "Too late. They're gone."

Rory's arm tightened around her shoulder. "It's all right, Seven. You drove them back. It's over. We won."

She clutched at Joe's limp body, feeling the slow, even rise and fall of his chest. Despair filled her own.

No, she thought numbly. *I failed.*

CHAPTER 23

He found her down by the lake, huddled on a log. The distant lights of the hotshot base gleamed from higher up the mountain, barely visible through the thick pines.

"Hey." Joe sat down next to Seven. "You disappeared from the party. Well, if you can call a group of exhausted, filthy firefighters trying not to fall asleep over non-alcoholic beverages a party. Then again, I'm pretty sure I saw Callum nearly crack a smile. That alone makes it a wild shindig."

Seven didn't turn her head. "You should not be this far out from Wystan's wards."

"I'm safe enough." He leaned into her a little, shoulder to shoulder. "Got my bodyguard with me, haven't I?"

Seven continued to stare blankly out at the gentle, moonlit lake. Her legs were drawn up; arms around her shins, chin resting on her knees. She still had her armor on. Dark smudges of soot marred the usually immaculate leather plates.

"Have you seen anything?" she asked, abruptly.

Not you too. Joe was getting really tired of being asked that question. Still, he couldn't blame everyone for being anxious.

"Nope." He gazed into the dark, rippling waters. The surface of the lake glittered at him like a broken mirror, for once devoid of the future. "I've been checking, but it seems fate hasn't got anything to show me at the moment."

Seven hugged her legs, staring into the lake herself. "Is that a good sign or an ill omen?"

"Well, it's a distinct improvement over hallucinating chains around my wrists and a towering evil monster eating my mate, so I'm gonna go with 'good.'" He bumped her with his shoulder again. "I know you've been brooding over that Lupa woman getting away, but maybe that doesn't matter. You guys kicked hellhound butt. Maybe they've given up. Maybe we're safe now."

"Maybe," she echoed. "'Maybe' is not good enough, Joe."

Just the light touch of her hip against his made his body tighten in need. He let out a long, slow sigh, shifting position to put a fraction of an inch of space between them.

"No," he admitted. "Not when it comes to your safety. It's just about killing me, but we can't mate yet. Not until I know for certain that it won't put you in danger."

She bowed her head. She'd untied her braids from her warrior's knot, letting them hang free. They shadowed her face, hiding her expression.

"This is all my fault," she said in a low, defeated voice. "I failed you."

"Hey. You were magnificent. I'm the one who failed." He slid off the log, kneeling on the ground in front of her. He took her hands. "I should have been able to see more. I shouldn't have let the squad walk near-blind into such a dangerous situation. It's only thanks to you that I'm not waking up in chains right now."

She shook her head. "I am not fit to be your bodyguard. If you'd had a true knight at your side, a *dragon* knight, your enemy would not still be at large."

Something about the way she'd phrased that snagged his attention. "Hang on. Seven, do you think Lupa got away because you aren't a sea dragon?"

She stared down at her hands, pale and small in his own. "A dragon could have protected you better. The others *did* protect you better.

The hellhounds stopped fighting me the instant Rory and Callum shifted."

"Which left you free to save me, and I bet the whole pack is kicking themselves tonight about that." He tightened his grip, wishing that she would lift her head and meet his eyes. "Seven, you sensed the ambush even before Callum did. And Rory told me how you detected when that guy ran out of poison darts. You saved me today *because* of your animal, not in spite of it."

She jerked away from his touch. "I am not a child, to be comforted by unearned praise. I didn't sense the hellhounds early enough to protect Wystan. And Rory and the others would soon have worked out that that man was bluffing. The truth of the matter is that I would have been more useful today if I was any other type of shifter."

"If you weren't a shark, you wouldn't be *you*."

"*And that would be better!*" She struck her breastplate with one fist, her face twisting in shame and self-loathing. "Damn it, Joe, I can't even shift on dry land. Stop pretending that I'm perfect just the way I am!"

He sat back on his heels. He studied her, noting her bared teeth and rigid, trembling hands.

"How long has it been since you last shifted?" he asked.

She stiffened, eyes going wary as though suspecting some kind of trick. "I...don't know. A couple of months, I suppose. What does that matter?"

"A couple of *months*?" He'd known she couldn't have shifted since she'd found him in Vegas, but that had only been just over a week ago. "I thought you were in Atlantis before we met!"

"I was. In human form. I always stay in the air-filled parts of the city." She said this matter-of-factly, as though it should have been obvious. "Lord Azure was gracious enough to assign me duties that fit my limitations."

"What limitations? You're a shark, for sea's sake. You can breathe underwater."

"So can herring. That does not make a fish equal to a dragon."

"Exactly. My kind are descended from land-dwelling creatures that got a whim to paddle about underwater. Compared to you guys, we're only half-assedly adapted to the ocean."

"But you are still *dragons*. Far bigger and stronger than any shark."

"So? Size isn't everything. I'm ten times bigger than Rory, and I still wouldn't want to take him on in a fight. You can swim faster than us, dive deeper, sense prey at a greater distance…for the love of sweet little fishes, I don't think there's *anything* that a sea dragon can do better underwater than a shark."

"I can," she snapped. "Not alarm the citizens of Atlantis. Sea dragons would be horrified to see a shark wearing the tokens of the Order of the First Water."

"And making sure they continue to *not* see a shark knight is meant to help them get used to it…how?"

Her mouth hung ajar for a second. Then her shoulders hunched. "You would not understand. You are a sea dragon. People don't stare at *you*."

"Hello? Crown Prince of Atlantis here?" He held up his hands in apology, forestalling her angry retort. "Sorry. I know, it's not the same thing at all. But I do get why you'd be self-conscious about going about your duties in public in shark form. What I *don't* get is why Lord Azure and the other knights were happy for you to just hide yourself away. It's a criminal waste of your talents."

She withdrew further, her armor making her look somewhat like an armadillo curling into a ball. "That is not Lord Azure's opinion."

"My opinion of Lord Azure's opinion can only be expressed with four-letter words, so let's not get started on that topic. Look, even if he was idiotic enough not to recognize the many benefits of having a shark in the knights, why in the sea would that stop you from shifting at all? Surely he didn't have you on guard duty every minute of every day. You must have been able to let your shark out for a swim *sometimes*."

"Any time I was not on duty, I spent training," she said defensively. "A knight must be continually striving to improve herself, resisting all temptations that might distract from duty. Swimming would be mere indulgence. Lord Azure commanded me to practice discipline in such matters."

"Discipline, my *ass*. That bullying, bigoted little—" Joe stopped himself, drawing in a deep breath and commanding his dragon to settle. "Seven, at some point we need to have a serious conversation about your Lord Azure, but not until my mom is present to hear every word. Stand up."

Reflexive obedience made her rise, though once she was on her feet she hesitated, looking suspicious. "Why?"

"Because you are going to indulge yourself. And me."

Her eyes narrowed—and then flew open as he pulled his shirt over his head. "What are you *doing?*"

"Undressing," he said, from within his shirt. He emerged from the garment, tossing it to the ground. "Because we are going for a swim."

"Now?" Her voice shot up. *"Together?"*

"Yep." He kicked off his shoes. "Because you are wound up so tight, I'm scared to make a sudden noise in case you fire yourself clear over the horizon. And it's no wonder, if you haven't shifted for so long. You are going for a dip if I have to *throw* you into this lake."

She eyed the placid water as though it was boiling lava. "It's freshwater. I'm a Great White. If I shift in there, I'll suffocate."

"Just trust me." He undid his belt. Seven made a very gratifying, wordless noise, and spun abruptly on her heel to put her back to him. "Now are you going to take that armor off, or am I going to have to shuck you out of it like a lobster?"

She cast him a searing glare over a shoulder, but reached for a buckle. With a few deft motions, a piece of her armor—it probably had some kind of fancy name, but he had no idea what—came free. The curved leather plate fell to the ground with a thump, exposing the elegant line of her shoulder-blade.

Now *he* was the one who had to fix his gaze elsewhere. He occupied himself with pulling off his socks, trying to ignore the soft rustles and thuds from behind him. His imagination, however, insisted on filling in every detail. *That* was the slight sound of her bending to unlace her leg guards, showing off the high, tight curve of her backside…and now the sensuous sigh of leather through a buckle, freeing her breasts…

He abruptly reconsidered his plan to strip down to his boxers. Swimming in wet denim was hard, but not as hard as what was going on underneath his jeans.

"There." Seven moved back into sight again, arms folded defiantly across her chest. She was down to nothing but a white sports bra and boy shorts that clung to her muscled body. "Satisfied?"

Satisfied was the exact opposite of what he felt at that instant. He could only stare at her, his entire body on fire.

Her tongue darted out, moistening her lips. It was all he could do not to ravish her on the spot. "Well? Are we swimming or not?"

"Guh," he managed to get out, eloquently. "No. I mean yes! Water. Great idea. Yep."

He stumbled into the shallows. It was a miracle the entire lake didn't instantly turn to steam. The summer-warm waters did absolutely nothing to counteract the effect Seven was having on him. Then again, *arctic* waters wouldn't have been able to do that.

He waded out into the lake, kicking off from the bottom as soon the water was deep enough. Seven followed, considerably more gracefully. She barely seemed to need to flick a finger to stay afloat. Her pale body cut through the water without a single ripple. He was no slouch at swimming—he was practically amphibious, having been raised as much in the sea as on land—yet he felt like a dog thrashing along next to an otter.

He grinned to himself. *Hah. I was right. She* is *way more awesome than me in the water. At everything, really.*

Now if only he could convince *her* of that.

When he judged that they were far enough out from the shore, he rolled to float on his back. Seven hovered at his side, holding herself in position with slight, distractingly erotic undulations of her legs. Water darkened her hair from silver to pewter. Her mouth was still set and stubborn, but some of the tightness had eased from around her eyes.

"Hmph." She rolled to copy his posture, drifting on her back next to him. "I hate to admit it, but you were right. I needed this."

"I can make it better." He caught her hand, drawing her closer. "Come here. I'm not sure how far this will work."

Trying his best to ignore Seven's bare, slick skin against his, he closed his eyes. He hadn't done this since childhood, but he could still remember his mother's voice, her arms around him...

We are the Heart of the Sea, she'd whispered in his ear. *Where we are, so is the ocean. We are connected to the water and the waves, always, no matter how far we may go. Remember, my love. Wherever you are, you are always home.*

Seven's gasp made him open his eyes again. She brought her fingers to her lips and then stared at him in wonder.

"Salt," she whispered. "Salt water."

"It's an Imperial bloodline thing," he managed to get out, past the roar of the waves crashing through his blood. It was like holding up a seashell to your ear to hear the sound of the ocean, except *he* was the seashell. "Heart of the Sea. We don't sit on the Pearl Throne just because we've got a big treasury and a bigger army, you know. The spirit of the ocean kinda follows me around like a needy puppy. Mostly I just ignore it, but I can make it do a party trick or two."

The moon reflected in her wide eyes. "This is more than a mere trick, Joe."

He shrugged as best he could while floating. "Hey, you should see what my mom can do. She's the *actual* Heart of the Sea. I'm just her understudy. Anyway, she taught me how to do this when I was little. My parents insisted that I went to a human school, which meant living on land for most of the year. I was horribly homesick for Atlantis."

Seven cast him a perplexed look. "But from what I've heard, you hardly ever go to Atlantis now. You haven't been seen in the city for years."

"Yeah, well." He flicked a few drops of water at her. "I had my reasons for avoiding the place."

She gazed at him for a moment, eyes darkening. "And not only because you knew I was there."

She always saw right through him. "That was a big part of it, but yeah. Not all. Anyway, my mom taught me that the ocean was always with me, so I never needed to be homesick. Never tried to do this on anything bigger than a bathtub, though. How far out does it go?"

Seven dove fluidly underneath him, her back brushing his. Even when she moved further away, exploring the limits of his power, somehow he could still feel her. It was as though she swam through *him*, not the water. His awareness caressed every curve and angle of her body, from her parted lips to her spread toes. It was simultaneously the most erotic thing he'd ever experienced, and also the most disconcerting.

"About ten feet in all directions," Seven reported, resurfacing. "Centered on you. It's bizarre. It's like there's an invisible bubble holding the seawater in. It doesn't mix with the freshwater at all."

"Just as well, since I really don't want to poison all the poor innocent fish in this lake." He rolled over to face her, treading water. "They're going to be startled enough by having a shark in their midst. Promise you won't eat any of them, okay?"

The awe on Seven's face was abruptly snuffed out, replaced by something he couldn't read. "You want me to shift."

"That was kinda the whole point of this, yeah." He spoke through gritted teeth, trying to ignore the siren song of the sea. It was getting louder, more insistent, calling to him with every beat of his heart. Hungry currents curled around his ankles, trying to tug him down into the lightless depths. "And if you could hurry up, that would be awesome. This isn't entirely comfortable for me."

She hung motionless in the water. There was a kind of hungry longing in her face, like a dieter eying up a dessert cart. For an instant, he could see her waver, tempted.

Then she shook her head. "No. I can see that doing this is stressful for you. I'm touched by the effort, but there's no need. I am perfectly fine now."

"Seven—"

"I said no!" She kicked her feet, propelling herself out of his circle of sea in one savage motion. "Stop it, Joe! I don't want to shift, not ever! Stop trying to make me!"

No, his dragon said in his soul. *Dive deeper. Wrap her in the ocean, in the heart of the sea. This is who she is, no matter how she denies her soul.*

The ocean's tides pounded through his mind, drowning out all other thought. He clung to his human self like a bit of flotsam, fighting not to be swept away entirely.

But this is who we are, his dragon whispered, through the roar of the waves. *Why do you both resist your natures?*

With an effort, he walled himself off from the sea's insistent pull once more. His awareness shrank back to his own senses.

"It's okay." Even without tasting it, he knew that the water lapping against his chin was merely the lake once more. "It's gone now. I'm sorry. I won't pressure you about shifting again."

Seven edged back toward him, as cautiously as if expecting a whirlpool to open up beneath her at any moment. "Promise?"

"I promise." He stretched out, floating spread-eagled on the surface of the lake. He tipped his head back, gazing into the star-strewn sky. "But I wish that you would tell me why you're so scared of your shark."

She was silent for a long moment. He just drifted, not looking at her. Giving her space.

Then Seven's cool, sleek body brushed his side. She rested her head on his shoulder, her smooth legs entwining around his own. He drew her closer, stretching out his free arm to keep them both afloat. They lay together on the lake as if on a bed, ripples rocking them gently.

"My father," Seven said, very quietly, "was not a good man."

When she didn't go on, he prompted, "I take it you got your shark side from him."

He felt her nod. "I never actually knew him. My mother…worked very hard to ensure that. She only found out what he truly was after I was born."

"He didn't tell her he was a shifter, even when she got pregnant?"

"No. But that's not what I mean." Seven drew in a long, shaking breath. "My mother never wanted to talk about him much. But she isn't a fool. I think he must have been charming enough while he was wooing her, in an alpha, commanding sort of way. And he was rich—like, private island, luxury-yacht rich. He spun my mother a story about being a hedge fund manager, but really his income came from organized crime."

Joe hissed through his teeth. "Lot of sea shifters who don't like the Pearl Empire end up in that area."

"Yes. Especially sharks. My father had a whole crew of renegade shifters, that he hired out to anyone who could pay high enough. The mob, the cartel, pirates…no job was too dirty. When I was a baby, my mom finally found out the truth. She didn't want any part of it. And when she confronted him, he just laughed at her. Told her she was welcome to leave, that he was tired of her anyway. But that I was staying with him. Because I belonged with my own kind. And then he showed her what he meant."

"He shifted?"

"Partially. Just his head. He turned into a monster, right in front of her eyes." Seven stopped for a moment, her legs tightening around his. "She was so terrified she fainted. Which saved us both. Because it made my father think she was weak. He locked her in their bedroom, but didn't bother to assign anyone to watch her. And he left me in there with her, because my crying annoyed him. When my mother woke up, she grabbed me and escaped out a window. She went on the run with nothing more than me and the clothes on her back. My father sent his sharks out to track us down, but my mother managed to evade them all, for years and years. All his money, all his mob power and shifter magic, and he still couldn't defeat her."

He stroked her rigid shoulder with his thumb, a feather-light caress. "Y'know, I'm beginning to realize you don't get your toughness from your animal."

"My mother is the strongest woman you'll ever meet." Pride warmed Seven's voice. "She runs a homeless shelter now, near Boston. She keeps other women and children safe, just like she kept me safe."

"She sounds a lot like my mom. Just without a crown. Do you get to visit her much?"

"Not for a long time. My duties mean I'm rarely free to leave Atlantis. And..." She hesitated, a catch in her voice. "It would hurt my standing in the Order if I asked to visit her. All of the knights are native sea shifters, as are all the other squires. They don't understand why anyone would want to spend time on land."

It didn't take a genius to guess that there was one knight in particular who disapproved. Joe privately added yet another item to his ever-growing mental list, 'Reasons to Punch Lord Azure in the Face.'

"Well, I really want to meet her," he said. "And I don't see any reason why we couldn't go hang out in Boston after fire season finishes."

Assuming we both live that long. The thought scuttled across his mind like a cockroach. He stomped on it, hard.

"I'd like that," Seven said softly. "I think the two of you would get on well together. You're both alike, in some ways. Always able to smile, no matter what else is going on. Even when she was bone-tired from working three jobs, even when she was sick and stressed and scared, she could still always make me laugh. She gave me a proper childhood. We never had much, but I never lacked for love."

He lifted his head so he could gaze at her profile. "Were you happy?"

She was silent for a long, long moment, staring up at the full moon. A silvery trail of water gleamed on her cheek. He didn't think it had come from the lake.

"No," she said at last. "And it made me feel like the most ungrateful, awful child in the world. My mother had told me just enough about my father—that he was a bad man, a criminal, and that was why we had to kept running—that I understood how much she'd sacrificed for me. I knew she loved me. But somehow, I always felt like there was something missing. That I was...incomplete. And different from everyone else."

"Well, you were." Then he started, accidentally dunking Seven. "Wait. She *didn't tell you?*"

"That I was a shifter? Of course not." Seven sounded surprised at his surprise. "She was scared that if she did, I would be foolish enough to want to go to my father. She did everything she could to raise me totally human. She kept me away from the ocean, as far inland as possible. She didn't even allow me to go to swimming pools. She managed to keep me from shifting until I was twelve."

He inhaled lake water, and lost a few moments to undignified spluttering. Seven trod water at his side, calmly, as though she hadn't just revealed years of appalling trauma.

Many types of shifter didn't experience their first change until near puberty...but not sea shifters. Sea dragons, sharks, seals, dolphins...they were all, by necessity, born with the ability to shift. Their animals were fundamentally woven through their souls. They were *supposed* to shift.

To grow up being prevented from expressing that side of her soul *at all,* prevented from even knowing it existed...it was incredible that Seven was even sane.

"That," he wheezed, when he could speak again, "is utterly horrible. I get that your mom was scared, and that she had the best of intentions, but couldn't she see what she was doing to you?"

Seven stiffened at the implied criticism. She flicked her hands, opening up a few feet of space between them. "She was *protecting* me. From my inner beast, as much as from my father. As far as she knew, she was stopping me from turning into a monster. In fact, she did. It's thanks to her that I can pass as human as well as I can."

Now he understood her perfect, even teeth. If she'd never shifted before losing her baby teeth, her shark would have been too weak and repressed to influence the shape of her adult set. Her human smile had been bought by years of pain.

He'd only seen her shark-teeth, her *real* teeth, once. He remembered the feel of those sharp, deliciously dangerous points press against his lips. Showing that she was totally in the moment, all control abandoned...

With all his heart, he longed to awaken that side of Seven again. But insulting her beloved mother wouldn't help. And he *could* sympathize with the poor woman's impossible predicament. Given her first and only exposure to the entire concept of shifters, it was no wonder she'd done everything in her power to stop her daughter from discovering her true nature.

"I'm sorry," he said, meaning it. "I can't imagine how hard it must have been for your mom, as well as for yourself."

Seven's defensive, cold glare softened. She swam back to him again, her hands slipping around his waist. Gently, he enfolded her in his arms. Their legs moved in perfect, effortless unison, keeping their shoulders and heads above water.

"Tell me what happened when you were twelve," he murmured in her ear. "How you found out at last."

CHAPTER 24

Almost, she refused him. The memories of that day—*the* day—were too powerful, too personal. She'd never shared them with anyone.

But Joe's arms were warm and gentle, fingertips resting featherlight on her skin. He held her as though she was some fragile, impossibly precious treasure. Something intricate and delicate, that he was terrified of breaking.

Did he think her weak, like Lord Azure did? Before, he had always respected her strength, her honor. But now that he knew her past, was that all he saw? A confused, lost little girl?

She didn't want him to hold her like spun glass. She wanted him to see her as a partner in battle. She wanted him to hold her like a sword.

If he was ever to trust in her strength, her resolve, she had to tell him about the day that she'd changed. The day that everything had changed.

The day she'd found her destiny.

"We'd just moved again," she said. "It was the middle of summer vacation, thankfully. I always hated when we had to move halfway through school. We were living out of our tiny, run-down motorhome. I was supposed to stay inside while my mother was out working, but it was so hot I couldn't stand it. I only meant to find some shade, but I found myself walking down the road. It was...I can't describe it. Like something was *pulling* me on."

He drew back a little from their embrace to gaze at her. In the moonlight, his eyes were dark, all their sparkling turquoise laughter masked in shadow. "Your shark?"

Her wet braids clung to her shoulders as she nodded. "I didn't know that, then. I just knew that I *had* to keep going. I stumbled through the town, like I was sleepwalking, until I heard voices. Children's voices. Laughing and hollering and whooping. Normally that would have had me running straight for home again. Even...even as I was, back then, other kids could always sense that there was something wrong about me. Children are more perceptive than adults."

"And crueler," he said, softly.

"Yes," Seven said, and had to stop there.

He pulled her close again, without saying anything. The strong, even beat of his heart steadied her own. She closed her eyes, concentrating on his warmth—not only against her skin, but in her soul.

His gentle, steady presence gave her the strength to swallow the razor-edged memories, and find her voice again. "But something called to me, drowning out my fears. So I pushed open the gate. I went through. And found myself in the middle of a party. A pool party, in someone's backyard. Kids running around shrieking, cannonballing into the pool, squirting water guns at each other...I just froze, trying to understand what I was seeing. It felt like I'd stepped into a whole other world."

The baking heat of the patio through her worn flip-flops. The smoky, mouthwatering scent of the barbecue. It was all burned into her memory, so intensely that even now, years later, she could see every detail. The bright patterns of the women's sundresses, the men's shirts. The rainbow spray of water into the air.

And...*him*.

Words came slowly, inadequate to explain the enormity of that moment. "As I stood there gaping, I slowly realized that a man was watching me from across the yard. An old, old man, bald and wrinkled, but still huge. He should have been absolutely terrifying...but somehow, he wasn't. I'd never seen him before, but I felt like I'd known him all my life. And, more than that, I felt that he knew me. Better than my own mother did. Better than *I* did."

Joe let out an ear-splitting whoop, nearly scaring her out of her skin. Apparently entirely forgetting where they were, he thrust his arms in the air, and immediately sank like a stone. Seven made a grab at him as he disappeared, but not quite in time to save him from a dunking.

Joe re-emerged with lake water streaming from his broad grin. "I will bet you a week of bacon that I know what town you were in."

Understanding dawned at last. Her heart was still hammering from the fright he'd given her, but she grinned back.

"No bet." On a sudden playful whim, Seven splashed water at Joe, making him splutter. "You already told me he's your godfather, remember."

"Curses. Foiled by my own tongue." He chuckled, shaking his head. "I am very put out, you know. Here I was, eagerly looking forward to introducing you to the Master Shark, and it turns out you've already met him."

"Only that once. And I didn't know who or what he was until much later. At the time, all I knew was that there was something about him that made everything else..." She groped for a way to explain it. "Disappear. Like he was the center of the world."

"Yeah, he has that effect on people. Especially other sharks." His grin shifted into a smirk. "Not to me, though. It's hard to be in awe of someone who used to give you piggybacks round the backyard while making train noises."

She stared at him.

Joe shrugged. "I was four. At that age, if it didn't go 'choo-choo', I wasn't interested. I'm guessing he didn't do that with you, though."

The mental image of the most dangerous shifter in the sea jogging in circles while intoning 'choo-choo' was...arresting. With an effort, she wrested her mind back to her story.

"He came over to me," she said. "I thought he was going to yell at me, demand to know who I was, what I was doing gate-crashing the party. But he just nodded to me, as though we saw each other every day. He asked me if I wanted to swim. I told him I didn't know how. He looked at me a moment longer, then got down on one knee, stiffly, so that we were eye-to-eye. And he said, '*Yes. You do.*'"

She could see his face as clearly as Joe's, in front of her now. Every weathered wrinkle; every pale, faded scar. Those old, old eyes, as deep and ancient as the ocean itself.

"When he said that, he was close enough that I could see that his teeth weren't human." Even now, the memory still made her feel cold, an echo of the jolt of pure terror that had shot through her at the sight of those pointed, serrated rows. "I screamed and shoved him away. I ran for my life. Just like my mother had told me to do, over and over, if I ever saw someone with teeth like a shark."

Joe blinked at her, looking nonplussed. "Hold up. You said she didn't tell you about shifters."

A short, painful laugh escaped her tight throat. "No. She told me that my father's gang members filed their teeth into points. So I just thought that he was working for my father. That he'd found me at last, and was going to snatch me away from my mother. So I ran. I thought the man would pursue me, but he didn't. He just watched me go."

"Well, he *is* something like a hundred years old," Joe said, sounding oddly defensive, as though she was attacking his godfather's honor. "I expect he *wanted* to sprint after you. He found you later, right?"

"Not exactly. I ran all the way to the diner where my mom was working as a waitress, screaming and sobbing the whole way. When she finally calmed me down enough to get me to choke out what had happened..."

Seven had to stop again. *That* was another face that was burned in her memory—her mother's expression in that moment. It had been the only time she'd seen her mother's smile crack. The first time she'd realized that her mother could feel lost and terrified too.

"She took me by the hand," she said, living it again as she spoke. "She marched straight out without even a word to her manager. We left Ochre Rock within the hour. By the time night fell, we were halfway across Arizona. We thought we'd gotten away. And then, the next evening, there was a knock on the door of our motorhome. My mother answered it with her shotgun loaded and ready."

A kind of crazy hilarity bubbled up inside her, at the bizarre workings of fate. Of all the people who could have knocked on her door that night…she hung onto Joe's neck, fighting to control a sudden fit of giggles.

"And that," she concluded, "is the story of how my mother nearly shot your father."

"My *dad?*" Joe yelped—and the rest was lost in bubbles, as the water closed over both their heads.

Seven kicked her way back to the surface, dragging Joe with her. "For the Crown Prince of Atlantis, you are remarkably bad at swimming."

"Hey, you're the one who keeps dropping these depth charges on me." He shook water out of his eyes, grinning at her ruefully. "But yeah, we'd better continue this conversation back on land. I need solid ground under my feet for this."

He ducked away, his long, lean body cutting smoothly through the waters. He certainly *could* swim, when he remembered to. Seven couldn't resist dropping back a little, the better to admire the flex of his muscled back.

He got to the shore first, and turned to offer her his hand, bowing like an old-fashioned gentleman helping a lady out of a carriage. He even mimed sweeping off an imaginary top hat. She rolled her eyes at him, but felt a smile tug at her lips anyway. She took his hand, letting him escort her out of the water.

She squeezed out of her braids, holding them away from her skin. "We should have brought towels. I can hardly parade through the base in my underwear, but I can't put my armor back on while I'm dripping wet."

"It's a warm night. We'll dry off soon. Just have to wait a little while to get dressed." Joe's voice dropped a little, taking on a hungry, feral edge that sent a delicious shiver down her spine. His heated gaze swept over her, slowly, from head to toe. "What a pity."

His wet jeans clung to him, leaving absolutely nothing to the imagination. Seven dragged her own eyes up to his face. "I'm afraid that if you want to hear the end of the story, you're going to have to put a shirt on. Whether you're dry or not."

His mouth quirked in a cocky, masculine grin. "Hey now, not fair. You can't expect *me* to put clothes on over wet skin if you aren't going to. Anyway, I don't see what your problem is. I'm just standing here."

He flexed, abs rippling in a way that got Seven's *full* attention. She found herself taking a step toward him, her hands reaching out as though drawn by magnets.

The playfulness vanished from his face the instant her fingertips made contact with his skin. In a swift, sudden movement, he captured her hand, pressing her palm against his hard chest. A jolt of heat shot down her arm, straight to her core.

"Sea." He breathed the word as though it was a curse. "I want you."

He dragged her unresisting hand downward. Everything else flew out of her head. Her pulse pounded between her legs as he guided her over his ridged muscles, under the edge of his waistband, down further—

He hissed another curse, yanking her hand back up again. She couldn't help the muffled sound of protest that escaped her lips.

"Sorry." He released her, stepping away. He adjusted his jeans. "Got—got carried away. I think *you'd* better put my shirt on."

"That really wouldn't help," she got out through the waves of desire pounding through her blood. "Not me, at least."

He flashed her a pained grin. "And considering that we've established that you can turn me on in turn outs, it probably wouldn't help me all that much either. But much as I want you, I also want to hear the rest of your story." He flopped down onto the grassy lakeshore, flinging one arm across his eyes. "Okay. I'm listening, and not looking. Talk fast before I run out of willpower. You said that my dad found you and your mom?"

She sat down next to him, doing her best not to look at him either. "I found out later that the Master Shark had called him. Told him what had happened, and where to find me. The Imperial Champion must have dropped everything and travelled without rest to catch up with us. All for one confused, scared little girl."

"Yes," he said softly. His arm still hid his eyes, but his mouth curved in a small, fond smile. "That sounds like my dad."

"He turned up in full armor." She smiled as well, thinking of that tall, shining figure incongruously framed by the door of their motorhome. "I think that was the only reason my mother *didn't* shoot him. He looked like he'd stepped out of a fairytale. He was too unreal to be a threat. He bowed to her, as though she was a queen, and he told her he was a knight of the First Water. And that he had come to protect us."

She remembered his gauntleted hands, holding out his sword to her. Her own fingers had looked tiny and frail in comparison. She hadn't understood then what he was doing, what a sea dragon's oath meant, not even what a Knight of the First Water was.

But when she'd touched the worn hilt of the sword, when she'd looked into his indigo eyes, when she'd heard his voice…she'd known that he was speaking the truth. That he *would* protect them, just like he said, to his dying breath. That she and her mother were safe at last, because he was strong enough to protect them from anything.

And she could still remember, with utter clarity, thinking: *I want to be like that.*

She glanced at Joe and found him watching her from beneath his arm. His eyes were steady and thoughtful, as though he'd heard what she hadn't said.

She cleared her throat. "Anyway, that's pretty much all there is to tell. The Knights of the First Water took care of my father and his thugs. The Sea Council worked out an arrangement with my mother. She let me come to Atlantis so I could learn about my shifter side."

Joe was still watching her with that intent, unwavering focus. "The Sea Council tried to foster you with a shark family, right?"

How had he guessed that? "Yes. But I wouldn't go. I'd already decided that there was only one path for me. I was stubborn enough that they eventually relented, and let me join the preliminary training classes for sea dragons aspiring to join the knights. I suspect your father had something to do with that. They would never have accepted a shark without some quiet pressure from the Pearl Throne."

"Hey, don't give him too much credit. He might have got you in the door, but *you're* the one who earned your place. I know the knights only pick about one in ten aspirants to become novices." A swift, sudden grin flashed across Joe's face. "My youngest sister is in training now. She's hoping to be good enough to be chosen as a squire next year. She's a nervous wreck about it. Maybe you can give her some tips."

Seven privately thought that a royal princess of the Pearl Throne had very little need of her advice. The knights were *supposed* to be blind to bloodline when deciding who was worthy to join the Order... but there were a suspiciously high number of noble-born squires.

"Anyway, the rest you know." She waved at her discarded armor and stun sword. "And that's why I am the way I am. You accused me of being afraid of my animal, Joe. I'm not, truly. I just take no pride in it either. I wasn't raised as a shark. It doesn't form part of my identity, not the way that your own animal does for you. Can you understand that?"

"Yes." Amusement fell away from his face. "I think I understand now. You want to be a sea dragon knight. *That's* your identity."

"Exactly," she said, relieved. "My shark is just a handicap to overcome. I refuse to have my destiny determined by some accident of bloodline. You of all people should understand—"

"No," Joe interrupted. He propped himself up on his elbows, his gaze holding hers. "I mean, you want to be a *sea dragon* knight. Seven, if Lord Azure appeared right now, this instant, and knighted you at last, would that be enough? Would you be the person that you want to be? Would you finally be happy?"

The words struck her harder than any blow she'd ever taken in combat.

Because the answer was: *No.*

Lord Azure could knight her. Her hair could be weighed down with golden honor-tokens. The entire city of Atlantis could hail her as a hero.

And it would still never be enough.

She looked down, shredding bits of grass between her fingers. "You must think me very foolish."

"Oh, Seven." Joe sat up, hitching himself closer. He put an arm around her shoulders, drawing her against his side. "I get it, you know. I really do. When I was a kid, I wanted more than anything in the world to measure up to my mom and dad. I know how much it hurts to want to be like someone, with all your soul, only to discover that you never can."

She leaned into his warmth. His salt-sea scent wrapped around her like a quilt. "You didn't keep dashing your heart against an impossible dream, though."

She felt him let out a long, heavy sigh. "No. I kinda went the other way. I couldn't live up to my role models, but I sure could be their exact opposite. I'm not claiming that's any better."

She closed her eyes against the burn of tears. "When I was a child, a magical knight in shining armor rescued me from a monster. He whisked me away to an enchanted underwater kingdom. I learned that dreams could come true."

She longed to keep clinging to him, drawing strength from his strength...but she straightened her spine, pulling away. The warm summer night suddenly felt much colder on her damp skin.

"I never learned that not *all* dreams could come true," she said. "You are right. I need to finally face reality, and find new dreams. I will never be a sea dragon."

Joe started to speak, but she put a finger against his lips, stopping him. For a moment, she let her hand linger on his face, feeling the softness of his mouth, the slight rasp of stubble on his jaw.

Then she let him go. She sat back, set her shoulders, and made herself say what she must.

"And I will never be a knight, either."

CHAPTER 25

"What?" He stared at her, trying to work out how in the sea she'd come to *that* conclusion. "Seven, you're already more of a knight than most of the knights I know."

"But I am not a knight. No matter how I act, how I feel, I cannot take that title for myself. It can only be given to me by another knight." Seven sat very straight, her shoulders squared. Only the slightest tremble to her lower lip betrayed how hard she was fighting to keep her composure. "And Lord Azure will never do that. Because I am abandoning my quest."

"You mean your assignment as my bodyguard?" Joe wanted to reach for her, but something about her tight, rigid posture warned him off. "Seven, I thought we'd been through this. You didn't fail today because you aren't a dragon. You *saved* me."

"Yes. Today. But tomorrow, or the next day, or the next, I will not." Her grey eyes flashed, stopping him as he tried to object. "You *saw* it, Joe. Over and over again. You knew that it was a warning that I could not stand by your side. Do not try to claim otherwise now."

"But I'm not getting that vision anymore." Joe waved at the lake, which still showed him nothing but the reflection of the moon. "We didn't need to capture Lupa after all. By driving the hellhound pack off today, you changed that future."

"No. That is not what changed the future." Seven rose—not with her usual fluid grace, but jerkily, as though her own body was fighting her. "*This* is what changed it."

She turned, picking up her discarded stunsword. He hadn't the faintest clue what she was doing...until she went to both knees in front of him, offering him the weapon.

Not across her palms, in the manner of a knight swearing an oath.

Hilt-first.

Every sea dragon knew *that* gesture. It signaled deepest shame, an admission of utter loss of honor. In ancient times, a knight who offered their sword like that expected the recipient to draw it...and strike off the failed knight's head.

These days, the ritual gesture wasn't treated as a literal request for assisted suicide, but he still scrabbled back as though the pearl-inlaid pommel was a live viper. "No. No, Seven. I'm not touching that."

"You have no choice." She laid the weapon at his feet, gently, carefully. "I swore an oath to stand by your side. That cannot simply be retracted. It can only be undone by death, or dishonor. You must take my sword, Joe. It is the only way that I can stand aside, so that someone worthier can take my place. Someone who will be able to succeed where I would have failed. Someone who will be able to protect you in the battle that still lies ahead."

To touch the sword would be to accept her self-proclaimed dishonor. He made futile flapping gestures at the weapon, as though it was a chicken he could shoo back to Seven. "There's no one worthier than you. I want you at my side, guarding my back. I *need* you."

"Joe." Seven circled round the sword to crouch in front of him. She took his head between her hands, making him meet her steady, certain gaze. "I need you too. I need you to be *safe*. You told me yourself that I was not going to be able to protect you, but my pride and dreams of knighthood deluded me into trying anyway. I know better now. I have to return to Atlantis, so that someone stronger can take my place as your bodyguard."

"But your knighthood." His distress distorted the human words, blending them with a sea dragon's keening cry of grief. "Your dream."

She bent over him, her braids swinging to curtain them both. Gently, so gently, her mouth brushed his. He closed his eyes, tears leaking from under the lids, as she kissed him; softly, sweetly.

"It was a false dream," she whispered against his lips. "Just a delusion. You have shown me the truth. *You* are my dream now. And this is the only way I can keep you safe."

He couldn't let her do this. He *couldn't*.

But if he did…

She would go back to Atlantis.

She would be safe.

NO! his sea dragon bellowed, shaking the foundations of his mind. *She is our mate! We need her at our side, always!*

He drew back from Seven a little. "Can—can you give me a second?"

She must have guessed his intentions. She nodded, releasing him.

His dragon fought him all the way to the water. He ignored its furious roars, locking it away behind the sea-wall that divided his soul. Seven didn't let her shark rule *her* decisions. There were times you had to think with your head, not your heart.

At the edge of the lake, he stopped. He closed his eyes for a moment, gathering his will.

Please, he silently begged fate, or destiny, or the sea itself. *Show me what to do.*

He looked down into the lake.

∽

Joe stood still and silent. The minutes stretched out, long enough that Seven began to wonder if he *was* having a vision.

But his eyes didn't flicker to follow the ghosts of the future. His scent didn't change, either with distress or relief. He just stared down into the water, absolutely motionless.

And she knew, in her heart of hearts, that he saw nothing but his own reflection.

He turned away at last. The agony in his eyes nearly broke her. She lifted her chin, forcing her own expression to remain calm and certain. He had to make the right decision. She had to make this easy for him.

"You promise you'll go back to Atlantis?" he asked, voice hoarse.

"I will. I would stay at your side if I could, even in dishonor, but you will be safer without me. As long as I am on land, there is a risk that our enemies could capture me." She smiled at him, to hold back her tears. "I know only too well what you would do in that situation."

He made a sound that was half acknowledgement, half pain. "Serve myself up on a silver platter with an apple in my mouth. Oh, sea. I hate this." He scrubbed his hands across his face. "Damn us sea dragons and our stupid customs and our stupid, *stupid* honor. What idiot came up with the concept of a binding vow, anyway? People shouldn't be shunned for changing their minds. And you shouldn't idolize sea dragons. We *suck*."

She picked up her stunsword, for the last time. Once more, she offered him the hilt, laid across her forearm.

"Please, Joe," she whispered. "For me. For us."

His hand hovered over the hilt. He reached for it, then jerked back. His mouth twisted in misery.

With a low, animal sound of pure pain, he put his palm on the pommel. He barely touched it, yet Seven felt the jolt of it all down her arm. It was as intimate as if he'd laid his hand against her naked skin; more than that. It felt like he was holding her exposed, beating heart.

"My prince," she said formally, fighting with every ounce of willpower not to break down. "I leave your service. I forsake my vow and break my oaths. My hand dishonors this blade. I relinquish it to you in reparation for the harm I have caused. May you find one worthier to bear it."

Slowly, carefully, he took her weapon from her. It was like losing a limb.

"I accept your blade." He put it down, carefully, as though it was a sleeping infant. When he straightened again, his eyes were fierce, blazing with an emotion she'd never seen there before. "But only for now. Because what you have touched, no other may claim. I will guard what is yours until you return to take it up once more."

That wasn't part of the ritual. Her breath caught as she realized what he was trying to do.

Trust Joe to attempt to bulldoze over millennia of tradition. Unfortunately, in this case, sea dragon customs were stronger than even Joe's stubbornness. She was touched by the gesture, but she knew it was futile.

"It doesn't work like that," she said, gently. "The knights won't accept—"

"Oh, they will accept." His deep, growling voice shook her soul, drowning out her doubt. He took a single swift, abrupt step forward, catching her chin in his free hand. "Because you will *not* go to Atlantis in dishonor or disgrace, Seventh Novice of the Order of the First Water, Guardian of the Sea's Heart. You will go in triumph, with celebrations and fanfare, to present yourself to the Pearl Empress as tradition demands. You will go as a Princess of Atlantis. You will go as my mate."

Trapped in his grasp, she could only stare at him, dumbfounded. He didn't wait for a reply. He bent to capture her mouth, roughly, savagely. Heat crashed through her as his tongue thrust past her startled lips, claiming her ruthlessly.

He bore her backwards, down to the grass, never breaking the kiss. The world spun around her head. She couldn't have said which way was up or down, whether she was on solid land or still floating in the lake. His powerful arms bracketed her, muscles rigid, pinning her in place. His scent filled her lungs. She was consumed by him, by the dizzying need to be filled by him.

She broke off the kiss, wrenching her head to the side. She put her hands flat on his chest, but couldn't muster the strength to push him away.

"W-we can't," she gasped, fighting for control. "Your vision—"

He wound her braids round one hand, forcing her to face him. He was breathing as hard as if he'd just run an ultramarathon. There was no playfulness in his turquoise eyes now. They were dark with raw, animal desire, focused on her with the utter concentration hunting predator.

"Swear to me you'll go." He gave her a little shake to emphasize the words—not hard enough to hurt, but emphatic enough that the show of dominance sent a fresh wave of heat gushing between her legs. "Swear on your honor you'll leave me here. *Swear it.*"

This was a side of him she'd never seen...and she liked it. It scared her, how much she liked it. This was how sharks mated, after all; teeth to teeth and bite for bite, grappling to a fierce, savage climax. The core of her soul resonated in response to his aggression.

"I swear." She could barely get the words out through the desire pounding through her. "On my honor."

His white teeth flashed in a fierce, triumphant smile. "Then you're mine. *Now.*"

He pulled her head back further, exposing her throat. She gasped as his hot mouth fastened on her neck. He kissed his way from her jaw to the hollow of her throat, open-mouthed, biting. Every rough scrape of his teeth against her skin had her bucking upward, desperate for more.

He went lower still, nibbling along her collarbone. He released her hair at last, freeing his hands so he could yank down the straps of her bra. She arced up to give him access to undo the garment. Her nipples were already drawn to hard points. The slight breath of the warm, gentle night breeze only made them stiffen further. She needed his tongue *there*, now, or she might explode with frustration.

She wanted to tell Joe what she wanted, but she'd lost all words. There was nothing in her head but pleasure and pounding desire. She writhed, yanking at his neck, silently urging him lower.

Joe's mouth curved against her skin. With maddening slowness, he ran his tongue in a teasing spiral over one breast. She tried to thrust up into his mouth, but his strong hands pinned her shoulders, holding her down. He savored her skin as though she was a rare wine to be sipped at leisure. She could only submit to the exquisite torment of his languid, unhurried exploration.

When his mouth finally closed over her nipple, stars shot through her. Her whole body came alive, electric with sensation. Every pull, every suck, made her core pulse in response. She wrapped her legs around him, hips jerking in helpless need.

His tongue swirled, teasing her, bringing ever-increasing waves of pleasure. He gripped her other breast in his hand, hard, rolling and pinching her nipple. The contrast of the softness of his mouth on one side, the roughness of his work-hardened hand on the other—she shattered. Ecstasy swept over and through her, blinding.

"Sea," he said hoarsely, releasing her nipple at last. "I've wanted to do that for so long. I could listen to you come all day."

She'd been lying boneless, adrift on the slowly receding tide of her orgasm, but his words brought her back to herself with a jolt. What ugly, animal noises had she been making? She was suddenly, horribly aware of her teeth, sharp and jagged in her mouth—

"Hey." Joe surged up her body, so that his face hung over hers once more. His hands cupped her face. "Stay with me. Stay with me, Seven. I need you. All of you."

His eyes filled her world. Dark pools of desire, filled with love.

He wanted *her*.

All of her.

He dipped his head, kissing her forehead, her eyelids, her cheeks, murmuring her name breathlessly between each one. He kissed her mouth—not as roughly as before, but still with that steely, irresistible command. A little twist of apprehension shot through the heat building in her…but she opened to him anyway, letting him in.

His strong, sure tongue stroked into her, banishing her lingering self-consciousness. She had an intense, aching desire to explore his mouth in return—but she didn't dare. It would be too easy to lose control, to hurt him. She held her head still as his tongue ran over her sharp-edged teeth.

Still, she couldn't help her body arcing. His taste, his touch, every movement of his mouth on hers, it all reignited the fire deep in her lower belly.

She ran her hands down the smooth, intoxicating curve of his back. She worked her fingers under the tight waistband of his still-damp jeans, and was rewarded by a heartfelt groan and a flex of his hips. His solid bulge ground against her thigh, making her core throb in response.

He was too damn *tall*—kissing her like this, face to face, she couldn't get his hardness where she needed it. She squirmed under him, trying to work her way lower, or pull him higher.

He broke off the kiss, bracing himself on his arms. His chest and abs flexed, taking her breath away. He rolled upright, to his knees, straddling her. The buttons of his jeans strained, barely able to contain his erection.

He fought to undo his pants, face twisted in a frustrated snarl. With a savage jerk, he ripped the top two buttons off entirely, giving himself enough space to loosen the rest. He didn't waste time trying to peel his pants off. He just shoved the wet denim down his lean hips. His cock leaped free at last.

Her pulse pounded even harder at the sight of his hard, straining shaft. His erection was in proportion to the rest of him—which meant it was *enormous*. She didn't feel the slightest bit intimidated, though. His size only made her more dizzy with desire, fresh wetness welling between her legs in readiness.

She reached for him, but he caught her hand. He raised her wrist to his face, inhaling her scent. Her breath caught at the light press of his teeth against her skin.

"Don't touch me." His voice was a growl, his breath as ragged as hers. "Not yet. Sea, you're so gorgeous. I'll come if you touch me, I won't be able to help it. And I need to come in you. Buried deep in your beautiful, beautiful body, feeling you shudder and clench around me. Oh, sea, I need you. Seven. *Seven.*"

He lifted his weight off her. Still murmuring frantic, filthy things, he tore her shorts off. One of his legs nudged her knees apart. She opened for him eagerly, spreading wide. She heard his breath catch in a gasp that was nearly a snarl, an animal sound of pure want. His cock jerked, liquid beading at the tip.

"Oh sea, Seven. Do you know what you're doing to me?" His palms skimmed over her inner thighs, making her tremble. "Let me look at you. Sea, let me just look at you."

He ran his hands down her legs, lifting them, spreading her wider. He hooked her ankles over his broad shoulders, and grabbed hold of her hips, tugging her up onto his lap so she was even more exposed to his hungry, avid gaze.

"Beautiful," he breathed. "So beautiful. My beautiful mate."

He ran one finger lightly over her sex. She bucked at the first contact, fireworks shooting through her. He traced her slick, swollen folds, every touch electrifying.

"Yes," he growled in approval. "So wet for me."

He pushed two fingers into her, and her vision blurred. She tightened around him, convulsively, yearning for more—but he drew back instead, leaving her empty and aching.

"Wait. I need this first." He put his fingers into his mouth, tasting her juices. His eyes closed, as a low groan escaped his lips. "Sea, you're sweet. So sweet. My Seven. My mate."

His hand dove back down, plundering her once more. This time he went further, harder, curling his fingers up so she saw stars. Words fell from his lips in time with each thrust.

"I want to keep tasting you so badly." His voice shook with need. "Soak my tongue in you. Lick you until you're overflowing, drink every drop as you come."

Despite his harsh, hungry words he didn't dip his head to replace his fingers with his mouth. He just kept stroking her rhythmically, coaxing her to higher bliss with each thrust. He added a third finger, stretching her even wider, filling her up even more deliciously.

"But if my face is buried between your thighs, I can't watch you." His thumb found her plump, swollen nub, and lightning shot through her entire body. "And I need to watch you. I need to see you come. I want to see you shatter for me, Seven, my Seven. I'm too hot, I'm going to explode the instant I slide into you. I'm going to come in you so hard, I won't be able to see, won't be able to see your face as you come too. I want to see you. Yes, that's right, like that. Show me."

How was he still *talking?* She had no idea, but she didn't want him to stop. His words caressed her as much as his strong hands, intensifying every sensation. His voice lifted her like the sea itself, buoying her up, whispering encouragement, until she was weightless, floating out of the world, tumbling upward into infinite stars—

"Yes," he breathed. "Like that. Now. *Now*, Seven."

She lost herself entirely, becoming nothing but rolling waves of pleasure. He held her through the storm, supporting her, murmuring the whole time.

"Oh, sea. Yes. Beautiful." He was still muttering broken, disconnected fragments as she came back down, his voice rough and desperate. "My beautiful shark. Mine. My mate. Mine."

He withdrew his hand. She could feel her own wetness slicking his fingers as he grabbed her hips. He lifted her as effortlessly as if she was a doll, shifting their positions so that her legs wrapped around his waist. Her core was still fluttering from her last orgasm, but a fresh pulse went through her as his hardness pressed against her.

His fingers tightened. His eyes met hers, blazing rings of turquoise fire. He bared his teeth in animal triumph.

"*Mine*," he said again.

He slid into her, burying himself to the hilt in one fierce thrust. She'd thought herself wrung out and spent, at her limit—but he crashed through her like a tsunami, sweeping her back into bliss with shocking suddenness. It was more than just the powerful surge of his body into hers, glorious as that was. *He* was in her, in her mind, her soul.

True to his word, Joe went rigid at that first thrust. He was so deep she could feel every pulse, every twitch, as he fought for control. His face twisted, tendons standing out in his neck.

She didn't want him to hold back. She wanted all of him, now, pouring into her without restraint.

She ground against him, making him gasp and swear. Still he held on, though sweat stood out on his brow. His arms flexed, pulling her upright so that they were pressed together, skin to skin, torso to torso. She didn't realize what he wanted until his hand tightened on the back of her head.

"Mine," he gasped, pulling her mouth down to his hard, hot shoulder. "Yours. Always. Claim me."

His salt-sea scent filled her lungs. His body filled hers. Nothing else existed, nothing else mattered. Everything was bright and simple and clear.

She bit him.

With an ecstatic groan, he spilled into her at last. Somewhere in the sea of bliss, their animals swam to meet each other. His dragon's coils entwined around her shark. They spiraled higher and higher, in perfect unison, until together they broke through into brilliant, blinding delight.

∽

Seven was quiet, after. He held her close, feeling the slow beat of her heart against his chest. The mate bond rippled between them, as calm and deep as the moonlit lake.

She stirred first. He could have lain there forever, wrapped in wonder, but she sat up, disentangling herself from him.

"How bad is it?" she asked.

It took him a second to work out that she meant the bite. He ran a finger over the neat circle of triangular puncture marks. They were already scabbing over, his shifter healing kicking in. Even so, it was deep enough to scar. He would carry her mark on his body for the rest of his life.

"It's perfect." He sat up too, capturing her mouth for a long, lingering kiss. "Like you."

She let out an aggrieved huff, but kissed him back. Her teeth were human again now, but no less intoxicating. He lost himself in exploring her sweet mouth.

"I've just realized," he said, pulling back. "You were born on land. You must have a human name."

She tensed. "No. Not anymore. I'm Seventh Novice now. That's my *real* name. The one I've earned."

"Yes, but—"

"We should still get back to the cabin," she interrupted. She reached for her armor, starting to strap her breastplate back on. "You need medical attention."

The faint throb of pain in his shoulder felt very distant. The gathering ache in his groin as she bent over to pull on her leggings was of far more pressing concern.

She narrowed her eyes at him, past her legs. "Stop that."

"Can't." He pushed himself to his feet, embracing her from behind. She gasped as he pulled her back against him. "I have the most beautiful mate in the world. I'm pretty sure it's physically impossible for me to tear myself away from you long enough to let us get back to the base. Resign yourself. We live here now."

Her short, breathless laugh was more addictive than any drug. Sea, he hadn't heard her laugh enough. He wanted to make her laugh again. And to gasp, and sigh, and scream—

"I *said*, stop that." With a wriggle that sent liquid fire shooting through him, she twisted free. She backed off, stooping to collect the rest of their clothes. "We have a lot to do."

He was fully hard again already. He'd always assumed that being fully mated would lessen his driving need for her, but no one seemed to have informed his cock that. "Yes. And you're top of my list."

She tossed him an exasperated look, along with his shirt. "We have to bandage that wound, no matter what you say. We need to get some rest. And..." Her voice wavered fractionally, something raw and vulnerable flashing across her face. "And we need to contact Atlantis."

The thought hit him like a bucket of ice water, sobering him up. "I can do that now. I'll contact my mom through the lake. I'm no good at most forms of communication-scrying, but I can always reach her. Another Imperial trick."

Seven bit her lip. "What...what will you tell her?"

"The truth." He stepped forward, taking her hands. "That I'm mated to the most incredible woman in or out of the sea. That you've agreed to go home because I can't stand the thought of you putting yourself at risk for me. That I need her to send another knight to guard me instead."

Her eyes searched his face. "But not about your talent?"

A guilty twinge shot through his chest, but he shook his head. "She doesn't need to know about that. Just the fact that you're my mate will be enough to explain why I can't have you as my bodyguard."

Her lips tightened, but she didn't try to argue further. She turned away, reaching down for her stunsword—and froze. He felt the sudden thud of her heart down the mate bond. She straightened again, slowly, never taking her eyes off the weapon.

"You'll have to carry that," she said, very quietly.

"Seven." Her silent agony made his own heart tighten. "It's still yours. I don't care what oaths you swore."

"But I do." She jerked her gaze away from her sword, fists clenching. "Take it, Joe. Please."

He wanted to hold her, but he knew it wouldn't help. Nothing he could do would help.

He pulled up his jeans, buttoning them. Then he bent to collect Seven's stunsword. He juggled the pearl baton awkwardly for a moment, trying to work out the most respectful way to carry it, and then gave up and just shoved it through a belt loop. It would serve him right if it went off unexpectedly and zapped him in the ass.

Seven had finished strapping on her armor. For a moment, her hand hovered oddly in mid-air, trying to rest on a hilt that wasn't there anymore.

She let it fall to her side instead. "I'll see you back at our cabin after you've talked to your mother. Don't be too long. We still need to bandage that bite."

"Seven," he called after her, desperately searching for words to make things better. "My mom will understand. She won't let anyone shame you. I'll make sure of that. Everything's going to be okay now. You'll see."

CHAPTER 26

The sky was blood red. A ceiling of smoke hung over the forest, reflecting the light from the smoldering fires below. In a clearing surrounded by towering, ancient pines, a woman's voice rose, harsh and desperate.

Not laughing. Not cold and triumphant.

"No." Lupa spun on her heel, fists clenching. "No! I won't let you do this."

No chains around his wrists. He wasn't there. For the first time, he wasn't going to be there.

But someone else was.

The hunched, ice-white shape of the wendigo faced Lupa across the clearing. Its skull-head lowered, like a buck about to charge. It took a step forward, leaving a frost-filled footprint in its wake.

"I said no!" Lupa lunged at the beast, pressing both hands to the center of its broad, shaggy chest. "Stop, Mort! As your alpha, I command you!"

The great beast's paw froze in mid-air. The burning blue eyes regarded Lupa steadily.

Then the monster melted into a man. An older man, his gaunt face lined with grief, hair gone to frost. But his eyes were the same, pale blue, gentle and certain.

"Lupa." The man took her shoulders, embracing her like a daughter. "We always knew it would come to this."

The raven-haired woman shook her head fiercely, pressed against the man's chest. "Just a little more time. Just one more day. Please, Mort."

"We're out of time. The queen's getting impatient." The wendigo named Mort gently pushed her away again, holding her at arm's-length. He brushed Lupa's hair away from her face, exposing the mark on her forehead. It stood out on her pale skin, livid as a fresh wound. "I know what she's doing to you."

Lupa tossed her head, making her hair cover the mark again. "I can take it. I'll talk to her. Persuade her to be patient. We can still pull off plan A. The hotshot crew are here now, all of them, working the fire."

Mort let out a pained breath of laughter. "And isn't *that* ironic."

"No, it's destiny. Fate is on our side. The sea dragon is with them, he could still take your place. I have Wulfric shadowing the crew's every move. All we need is a single opportunity—"

"They aren't going to give us that. They're onto us now. And it's taking everything the pack's got just to hold off the Thunderbird, now that *it's* wise to us. If it gets through and burns the sacred ground before the king can rise, it'll all be over. You know what she'd do."

Lupa's face paled, but her jaw set stubbornly. "It won't come to that. I'll make the pack stronger. I'll go tonight, find more men, turn as many as we need. They'll do what I tell them to. And so will you."

"You are my alpha, but you don't control me like you do them. And I won't let you risk yourself for me." The old sorrow in Mort's face deepened. "I promised your father I'd protect you."

Lupa started to reply, then gave a cry of pain. She bent over, her hair swinging to shadow her face. Both her hands pressed against her head as though she was having to hold her skull together.

The wendigo's face twisted in matching, helpless agony. He hugged her again, holding her close, until her spasms passed.

This was wrong, all wrong. He was supposed to be there. There were supposed to be chains around his wrists. This wasn't what was meant to happen.

"Lupa." Mort bent his grey head, pressing his cheek against her sleek hair. "Little one. It's time. Let me do this. For your father's sake. For you."

Lupa's breath came in harsh, hitching sobs. Her arms tightened around him. "But you'll be *gone*. If you're a willing sacrifice, it will eat your soul instantly."

He wouldn't have been a willing sacrifice. He would have fought, to the last breath in his body. It was supposed to be him.

Lupa's voice cracked, broke. "We won't—we won't even have time to say goodbye."

"So we'll say goodbye now." Mort kissed the top of Lupa's head, tenderly as a father tucking his child into bed. "Goodbye, little one. I love you. Never forget that."

The hellhound alpha's voice was barely audible. "I won't."

For a moment, Lupa just clung to the wendigo shifter, like a lost little girl. Then she let him go. She knelt, pressing one palm against the rich, dark soil.

"Father of Serpents." The mark on her forehead lit up, pulsing with a sickly red light. "Blood calls to blood. The world turns, the storms fade, and the time of snakes and shadows comes once more. Rise, horned consort, the ever-hungry one, the one who gnaws at the roots of the world. Accept...accept this..."

Her voice faltered. Mort put a hand on her shoulder. His fingers tightened, squeezing, once.

"Accept this willing sacrifice," he said softly.

"This willing sacrifice." Lupa closed her eyes. A tear trickled down her cheek, but she went on, her voice gathering strength once more. "His heart awaits you, shadow-snake, eater of mountains. Come, devour, and grow strong, that you may serve your queen. On her behalf I call you by name: Unktehi, crowned serpent, mighty consort. It is time. The way is open. Rise."

The ground split apart. Thick black smoke poured upward, taking the form of an enormous serpent. Sharp horns curved from its broad forehead. Slits opened in the inky darkness; twin chasms of burning, malevolent lava. The demon hung above Lupa and Mort, taller than the trees, old as night.

It was supposed to be him. He *was supposed to look up into those hellfire eyes, see them fasten on him in bottomless hunger. See the fanged mouth open—*

Lupa's face twisted as she stared up at the towering evil she'd summoned. She scrambled to her feet, starting to fling her arms wide in front of Mort—but if she'd had a change of heart, it had come far too late.

The horned serpent struck, slamming straight into Mort's broad chest. If it had been a physical creature, the impact would have crushed even the massive wendigo shifter into a thin smear—but he just gasped, mouth and eyes opening wide, his whole body stiffening.

The serpent poured into him like water into a cup. Crimson fire filled his pale eyes. In seconds, the shadowy creature was gone. Only Mort remained.

Or rather, his body.

Its hands twitched, flexing like claws. It let out a long, satisfied breath, looking down at itself.

"Such strength." The hissing voice wasn't Mort's. "Such power."

Tears streaked Lupa's face. "This sacrifice pleases you, serpent-father?"

"It pleases me very much." Ice crystals flurried through the air. Frost was forming where it stood, spreading out from its feet. Lupa shivered. "With this host, I can freeze the world. You have done well, child."

Lupa hugged herself. Her lips were already blue with cold. "Devourer, even now my pack holds your enemy at bay. They give their lives for you. If it pleases you, will you join the fight?"

"The last Thunderbird's feathers shall fall like snow." The abomination's thin lips stretched, exposing teeth that were already sharpening into fangs. "My queen shall rise again."

It wasn't right. It wasn't right. *It was supposed to be him, he was supposed to be there, HE WAS SUPPOSED TO BE THERE—*

Someone was calling his name, shaking him. The vision broke, shattered. As the swirling shards evaporated like morning dew, he caught one last snatch of the demon's triumphant, hissing voice.

"And together, we shall feast."

~

"Joe! *Joe!*"

He bolted upright, heart hammering. For a terrifying moment, the darkness enclosing him was the demon's inky blackness—and then his eyes adjusted to the faint dawn light. The slice of sky visible through the small window was clear and untroubled by smoke; the faint woody scent came not from towering pines, but from the familiar log walls of his own cabin.

Seven's arms slid around his waist. She hugged him from behind, her bare skin pressed against his. He leaned back against her soft curves, her solid strength. Her soul embraced him as much as her body. Gradually, his racing pulse slowed.

Seven rested her chin on his shoulder. Her voice was soft in his ear. "That wasn't your usual vision, was it."

"No." The word came out as a croak. He moistened his dry lips. "Something new."

Her strong, calloused hands started to knead the tension out of his knotted back muscles. "I thought you didn't get visions after sex."

"I never have, before." He moistened his dry lips. "Did I...did I say anything?"

"Not much. Mostly, you were just twitching. Then you started muttering something about how you were supposed to be somewhere. You seemed so concerned about it, I was worried that you were about to try to walk there in your sleep. So I woke you up." She pressed a gentle kiss to his bare shoulder blade. "So you could at least put some pants on first."

"Thanks." He was still drenched in cold sweat, but he forced a chuckle. "Turning up bare-assed at a forest fire would be unprofessional even for me."

"Is that what you saw? The crew's next fire?"

"More the one that we're already on. Or at least, the human half of the crew are there. The Kootenai wildfire." He rubbed at his eyes. They felt as red and raw as if he really *had* been standing in that clearing, surrounded by the smoke of an approaching wildfire. "That's where I have to be. I have to go right away. I know what I have to do now."

Her hands stilled. "But you must wait for your new bodyguard to arrive."

He'd had a lifetime of practice at appearing cheerful and carefree. He drew on all of that now, to hide his cold realization even from the mate bond. He turned, flashing Seven a bright, cheerful grin.

"Don't worry." He kissed her, swift and certain, and started to get dressed. "I'm not going to need a bodyguard."

CHAPTER 27

"I wish you were coming with us," Edith said unhappily.

Seven passed her the final box of supplies to load into the back of the crew vehicle. "As do I. But when I insisted on staying by Joe's side, his gift showed him nothing but disaster ahead. Now, at last, it seems there is a path to victory."

"Which doesn't make a lick of sense," Buck said from the driver's seat. He scowled at her through the open side window. "The way I see it, you staying behind just means I'm down a solid crew member for no good reason. Joe's really sure about this?"

Seven looked across the car park at Joe's tall, distant form. He was over by the mess hall, apparently talking to—or at—the Thunderbird. He had his back to her, but she could still read his emotions down the mate bond as clearly as if they stood face to face.

"Yes," she said. Joe's hard, unshakable certainty sat in her soul like a rock. "He is very sure."

Buck *hmphed*. "Motherloving shifter hocus-pocus. I still trust all this about as much as a magazine horoscope. At least I can wipe my ass with one of those." He leaned on the car horn, raising his voice. "Come on, you slackers! Are you shifters or slugs? Get a move on!"

Seven stepped back to allow the rest of the squad room to pile into the vehicle. Edith surprised her with a brief, bone-cracking hug, releasing her again before Seven had figured out how to respond. Rory gave her a more professional handshake, but his golden eyes were just as regretful.

"If you change your mind, there will always a place on the squad for you," he told her.

"Excuse me, who's crew is this, mine or yours?" Buck snapped. He fixed Seven with a ferocious glare. "Though there *is* a place for you here, if you ever come to your senses. You're a damn useful person to have around in a pinch, Seven. And a motherloving hard worker. If all sharks are like you, then I'll gladly hire half a dozen more."

Her throat closed, unexpectedly. It was more praise than she'd ever heard from Lord Azure.

"Thank you, sir," she said. "That means…that means a great deal to me."

Blaise and Wystan both had murmured farewells for her, along with a squeeze on her arm. Even Callum gave her an awkward, unexpectedly sweet smile that transformed his usually grim face.

"Will miss you," he mumbled as he slipped past and climbed into the waiting vehicle. "Was nice having someone quiet around here."

Fenrir's cold nose poked her thigh. *Should run with us, Deep Bitch. Pack hunts with pack.*

"Not this time." She knelt to look into the hellhound's copper eyes, hiding her face from the others. "Guard him well for me, Fenrir. Guard them all."

Will. Always. Fenrir's broad pink tongue gently licked the tear from her cheek. *Once pack, always pack, Deep Bitch.*

Buck honked the horn again. "This motherloving bus is leaving, Joe! Stop chatting up that bird and get your long scaly ass in the truck. Unless your crystal ball has changed its mind?"

Joe jogged over. The Thunderbird watched him go. Its blank white stare was as enigmatic as always, but there was a thoughtful stillness to its stance.

Buck looked from the Thunderbird to Joe with narrowed eyes. "What was all that about?"

"Just checking that the big guy is ready to do his part," Joe replied. "Chief, can I get one last moment with Seven?"

"Depends on what you're planning to do with it," the Superintendent grumbled. "Fine. But make it quick. The Kootenai fire isn't going to contain itself."

Buck put the crew vehicle in gear. Gravel crunched under the tires as the transport inched forward a few feet, leaving her alone with Joe.

For a moment, he only gazed at her, as intently as though he was trying to memorize her face. His own was set and solemn, his turquoise eyes deep and dark. He wore his battered firefighter gear as if it was a knight's armor. He looked like some ancient warrior-prophet on the eve of battle. He looked like a prince. He didn't look like himself at all.

Then, without a word, he opened his arms. She stepped into his embrace, his salt-sea scent wrapping around her, and he was still Joe, her Joe, her mate. She closed her eyes, pressing herself against his hard chest, feeling the soft, steady thump of his heart.

"Promise me you won't take any risks," she said.

His hands tightened on her back. "Like I said, the hellhound pack are too scared and weak to come after me again. All I have to do is stick with the squad, and I'll be perfectly safe."

The mate-bond was as steady in her soul as his heartbeat was under her cheek. He was telling the truth, she knew he was telling the truth…and yet she felt as though she was floating on the surface of the ocean, surrounded by sparkling light, unfathomable depths gaping below.

"Seven." Joe leaned back a little, enough so she could look up into his eyes. "I promise you, this is going to work. I know exactly how to stop the demon. All the squad has to do is hold off the pack long enough for the Thunderbird to get through and set fire to it."

"Then why can't I be there?"

"Because it's not your destiny." He smoothed one of her braids back from her face. "I'm sorry, Seven. But this is the way it has to be."

"But only for now," she said, clutching at hope. "After—after all this is over, I can return to your side. We'll be together again soon."

His hand hesitated on her cheek. The faintest tremble went through the mate bond, like the distant ripple of some great sea beast stirring in dark, lightless depths.

"Seven." He pressed his forehead to hers. "You belong in Atlantis. That's where your future lies. You have to be there, where you can take care of my family for me."

"Your mother has all the knights of the sea at her command. She hardly needs *me* at her side."

"But I need you there." His voice hardened, in a way that she'd never heard before. "Seven, you gave me your oath. You have to stay in Atlantis. I can't bear the thought of you getting hurt. I can't live like this any longer, constantly terrified of the future, of what could happen to you. You can't come back to the squad. You'd only be in the way. You said it yourself, you can't even shift on land."

She *had* said it herself…and yet it still hurt to hear *him* say it. She released him, resorting to traditional etiquette to hide her sudden odd sense of betrayal. She gave him a formal bow, fist to heart. "May the sea guide you to victory, my prince."

His expression didn't so much as flicker, but she felt a strange reflection of her own pain down the mate bond, as though her words had stabbed him just as deeply. He echoed her salute, clumsily, with entirely the wrong degree of respect given the vast difference between their ranks.

"It already has," he said. "Seven…"

He trailed off, words evidently failing him for once. He kissed her instead, long and deep and lingering. She stretched up to him, answering him in the same silent language.

All too soon, he pulled back. "I love you."

Every instinct screamed to hold on to him, to never let him go—but she had sworn an oath. She made herself step back. "I love you too."

He hesitated, one hand reaching out as though he too felt that urge to cling to each other. Then he let his arm drop again. Never taking his eyes off her, he walked backward until he reached the waiting crew transport.

"Joe!" she called after him as he swung himself inside. "Stay safe!"

He leaned out the window, flashing her a strange, brittle smile. "I love you," he said again.

That was her last sight of him—hanging out of the window, smile dropping away, craning his neck to keep her in sight as long as possible as the transport rattled away.

And then he was gone.

CHAPTER 28

The first day on a big fire was always an exercise in organized chaos. Navigating the impromptu tent-city of fire crews and first responders; finding a spot amidst all the other interagency hotshot vehicles; reunions with crews they'd worked with before, introductions to others; unpacking and organizing the gear while the Superintendent and squad bosses liaised with Incident Command to work out the best plan of attack. And all in the acrid smog of an active wildfire, barely a few miles away.

With all the constant turnover of tired firefighters returning from the lines and fresh squads heading out, it should have been a piece of cake to slip away unnoticed. And it *would* have been, if not for one thing.

Or rather, one person.

"Bro," he snapped. "I'm a big boy now. I can go to the toilet on my own. You don't have to hold my hand."

Callum still stuck to his heels like a red-headed shadow. "I have to go too."

Like the pegasus shifter had conveniently needed to go at the same time as Joe the last four times. He'd also insisted on accompanying him to the water station (twice), the food truck (once), and the random crew that Joe had invented a pressing need to greet (fortunately, it had turned out that he *did* know one of the squad bosses there. Even more fortunately, she'd informed him—after her initial surprised, pleased hug—that she had a boyfriend now).

Joe was surprised at how easy it had been. He'd thought he'd have to act a *lot* more suspicious to make Callum follow him.

Now Joe stomped through the camp yet again, taking care to be as loud and visible as possible. He put on an aggrieved tone. "Did Rory put you up to this? Does he think there's something I'm not telling you guys?"

"Is there?"

"I told you, the hellhounds have given up trying to kidnap me. You don't have to keep following me around like a—"

He'd intended to say *bodyguard,* but his throat closed around the word. For a moment, all he could see was Seven. Her beautiful grey eyes, the elegant line of her neck, her strong, intoxicating body. How she'd stood, straight-backed and alone, as he'd left her behind.

Callum's green eyes narrowed fractionally. Joe became aware that he'd just left his sentence dangling, and hastily added, "Uh, like the world's worst secret agent. Seriously, bro. I got this. Trust me."

Seven trusted him. She'd looked at him with such terrible, terrible trust, despite the awful things he'd said to her. In his desperation to make her let him go, he'd heartlessly exploited her insecurities, implying that she wasn't good enough to protect him…and yet she'd still trusted him.

When she found out…

He hoped she *did* hate him, later. Maybe that would help her. He had to cling to that, to his certainty of her strength. She would make a life for herself; achieve her dreams. She would be happy.

Callum, on the other hand, was looking even less happy than usual. He continued to dog Joe's steps. "Fool me once."

It took him a second to work out what the pegasus shifter meant. *Fool me once, shame on you, fool me twice, shame on me.*

"Would it kill you to speak in complete sentences every once in a while?" Joe snapped, then winced. *That* wasn't what he wanted his last words to his friend to be. "I'm really sorry, bro. I didn't mean that. I'm kinda on edge."

"I know." To Joe's astonishment, Cal reached out, awkwardly clasping his shoulder. It was just the briefest contact, but Joe couldn't remember the last time Callum had willingly touched *anyone*. "Joe. We're friends. Whatever is wrong, you don't have to face it alone. Talk to me. What's going on?"

For Callum, it was practically a Shakespearean soliloquy. Joe had to fight back a sudden mad urge to tell the pegasus shifter the truth. Maybe Cal would understand...

No. He couldn't risk it. He had to stick to the plan.

They'd reached the edge of the encampment. Joe drew Callum behind a parked bulldozer, glancing around. No one was in sight.

It was time.

He dropped his voice. "Okay, look. I admit it. There's something going on, something I couldn't tell everyone else. If we're going to defeat the demon, I need you to do something for me."

A blink was the only sign of Callum's surprise. "What?"

Joe drew Seven's stunsword out from under his jacket. "Hold this. Not like that," he added quickly, as Callum reached for the hilt. "This end, right here."

Callum shot him a puzzled look, but obediently clasped the blunt, retracted business end of the weapon. "Now what?"

"Now I'm really, really sorry," Joe said, and activated the stunsword.

He caught Callum as the pegasus shifter collapsed. He could only hope that he hadn't zapped him too hard. The mate bond had let him channel just enough of Seven's essence to fool the weapon into thinking he was its rightful owner, but he had none of her skill or finesse at controlling its magic.

"Sorry," he told Callum again. He rearranged the pegasus shifter into a more comfortable position. He tucked the stunsword under Callum's elbow like a teddy bear. "See that this gets back to Seven for me, okay?"

He struck out from camp, heading randomly into the forest. He had no idea where he was going, but that didn't matter. He thrashed through the undergrowth, making as much noise as he could.

Come on, come on. He took off his jacket, pretending to wipe sweat off his brow as if overheated. *Here I am. One sea dragon prince, ready and waiting. Come* on, *Wulfric, whoever you are—*

Something sharp plunged into his shoulder. Cold numbness filled him.

With relief, he closed his eyes, and surrendered to fate.

CHAPTER 29

Time had never moved so slowly. She felt like a ghost in the deserted compound, frozen in an unchanging moment, forgotten and fading. She kept trying to keep herself busy, but any task she started immediately felt wrong. How could she presume to tend to the spare tools or clean the communal areas? She wasn't a hotshot crew member.

She couldn't practice sword-drills, either. Even if she'd had her weapon, she had forfeited the right to step through the ancient, honorable forms of a sea dragon warrior. Though her dishonor was not yet public, she had already given up her name. She wasn't Seventh Novice of the Order of the First Water.

She wasn't anyone.

The Thunderbird watched her impassively as she drifted from building to building, bereft of purpose. Its still, silent presence was no comfort. The great bird seemed to be waiting for something, just as much as she was.

In the end, she gave up and went to the gym. For hour after hour, she lifted weights and ran through conditioning exercises, all while keeping half an ear out for the sound of an approaching vehicle. Joe had said that Atlantis would send someone to fetch her, but not when or how.

She'd expected a helicopter, or possibly a car. What she *hadn't* expected was for a tall, curvy, motherly woman to breeze into the gym without so much as a knock.

"Goodness, that's a steep mountain. And a long walk up from the lake." The woman settled her ample backside onto the end of the weight bench. She pushed back her long, tightly curled black hair, revealing a sweaty but smiling face. "Could I trouble you for a drink?"

Tongue-tied, Seven handed her water bottle to the Pearl Empress, Queen of Atlantis, the Heart of the Sea.

"Oh, that's better." The Empress took a long drink, then splashed a little water into her palm, patting it onto her forehead. She wasn't wearing a crown, or formal robes of state; just a simple silk sundress that clung to her generous curves. "I really don't know how you firefighters do it, you know. Just being outside in this heat has me melting into a puddle. I can't imagine working flat-out for twelve, fourteen hours, and then getting up the next day and doing it all over again. I'm sorry, we haven't met. I'm Neridia."

It took Seven two attempts to form words. "Yes. I know."

Neridia made a little grimace. Her eyes were exactly the same turquoise as her son's. "I suppose you do. Atlantis is a small place, after all. Please don't do that."

Seven, who'd been belatedly sliding off the bench to drop into a formal genuflection, froze. Feeling about as graceful as a newborn goat, she got to her feet, straightening into parade rest. "Your Majesty—"

"Oh, no." Neridia winced, just like Joe had done when she'd first addressed *him* by his title. "If I'm going to be your mother-in-law, we'll have to ditch some of the etiquette. Otherwise family dinners are going to be terribly stilted." She hitched over a little, patting the bench next to her. "Here. We need to talk. Sit down."

Seven did so. "I'm sorry," she blurted out.

Neridia's eyebrows lifted a little. "What for?"

"For...for being your son's mate."

Neridia gave her a long, considering look. "*Are* you sorry about that?"

Under the pressure of that penetrating, sea-deep gaze, the truth slipped out. "No."

Neridia's generous mouth curved upward. "Good. Then there's hope for you both." She leaned back on her hands, gazing thoughtfully around the shabby gym. "So this is where my son has been hiding from me."

Seven thought of Joe's deprecating words when he'd first shown her around the base; his flippant tone, and the clear love in his eyes. The warmth of the mate bond pulsed in her chest.

"He does miss you," she said. "And Atlantis. But he belongs here, too. Please don't make him give it up."

Neridia's face softened. "I would never ask him to give up something he loved." She let out a soft sigh, her voice dropping. "I wouldn't have to. He's far too good at doing that all on his own."

Oh, Joe's mother knew her son. "He—he is very certain that this is the right path for us."

"Yes, I know," Neridia said, rather dryly. "He explained it to me at great length, and with a great many words. He was very convincing." She pinned Seven once more with those unnerving, sea-colored eyes. "Now I want to hear what *you* think."

Seven couldn't hold the Empress's gaze. She dropped her own to her hands, fidgeting. "I trust him. If he says that this is right, it must be."

Neridia tilted her head. "Because he can see the future?"

Seven stared at her. "You...you know?"

"I have always known." Neridia's calm aura faltered. For a moment, she was just a mother, helpless to help her child. "Ever since he first started screaming in his sleep. But he always insisted they were just nightmares. He wouldn't..." Her folded hands tightened. "He wouldn't come to me."

On impulse, Seven put her hand over Neridia's. "I think he wanted to. But he was frightened. He thought that if anyone knew, he would lose his freedom." She hesitated. "You know that he doesn't want to be Emperor, don't you?"

Neridia was silent for a moment. A tear overflowed, running down her cheek.

"My biggest regret is that I didn't give him a normal childhood," the Empress said quietly. "I should have kept him out of the spotlight. But I couldn't bear to leave him with a foster family, or a nanny. I told myself that he was only little, he needed to be with me just as much as I needed to be with him. And the Sea Council was so thrilled that the Imperial bloodline would continue, and everyone in Atlantis loved seeing the adorable little Crown Prince toddling at my side...I should have done better. I should have protected him."

Her own mother's face flashed in her memory. "Nobody's childhood is perfect. The most important thing is that he knows what it feels like to be loved, unconditionally, just the way he is. That's the greatest gift you could ever have given him."

Neridia sniffed, wiping the back of her hand across her nose in a very un-regal manner. "I am so happy that you're his mate, Seven. And I would love to have you by my side in Atlantis. As a knight, and more. The Sea Council needs more diverse voices, voices like yours, if we are truly to do right for all the people of the Pearl Empire. But..."

Neridia drew in a deep breath, straightening. It was like she drew on an invisible robe of state as she did so. It didn't matter that she wasn't wearing a crown. She didn't need one.

"But first," the Empress said, meeting Seven's eyes, "I need you to tell me, honestly, that you truly believe that Joe is right. That your place is with me, in Atlantis, and not by his side."

Her shark circled around the glowing mate bond at the center of her soul. Seven reached for her animal, for her sense of Joe, for her heart.

She listened.

She shot to her feet. "I have to go. I have to go *right now*."

Neridia nodded, unsurprised. "I rather thought you might. Is there any way I can help? Any assistance I can offer?"

"No. Thank you," Seven added, belatedly. "Thank you for everything."

She didn't wait for a response. She was already running, out the door, past the startled Imperial honor guard waiting outside. She ran, through winds that were already starting to pick up, under clouds that were thickening and darkening every second.

And she could only pray that she wasn't already too late.

CHAPTER 30

He awoke with cold chains around his wrists.

It was so familiar that for a moment his mind rebelled, reflexively trying to break free from the vision. But there was no waking up. Not this time.

This wasn't a vision. This was real. It was finally happening, now.

Oh, sea. He'd been hoping to have the strength to meet his fate with a cocky grin and a witty quip. Now, he was just grateful for all those trips to the toilet. At least he would go out with dry pants.

He opened his eyes a crack, trying not to let on that he was conscious again. He was lying on his side, dry leaf litter against his cheek. Chains bound his arms and legs, uncomfortably tight. There seemed to be an argument going on above his head.

"I don't like this, Lupa." Joe recognized the deep voice of the wendigo shifter, Mort. "He walked straight into our hands. This has to be some kind of trap."

"He's bound and drugged. Wulfric injected him with enough basilisk venom to keep him from shifting for days." Joe felt Lupa's small foot nudge him in the ribs. He stayed limp, playing dead. "What could he possibly do to hurt me?"

"I don't know, and I don't want to find out." Mort blew out his breath. "Look, Lupa. I know you're only doing this for me, but I don't want any more innocent lives on my conscience. I'm begging you. Let him go."

"No," Lupa said flatly. "Go and help the rest of the pack. Keep the Thunderbird from interfering."

"Little one—"

"I said no!" Lupa's voice rose sharply. "I'm not losing you! Now go!"

Joe heard Mort stagger back, as though Lupa's power had physically shoved him. The wendigo hesitated, then let out another long sigh. Human footsteps turned into the *crunch* of giant paws, heading away.

Lupa kicked him in the ribs again, harder. "I know you're awake. Stop playing dead and get up."

Dying on his feet seemed more dignified than dying flat on his back. He sat up, wincing as the drug made the clearing spin around his head. He reached for his dragon, but it was still unconscious. He felt cold, naked without his animal. The mate bond was the only spark of warmth remaining in the vast, silent sea of his soul.

Lupa dragged him upright by his chains. He started to topple over again the moment she let go of him. Lupa made an impatient, annoyed sound, and propped him up against a tree.

"If this *is* a trick, it's not going to work," she informed him.

"No trick," he croaked out. "But you don't want to do this."

She folded her arms, glaring at him. "And why is that?"

"I don't know. I just know that you don't."

"You know *nothing* about me."

"I know that your name is Lupa." He jerked his chin in the direction the wendigo had vanished. "I know his name is Mort, and that you love each other like family. I know that you'd do anything to protect him. That's why you plan to sacrifice me instead of him to…" He struggled to remember the name she'd called in his vision, the name she'd used to summon the demon. "To Unktehi."

She caught her breath. "How do you know that name?"

"I know a lot of things. What I *don't* know is why you're doing any of this in the first place." His feet were sliding out from underneath him. He fought to stay upright, to hold her shocked stare. "But I know you don't really want to. Something's making you, something bad. You don't have to do this, Lupa. Whatever you're facing, my friends and I can help. Please. Let us help you. You've made some bad choices, but you can't be all bad if you can love someone like you clearly love Mort."

For a moment, he thought he had her. Her topaz eyes were wide, vulnerable. For a moment, she looked very young.

Then her face twisted. She tossed her hair, revealing the horned-serpent mark on her forehead.

"You think *love* is enough?" she spat. "You think that's enough to make someone a good person, worthy of redemption, no matter what else they've done? You know nothing. *Nothing*. You can't help me." The biting scorn in her voice wavered, just for an instant. "No one can help me."

With a final toss of her head, she turned away. She knelt down, pressing one hand to the ground.

"Father of Serpents," she began, just as he'd seen in his dream. "Blood calls to blood. The world turns, the storms fade, and the time of snakes and shadows comes once more."

He hadn't really expected to persuade her to trust him. He'd known it would come to this. Still, his guts clenched in fear as the mark on her forehead lit up.

"Rise, horned consort, ever-hungry one," Lupa went on. "The one who gnaws at the roots of the world. Accept this sacrifice—"

"Unwilling sacrifice!" He twisted his wrists together, futilely straining against his chains. "Very, very unwilling!"

"Be quiet," Lupa snapped over her shoulder. "Accept this sacrifice—"

He raised his hand—well, both hands, since they were chained together. "Sorry to interrupt, but can I clarify just how unwilling I am? I know I kinda walked right into your clutches, but I honestly am exceedingly unhappy to be in this position. I just want to make sure that's noted down. You know, formally. Just in case it matters."

Lupa stared at him as though he'd started speaking in sea dragon. "This is your big plan? Do you seriously think you can *rules-lawyer* your way out of a demonic ritual?"

He raised his eyebrows at her hopefully. "Can I?"

"*No.*"

"Pity. Well, it was worth a try."

It *had* been worth a try, but it wasn't his plan. His plan was very, very simple.

Just keep talking.

Long enough for the Thunderbird to battle its way through the pack and torch the place. Ideally, before the demon rose. Not because he was hoping to get out of this alive—he had no illusions about *that*. He'd never seen anything in his future past this day.

It was just that he had a suspicion it was going to be a whole lot harder to delay the demon once it was actually inside his body. The longer he could distract Lupa, the better.

He let the words flow, free-associating madly. "I mean, I did kind of get the impression that your giant snake-demon friend isn't real big on consent, but I'd still like it to be crystal-clear that I could not possibly be any more unwilling. You know, just for posterity. I'd hate for my gravestone to read *Here Lies Joe, He Was Dumb Enough To Feed Himself To A Demon, Good Riddance.* I'd die of embarrassment."

Lupa rolled her eyes. "Fine. Accept this unwilling and *exceedingly annoying* sacrifice. His heart awaits you—"

"It really, really doesn't. One hundred percent already taken, this heart. And I'm sorry to say that she's a lot prettier than Mr. Unktehi. But I'm sure there's someone somewhere who is just pining to give their heart to a giant horned snake. Has he tried online dating?"

"Do you *ever* shut up?" Lupa snarled at him.

"I'm not known for it, no. I mean, if it was a quiet and dignified demon-raising ceremony you were after, you should have abducted Callum to be your sacrifice." He kept one eye on the sky as he babbled. Was that a darker shape, amidst the swirling smoke? "Now there's a man of few words. Which is kind of weird, actually, because his dad and brothers are even more talkative than I am."

"The mind boggles," Lupa muttered. "Are you going to make me come over there and gag you?"

"Probably. Sorry. Well, not sorry. I mean, you are trying to feed me to a giant snake-demon. You can't really blame me for not being hugely cooperative."

Lupa started to stalk toward him, and then checked herself. Her head turned, nostrils flaring. His heart gave a great bound—but she was staring into the trees, not the sky.

A pair of men came into view, forcing their way through the tangled undergrowth. They were dragging a struggling form between them. Someone smaller, pale-skinned, with ash-grey hair...

He'd thought he was scared before. It was nothing compared to the utter terror that gripped him now.

"We caught her on the edge of the sacred grounds," one of the men said. The other one, a massive, black-bearded man, was having to use all his strength to restrain Seven. "The Thunderbird dropped her. She nearly snuck by while we were chasing it away."

The bearded man suddenly swore, yanking his hand away. "She bit me! The ugly bitch bit me!"

"We're out of darts," the first man said to Lupa. "Do you have any left?"

Lupa pulled an odd, snub-nosed pistol out of the pocket of her jacket. It had a gas chamber at the back, and a long, fletched dart loaded into the barrel. Sickly neon-green liquid shimmered inside the dart's chamber. Seven twisted even harder.

Lupa tapped the tranquillizer pistol thoughtfully against her palm, looking Seven up and down. Her lips pursed.

"No," Lupa decided. She holstered the gun again. "It's the last one, and it will be a while before I can harvest more serum. We need to save this in case any of the other, more dangerous shifters show up again. This one is just a shark. She's no threat to us."

"Beg to disagree," muttered the bearded man, sucking at his bleeding wound.

"Just hold her so she can't cause trouble." Lupa glanced at Joe, one eyebrow lifting. "Was *this* your master plan? Distract me so your pet assassin, or whatever she is, could sneak in and stab me in the back?"

"No." He could barely get the words out through the terror clogging his mouth. "She isn't supposed to be here."

Lupa's mouth twisted in a sneer. "Oh. Now I see. True mates." She shot him a last, searing glance before kneeling down again. "I told you love wasn't enough."

"I'll be willing, I'll welcome your demon with open arms, I'll do anything you want!" He tried to stumble toward Seven, but the world lurched sideways under his feet. He crashed to his knees, barely avoiding falling flat on his face. "Just let her go. Please!"

"No!" Seven flung herself against her captors' hands, straining to reach him. "Let *him* go! Take me! Sacrifice me instead!"

"You?" Lupa cast her a scornful look. "What would the king want with *you*?"

Seven's frantic eyes met his as Lupa started to chant again. He could feel her fear down the mate bond—not for herself, but for him.

I'm sorry, her voice whispered in his heart. *I thought I could save you. I thought I was strong enough. I'm so, so sorry. I failed you.*

Lupa's voice rose in a triumphant scream. "On your queen's behalf I call you by name: Unktehi, crowned serpent, mighty consort! It is time. The way is open. Rise!"

Just like in his dream, the earth split apart. The demonic serpent rose, blotting out the sky. The two men holding Seven screamed and fled. She lunged for him the instant they let go of her, but it was far too late.

"Seven, no," he begged, as her hands closed on his shoulders. He was far too big for her to carry, the demon far too close— "You have to leave me, save yourself! Seven!"

Somewhere in the darkness behind the demon, Lupa's shrill laughter rose, cold and triumphant. Death rose above them, horned and hell-eyed, a heartbeat away.

Seven's grey eyes looked into his, alight with love.

One last time.

"*Seven!*" he screamed, as she stepped in front of him. "*Run!*"

She ignored him. She faced the towering monster head-on, unarmored, unarmed. Unflinching.

She spread her arms.

And this was the point where the vision always turned to nightmare. He'd seen her die, over and over, a hundred different ways—quickly, slowly, bitten or burned or just flung aside like a piece of trash.

She knew what he'd seen. She knew she was going to die.

But still she stepped forward. Because she had nothing left to protect him with but her own body.

She couldn't even shift.

She couldn't even shift.

His dragon was still unconscious, useless. But there was more in the depths of his soul than just his animal.

He reached within, to the part of himself that he'd denied for so long. To the walls that he'd built to keep it locked away, locked out.

And he brought them all down.

CHAPTER 31

One moment, she was standing on dry ground, looking death in its burning red eyes.

The next, she was in the sea.

A great wave washed over her so powerfully, she staggered. Salt burned in her eyes. She instinctively held her breath, feeling the cool all-enveloping touch of the water. Her whole body was buoyed up, lifting, suddenly weightless. Her braids floated free.

The huge horned serpent had been gathering itself to strike, but now it hesitated. Its shadowy head cocked to one side. The taste of its sudden confusion and suspicion washed over her tongue.

"What magic is this?" Lupa demanded, through the roar of the waves.

How is she speaking? Seven wondered. *Why hasn't she been washed away?*

Yet the hellhound alpha was still standing there, just beyond the serpent. The sea that enveloped Seven didn't seem to touch either one of them. The ground was still bone-dry. Not a blade of grass stirred, despite the fact that currents tugged so hard at her own body that she could barely stay on her feet.

The sea wasn't around her.

It was *in* her.

Heart of the Sea, Joe had said.

He was the Crown Prince of Atlantis, the Emperor-in-Waiting. He was the Heart of the Sea.

And he'd given her *his* heart, just as she'd given him hers.

Now all his power roared through her soul. He'd opened the floodgates, holding nothing back. His love, his trust, his strength, his utter confidence in *her* strength, it all poured into *her*.

Black sparks danced in front of her eyes. She was growing light-headed from lack of oxygen.

But she could breathe underwater.

Her shark surged up. For once, she reached for it, embracing it, this sleek, deadly, beautiful part of her soul. Her clothing shredded, falling away. She was a creature of muscle and teeth, perfectly honed for a single purpose.

To *hunt.*

With a flick of her fins, she soared into the air. No—she *swam*, through a sea that was tangible only to herself. The serpent snapped uselessly at her. She evaded it without thought, as easily as breathing, and tore a great gaping bite out of its smoky hide.

The demon *screamed*, in a voice made from nightmares. It lashed out at her again, but it was big and clumsy and slow. It was no more adapted for dry land than she was. It batted at her like a sloth trying to swat a hummingbird, and with about as much success.

Again and again, she darted in. The creature's armor was strong, but a Great White had a bite strength that would shame a Tyrannosaurus Rex. Her teeth tore through the shadowy scales as if they were paper. Burning blood ran like lava down its writhing flanks.

"Seven!" Joe's shout cut through her joyous frenzy. He was trying to get to his feet, but he was still weak from the drug. "Look out!"

At the edge of the clearing, Lupa stood in a perfect marksman's stance. The barrel of her tranquillizer pistol tracked Seven through the air with utter precision.

Seven flung herself into a desperate series of twists, spinning through the air like a dolphin. The horned serpent took advantage of her distraction, lunging to intercept her. Its enormous fangs almost grazed her tail. Only a deft roll that left her spine aching saved her.

She couldn't keep this up for long. Either Lupa or the serpent, she could handle, but both together...

She could taste the serpent's sudden gloating triumph. She sensed Lupa's churning emotions focusing, narrowing, coming to a decision as sharp as a knife.

Lupa's finger tightened on the trigger.

Seven reflexively tried to evade...but it was pointless. The dart disappeared harmlessly into the dark, missing her by a mile.

The serpent roared in fury. It turned on Lupa, its eyes alight with vicious, vindictive rage. For a moment, it forgot Seven entirely.

She dove, sinking her teeth deep into its unguarded throat. She hung on, locking her jaws, as the serpent screamed and thrashed. Out of the corner of her eye, she glimpsed a white blur, streaking out of the forest. Lupa leaped onto the wendigo's back, and the pair vanished into the sky.

"Seven! *Seven!*" Joe was waving his arms. He pointed up, urgently.

For a moment, she thought he wanted her to chase after the fleeing Lupa...but then her snout prickled. With a sense that humans lacked, she could detect the electromagnetic fields around changing, swirling like the storm clouds gathering above. She could feel the ominous, gathering power.

She released her prey, swooping down toward Joe. He leaped, grabbing hold of her dorsal fin, locking his legs around her body. She soared back into the sky, carrying him.

Just in time.

Pure white light knocked her head-over-tail like a hammer blow from an angry god. The dying serpent vanished utterly, its darkness ripped apart by incandescent power. Every tree around the clearing went up like a firework.

Scorching heat licked against her belly. She spiraled higher, away from the devastation, carrying her mate to safety.

Behind them, the Thunderbird hammered lightning bolt after

lightning bolt into the corrupted ground, until there was nothing left but fire.

CHAPTER 32

As he rode a giant flying shark through the sky with fire and lightning exploding in their wake, Joe had only one thought.
This really needs a soundtrack.

One of Seven's small, dark eyes rolled to peer up at him.

Joe, her voice said in his mind. **Are you trying to sing* Ride of the Valkyries?*

"Dun dun-dun DUN dunnn!" he belted out at the top of his lungs. He flung his arms wide, tilting back his head. "DUN DUN-DUN *DUN* DUNNN!"

Sharks couldn't smile, but he could feel her laughter echoing down the mate bond. She shook herself a little, making him grab hold of her fin to avoid sliding off.

We should land and continue on foot, she said, sounding rather regretful. **There's too much risk of being seen.**

He leaned over to peer down at the forest. They'd left the new fire behind, and were soaring over the smoldering ashes of the old. Fire lines cut through the forest like scars, showing where crews were working to contain the blaze.

"Don't worry," he shouted into her ear—or at least, where he thought her ear probably was. He was a little unclear on the finer points of shark anatomy. "No one will notice us."

Her eye rolled again. *Joe. I am a flying shark. I think we may attract comment.*

"Everything's going to be fine. Trust me."

He put his hands flat against her hide, concentrating. He wasn't in animal form, but *she* was. With the mate bond weaving their souls together, the sea surging through them both, it was child's play to lend her the mythic shifter power to make herself invisible to normal humans.

Which didn't mean that *no one* could see them.

As Seven back-finned to hover in front of the rest of A-squad, Joe's wish for a boombox was replaced with an even more fervent desire.

"Someone lend me a phone," he demanded urgently. He slid off Seven's back, holding out a hand. "Someone give me their phone *right now*. I need to take a picture of all your faces."

Nobody moved.

"Oh, come on." Joe folded his arms, raising his eyebrows at them. "Haven't any of you guys ever seen a shark before?"

No, Fenrir said. The hellhound's mouth hung open, his tongue flopped out as though he'd forgotten it existed.

"Yes," Wystan said weakly. "But not in a forest."

"You. Uh. The." Rory appeared to have lost the ability to form a complete sentence. "What. How?"

Edith's hands suddenly flurried like confetti. She let out a loud, whooping cackle.

"That," she gasped, flapping with delight. "Was. *Awesome.*"

"I know, right?" Joe flung double horns at her. "Totally metal."

Seven nudged him with her blunt snout. *All right, enough fun. Poor Blaise looks like she's about to faint, and I think Callum may never speak again. Ask them if someone would kindly lend me something to wear. I'm not a mythic shifter. My clothes don't come with me.*

"Oh, right." Joe turned back to the squad. "Seven needs clothes. She can't parade into fire camp buck-naked."

There was a small moment of confusion during which Callum, Blaise, and Wystan all simultaneously tried to hand Joe their jackets. He was briefly buried in yellow Nomex.

"She doesn't need to construct an impromptu tent, guys." He plucked out Callum's jacket as being the biggest, and held it out in front of Seven so that she could shift without flashing the whole squad.

As she shrank back into human form, he let the sea recede as well. The ocean withdrew, leaving them both standing on dry land once more.

But he could still feel the waves, whispering deep in his heart. The sea would always be there. *Had* always been there. It was a part of him, as much as his animal.

As much as his mate.

"Thank you." Seven wrapped the heavy fabric around herself. Callum was tall enough that it covered her nearly to her knees. She glanced around at them all. "What are you all doing on the edge of the forest? Surely you weren't heading out to the lines at this time of night?"

"We, ah." Rory swallowed hard. "We...were coming to rescue you?"

"We saw the Thunderbird streak over fire camp, heading for the forest," Wystan said. "The hellhound pack turned it back. We were trying to help the Thunderbird break through when Cal regained consciousness and screamed that you were in danger."

"It seems you didn't need us after all, though," Blaise added.

"Nah." Joe slung an arm over Seven's shoulder. "Seven could handle it."

She leaned into his side. "*We* could handle it." She frowned. "Wait. Why was Callum unconscious?"

Callum held out Seven's stunsword, without a word.

She took it, looking puzzled—and then her eyes widened. "Joe. You *didn't*."

"Sorry. It seemed like a good idea at the time."

"It was a terrible idea." She smacked him lightly in the arm with the hilt of the weapon. "The whole thing was a terrible idea. Promise me you'll never do anything like that again."

He took her into his arms, protective coat and stunsword and all. He bent to press his forehead to hers.

"I promise," he whispered against her lips. "No more secrets. No more running from fate, or trying to fix everything on my own. As long as you promise to be at my side, always."

"Always," she murmured, and claimed his mouth.

After a long, long moment, Rory cleared his throat.

"We're all very happy for you both," he said. "Now will someone *please* explain what just happened?"

~

There were explanations. There were drinks (sadly non-alcoholic, given the restrictions of fire camp). There was food (terrible). There were more explanations.

And at the end of it all, there was his mate, in his arms.

She stretched out as much as she could in the limited confines of their pup tent. Normally they would have slept out in the open when on a job, but they'd wanted some privacy.

"I could sleep for a week." She let out a huge yawn. "How much time do we have until we have to get up?"

"About four hours." He traced the creamy curve of her bare shoulder, marveling at the contrast between soft skin and the hard muscle below. "Doesn't really seem fair. We saved the world. We should at least get the day off."

"That's the problem with saving the world. Most of the time, nobody realizes." She rolled over to face him, face to face, her hand sliding over his hip. "But *I* know what you did."

He kissed the tip of her nose. "You did all the hard work. I just had to stand there."

"You had to embrace the part of yourself that you'd feared." She traced light spirals up his spine, making his breath catch. "I know how hard that is."

"Yes," he said softly. "I know you do." He snugged her closer. "Know what else is hard?"

She laughed. Her hips flexed, deliciously. "Joe. We have to get up and cut line in four hours."

He sighed, releasing her—but she rolled, straddling him. Her hands pinned his wrists. She grinned down at him. Her sharp-edged smile sent a jolt of pure fire through him.

"So I'll be quick," she said.

She sank down onto him, capturing him in her wet heat. All thought fled. There was nothing in the world but her, riding him, hard enough to make him see stars.

"Oh, sea," he gasped, arcing up to meet her. "Seven. My mate."

She captured his mouth, silencing him. Her hips ground against him, getting just the right angle to rub her slick, swollen nub against his hardness. Her inner walls tightened. He could sense her own pleasure gathering like a tidal wave, increasing his own.

He couldn't hold back. Hot pressure built at the base of his spine. He spilled into her in ecstatic pulses, feeling her grip him tight in her own release.

She collapsed down onto him, breathing hard. She kissed the side of his neck.

"There," she said, sounding smug. "I finally found out how to make you stop talking."

"A mighty feat," he agreed. "You should add it to your name. You know, officially. *Seventh Novice, Slayer of Demons, Silencer of Joe.*"

"Guardian of the Sea's Heart," she said sleepily.

"That too." He held her close, hearts beating in unison, slowing. His thoughts were slowing too, turning fuzzy around the edges. "Actually, I guess you won't be Seventh Novice, will you? You fulfilled your quest. I'll have to get used to calling you Fourteenth Knight, or whatever number they're up to in the Order of the First Water."

"Seren," she mumbled.

"What?"

"It's my birth name." She nestled closer against him. "The one my mother gave me. I haven't used it in a long time, but now I want to reclaim my human side as well as my shark. You can call me Seren."

"Seren," he whispered. "Oh, yes. My Seren."

Sleep enfolded them both, softly as a blanket.

And all his dreams were good.

EPILOGUE

Even far under the sea, Atlantis glowed with light. The waters surrounding the city were filled with shimmering bioluminescence. Through the air bubble enclosing the Imperial Palace, the soft, constantly changing shades of blue and green looked like the Northern Lights. Vast shoals of glowing fish danced and darted in ever-shifting, living constellations.

Joe gazed up, watching a pod of young dolphin shifters playing in the waters outside the magical barrier. A sinuous sea dragon knight hovered a little way off, nominally on guard, but mostly just keeping an indulgent eye on the exuberant children. He breathed deeply, inhaling the sharp tang of salt.

A warm hand fell on his shoulder.

"It is good to have you home, my son," his father said.

"It's good to be home." He turned, leaning back against the polished coral railing. "Even if it's only a flying visit. I wish I could stay for longer, but we only get two days off every few weeks."

"We are honored that you chose to spend them with us." His father was in full formal armor. Light danced from the polished metal plates as he chuckled. "I must confess, most of the time when I finish a long shift of firefighting, all I want to do is sleep."

Joe grinned back. "Well, not going to say it wasn't an effort to force myself out of bed this morning."

"I suspect that had very little to do with sleep," his mother said dryly as she joined them. She adjusted the ornate crown perched on top of her cloud of dark curls. "Are you ready?"

He touched his own circlet. It was just a simple golden band, set with a single deep blue sapphire, but it still felt heavy on his brow. "As ready as I'll ever be."

His mother and father glanced at each other, in the silent communication of a long-mated couple. He smiled again, thinking of Seren. One day, that would be them, the bond between them only growing deeper and brighter with each passing year.

"I will see if the Princesses are finally dressed," his father said. A faintly pained expression crossed his face. "And not in ripped jeans and sneakers."

"Tell them that if I have to wear this stuff, so do they." Joe held up his hands, showing off his own formal, traditional attire—tight leather trousers, golden armbands, his torso bare but for a turquoise silk sash that matched his eyes. "At least I make it look good."

"I shall exhort them to live up to their big brother's shining example." His father hesitated, his eyes going suspiciously bright. "I am proud of you, my son."

A lump came to his throat. He shrugged, affecting nonchalance. "Hey, it's just an outfit."

His father clasped his shoulder again, fingers tightening. "I was not referring to the clothes."

"You don't have to do this, you know," his mother said to him as the Imperial Champion left. "Make it a public ceremony, I mean. Not if you don't want to."

"I do want to. I have the most amazing mate in the world. I want to show her off to everyone in Atlantis."

His mother stretched up to tap his circlet, the crown of the Emperor-in-Waiting. "You could do that without this, though."

He studied her. His mother, the one who'd held him and sung to him and kissed his bruises; all that still, and also every inch the Empress.

"I want to make you proud of me too," he said.

"I already am." She smiled, through the tears welling in her eyes. "I have always been proud of you."

He hugged her tight, resting his cheek against hers. "Seren told me that you knew. About my gift, I mean."

"I'm sorry," she mumbled into his ear. "It's not fair. I've given you so many burdens by being your mother."

"Don't be sorry." He stepped back, offering her the end of his sash to wipe her eyes. "I was scared of my birthright for a long time, but I'm...well, to be honest, I'm still scared. But I'm not running away from it. Any of it. Not anymore."

"If you wanted..." His mother stopped, sniffed, and went on. "If you wanted to renounce the throne, I would support you, you know."

"I know." He brushed his fingers over her crown. "But I know as well as you do that this is just a symbol. I was born with power. I could try to deny it, turn my back on it, insist that I was like everyone else...but it wouldn't be true. I was given a great gift, unearned. I have to pay it forward. Use it to help people who weren't so lucky."

He reached out to take her hand, squeezing it. "Just like you do."

His mother gazed at him for a long moment.

"Sea dragons have it wrong, you know," she said softly. "It's not our ancestors we have to try to live up to. It's our descendants."

He raised his eyebrows at her. "If that's a subtle hint about grandchildren, you'll have to take it up with my mate."

She burst out laughing. "I wouldn't dare."

"Pity. I was hoping you'd start crocheting tiny booties meaningfully in her direction."

"Riveting tiny war boots, possibly. Between your genetics and hers, one doesn't have to be able to see the future to predict that your children are going to be utter terrors." She sounded distinctly pleased by the prospect.

"I just hope they take after their mother." The mate bond brightened in his heart as he spoke. "Speaking of which..."

Seren stepped through the archway, joining them on the balcony. The underwater aurora shimmered from her armor, washing the curving steel plates in turquoise and emerald. The gems set into her silver bracers sparkled.

As always, his heart moved sideways in his chest at the sight of her. He caught her hand, lifting it to his lips.

"You look stunning," he breathed.

She made a small face, tugging self-consciously at one pearl-inlaid shoulder-guard. "I'm still getting used to it. My old leathers were lighter."

"Ah, the burdens of knighthood," he teased her. "I have something for you."

Her eyes flicked downward, and then to his mother. "Is this really the time?"

He laughed. "Not that."

Though *that* would come later, he vowed. Gorgeous as Seren was in her new armor, she would be even more gorgeous out of it. Naked, splayed across the royal bed, while he adorned her with gold and gems from his personal hoard...

He had to surreptitiously adjust the end of his sash. There were distinct disadvantages to the skin-tight leggings of traditional sea dragon male attire.

"It's a mating gift," he said, kneeling to open the chest next to him. "It's traditional for a Crown Prince to give his new Princess something from the Imperial treasury."

"It's not a crown, is it?" she asked, sounding a little apprehensive. "Or some other kind of heavy jewelry? I mean, I'm already clanking when I walk."

"Nope." He straightened, turning back to her. "I thought you'd like this best."

She gasped at sight of the gleaming sword balanced across his palms. "*Joe.* That's—that's—"

"Seafire," he said. The opal on the sword's pommel sparkled in response to its name, gleaming with frozen turquoise flame. "Yes."

"Forged by the Fourth Empress," Seren breathed. Her hand trembled over the hilt. "For her mate, the Founder of the Order of the First Water. Carried by knights of the Imperial bloodline for generations. Joe, you can't give me this."

"Actually he can," his mother said mildly. "I told him to pick whatever he wanted. And I thoroughly approve of his choice. The Guardian of the Sea's Heart needs a worthy weapon if she is to protect my son." Her smile softened, shaded with old sadness. "That was my father's sword. He would have been delighted to see her go to you. More than anything, he wanted to heal the rift between sharks and sea dragons."

"Take her," Joe urged, when Seren still hesitated. "You need a proper sword in order to be knighted. And look, she knows you. She's been waiting for a worthy wielder. Take her."

The glow from the opal was brightening, the colors within swirling faster. When Seren's hand closed on the hilt, the whole gem lit up in a dazzling flare. Her mouth curved in a stunned, joyful smile as she lifted the sword.

"Seafire," she said reverently, drawing it an inch to inspect the thousand-layered steel of the blade. "She's beautiful."

"Just like her knight." He claimed her mouth for a kiss. "Now come on. Atlantis is waiting for us."

There was still some confusion over her name, Seren noted with amusement as she rose. The Imperial scholars had been debating for weeks whether *Princess-Consort* should come before *Sixteenth Knight of the Order of the First Water,* or vice versa. Apparently, two eminent sea dragon historians from the Underwater Academy had even come to blows over whether *Guardian of the Sea's Heart* was indeed a formal title at all, or merely a fond poetic nickname that had been invented the one and only time previously that an Emperor-in-Waiting had ended up mated to his bodyguard.

The people of Atlantis, however, seemed to have made up their own minds. Even as the Knight-Commander of the First Water lifted her to her feet, formally welcoming her into the Order as a full knight at last, a single shout went up from the watching crowd.

"Demon-Slayer!" they roared joyously, in both human and dragon tongues. *"Demon-Slayer!"*

The Knight-Commander chuckled as they clasped forearms in the greeting of one warrior to another. "So much for scholarship," the tall, dark sea dragon woman murmured.

The Knight-Commander turned to address the assembled ranks of knights, gorgeous and gleaming in formal armor. "It is my great honor to present to you our newest sister in battle. All hail the Demon-Slayer, Sixteenth Knight of the Order of the First Water, Princess-Consort and Guardian of the Sea's Heart!"

The knights drew their swords, saluting her. Seren drew Seafire, marveling once more at the exquisite balance and beauty of the blade. The crowd cheered even louder as she lifted the sword high.

Only one person wasn't cheering. Lord Azure had drawn his sword as tradition demanded, but his salute was half-hearted at best. Technically, *he* was supposed to have been the one to knight her, but he'd relinquished that honor to the Knight-Commander. Seren had been secretly relieved by that. Lord Azure might have been forced to accept the success of her quest, but he clearly hadn't been happy about it.

Now he was glowering at her, the only scowling face amidst the beaming knights. He rammed his sword back into its sheath. She saw his lips move, muttering something.

She too far away to hear what he'd said, but sea dragon hearing was better than a shark's. A little ripple went through the knights, a kind of mass in-breath of shock.

"Lord Azure," Joe said from behind her, his voice silky-smooth. "Would you care to repeat that?"

Lord Azure twitched as everyone turned to stare at him. "It…it was a private comment, Your Highness."

"No, it wasn't." Joe stalked toward Lord Azure. The rest of the knights wisely scattered out of his way. "It was a very serious accusation. Repeat it, or retract it. *Now.*"

Lord Azure swallowed, throat bobbing. He glanced around as though for support. The crowd had fallen absolutely silent, riveted by the unexpected drama. Seren knew that a man as proud as Lord Azure would never back down in front of such a large audience.

The knight drew himself up, puffing out his chest in a show of bravado. "I shall repeat it, then. She would never have been knighted had she not been your mate."

The assembled shifters gasped. Seren's heart thudded as people's eyes moved from Lord Azure to her and back again.

They'll believe him. She could see it in their faces, hear it in the growing whispers. *At least some of them will believe it's true.*

"It is only the truth!" Lord Azure lifted his voice, emboldened by the crowd's response. He jabbed an accusing finger at her, playing to his audience. "I had no choice but to say that she was ready, for fear that the Crown Prince would unjustly and unlawfully take revenge on the entire Order. In truth, I would never have recommended her for knighthood. She is not worthy, will never be worthy! She dishonors the Order of the First Water!"

Pure fury washed over her, but she held herself back. She tore her eyes from the raving Lord Azure to seek out Joe. He was a single point of calm amidst the growing chaos. Despite his earlier anger, he now stood in a relaxed stance, thumbs hooked into his sash, head tipped back. He gazed thoughtfully up past the magical air bubble enclosing the plaza, into the deep blue of the waters above.

Then he looked at her. He winked.

"Lord Azure," she said loudly, instantly silencing the crowd. "You insult my honor. I challenge you. Will you accept or concede?"

"Accept," he snarled. "I have no fear of a mere shark."

She bowed to him, in the barest minimum show of courtesy. "Then the choice of weapons is yours."

"You have been given a blade." He drew his own, light running down the razor-edged steel. "Let us see if you can use it."

"Lord Azure!" the Pearl Empress said sharply. "You know I do not condone duels with live steel. Does honor truly demand that this is settled with blood?"

"Yes," Lord Azure and Seren said together.

Joe had moved to his mother's side. He touched her sleeve, whispering in her ear.

The Empress puffed out her cheeks, but nodded. "Very well then. But to first blood *only*, understand? My extreme displeasure will fall upon anyone who inflicts a serious injury on the other."

Seren saluted the Empress, then Joe. His sun-bright confidence in her filled her heart. She felt no fear, not so much as a single flicker of doubt as she took up her stance opposite Lord Azure.

She swept her sword round and up, formally saluting him. He sneered, and launched straight into an attack with none of the customary respectful preliminaries.

Seafire was an extension of her own body. The sword sang joyously through the air, turning aside Lord Azure's blow.

The whole world fell away. She danced in combat time, every part of her gloriously alive, focused entirely in this moment. For all the danger, there was delight, too. This, *this* was what she had dreamed of, what she had trained for, what she had been made to do.

Lord Azure had been a full knight for nearly a decade. He was arrogant, true, but it wasn't entirely unearned. He was good. She *knew* he was good.

And yet, as their blades clashed time and again, she could taste his rising distress. Despite all his experience, all his confidence, he couldn't penetrate her defense.

He was good.

And she was *better*.

She saw the moment he realized it, that he wasn't going to win. His guard faltered, just for an instant. Seafire darted in, swift as a dolphin. Lord Azure only managed to save himself with a frantic, clumsy leap back, barely evading her blade. He stumbled, off-balance, almost falling into the crowd.

She could have lunged and had him there and then, but she checked herself. There were too many people around, pressing too close, idiotically pushing each other to get a better view. There was too much risk of someone getting hurt.

She retreated to the center of the impromptu arena, giving Lord Azure space to do so too. "At your convenience, Lord Azure."

He glared at her, falling into stance once more. He was winded, clearly losing, and yet she still tasted a sudden sharp surge of triumph from him.

"I shall show everyone what you are," he hissed.

He spun his blade. It might have made sense as an attack if she'd been *behind* him...barely. Confused, she tightened her guard, wondering what in the sea he thought he was doing.

With a smile as though his bizarre action was some master move, he drew the edge of his sword across his own arm.

She blinked at him as his blood welled up. He continued to stare at her expectantly. When she finally realized what he was waiting for, she could barely stop herself from laughing out loud.

He thinks I'm going to fly into some kind of bloodlust frenzy. Just because I'm a shark.

"Lord Azure," Joe drawled. "You cannot claim the victory by drawing first blood on *yourself*."

Lord Azure's face darkened as titters spread through the crowd. He didn't seem to know what to do next. He just stood there, looking more and more foolish, as the giggles turned into full-blown roars of laugher.

She smiled sweetly at him, deliberately letting her teeth lengthen into sharp points. "Do you need to take a break for medical assistance, Lord Azure?"

He bared his own teeth in a furious snarl. He threw himself at her, no finesse at all in his attack. Calmly, she sidestepped, and smacked him across his backside with the flat of her sword. He went sprawling.

Before he could recover, she put a boot on his neck, pinning him down. She let the point of her sword kiss his skin, ever so lightly. She glanced at the Pearl Empress.

"I will draw blood if I must," she said. "But only if Lord Azure insists."

"Let him up, Demon-Slayer," the Empress said, laughing along with the rest. "Lord Azure has lost quite enough for one day."

Lord Azure climbed stiffly back to his feet, nostrils pinched in humiliated outrage. "It was not a fair duel! She is a shark! She has, has savage magics, strange senses! It was not a fair fight!"

The Knight-Commander stepped forward. Her voice was mild, but her eyes were arctic. "Interesting, Lord Azure. Earlier, you claimed that the Demon-Slayer was unworthy to join the Order *because* she was a shark. And now, miraculously, it seems that same animal makes her unfairly powerful. You cannot have it both ways. So which is it to be?"

Lord Azure stuttered for a moment. "I—I—I was only attempting to defend the noble traditions of our Order! I agreed to take her on as a squire because I knew that if she went to serve any other knight, her abilities would blind them to the threat she poses. We cannot have a shark in our Order."

"No." The Knight-Commander shook her grey-touched head. "We cannot have dishonor in the Order. Your sword, Lord Azure."

All the blood drained from the sea dragon's face. "Knight-Commander, no. You can't."

"If you cannot recognize your own dishonor, then it is up to me as the Knight-Commander to enlighten you." The stern, middle-aged woman held out her hand. "*Your sword,* former knight."

Lord Azure's head bowed in defeat. Without further protest, he handed her the weapon, hilt first.

The Knight-Commander bowed first to Seren, and then to the Imperial family, as a pair of knights frog-marched Lord Azure away. "My sincere apologies that this unpleasantness interrupted this joyous occasion. Rest assured, I shall take action to ensure that no such thing happens again."

The Empress glanced at Seren, eyes gleaming. "Oh, I do not think anyone in Atlantis will ever again be so foolish as to doubt that a shark can be a knight." She turned to the crowd, raising her arms. "Citizens, what say you?"

Seren felt a blush sweep over her face at the whole-hearted roar of approval. She sheathed her sword and bowed to the crowd, rather self-consciously.

"They'll stop soon, right?" she whispered to Joe.

"Nope. I predict that this party is just getting started." He nudged her, jerking his head. "I think you made quite an impression."

Seren followed his gaze. At the very front of the crowd, an entire class of small children was leaping up and down, waving flags and shrieking as though she was some kind of movie star.

One little boy caught her eye in particular. He couldn't have been older than six or seven. He stood rock-still, clutching a toy sword to his chest, staring at her in sheer adulation.

"Wave," Joe muttered to her out of the corner of his mouth.

She did so, making eye contact with the boy. His pale skin flushed bright red as he realized she'd seen him. Suddenly shy, he hid behind his teacher…but not before flashing Seren a sweet, sharp-toothed smile.

Joe chuckled in satisfaction. "You've started a trend. Next season, the knights will be inundated with applications from all sorts of shifters. Sharks, seals, dolphins…"

She kept waving and smiling at the crowd. "That's why you encouraged me to challenge him, isn't it? You saw what it would mean. You saw that I would beat him."

"Nope," Joe said brightly.

She turned to stare at him. "What?"

"Didn't see a thing." He caught her up in his arms, dipping her into a flamboyant kiss. His lips curved against hers as the crowd went wild. "I didn't have to."

∼

TWO MONTHS LATER

"So, Seren." Blaise wiped her filthy, sweaty brow with the back of her jacket sleeve. "When you were little and imagined being a princess, is this what you had in mind?"

She laughed, despite her own aching muscles. "I never imagined myself as a princess. I only ever wanted to be a knight. I dreamed of fighting monsters."

"This fire certainly qualifies as one of those," Wystan said. He was flat on his back at the side of the road, gazing up at the smoky sky. "This is even worse than the last one we fought in California. It feels like the whole state bursts into flame every time we turn our backs."

"Beat the last one," Callum grunted. They were all supposed to be taking a break, but he was still chopping back stray bits of vegetation with obsessive precision. "Beat this one too."

"Yup." Joe leaned on his Pulaski, looking down their newly cut line with pride. Anchored in rocky ground at the far end and the road at this end, it provided a solid barrier to prevent the fire from spreading any further. "We're the thin yellow line between civilization and destruction."

"Thin sweaty line," Blaise corrected, tugging at her jacket and trying to fan air underneath. "Very, very sweaty."

"Don't forget smelly," Edith added, wrinkling her nose.

Fenrir rolled luxuriously in a patch of dirt, paws waving in the air. *Nothing wrong with smells.*

"There is when we have to share a small enclosed space with you for hours," Blaise told him. "When we get back to base, you're getting a bath."

Seren leaned back on her elbows, letting the familiar good-natured bickering wash over her. After nearly two weeks on this fire, she was sore in parts of her body she didn't know could *get* sore. Not even the sword-drills of knightly training were as strenuous as wildland firefighting. She rolled her neck, trying to loosen taut tendons.

"Hey." Joe's strong fingers kneaded her shoulders. "Wish you'd stayed in Atlantis?"

She closed her eyes, letting out a groan of appreciation. "Never."

Despite her exhaustion, his touch sent sparks tingling through her. It always did, and she suspected it always would.

He let out a low, pleased chuckle, sensing her response. He dipped his head to nibble teasingly at her neck. "Just got to wait for the transport to pick us up and take us back to base, and then I'm all yours. Of course, we don't *have* to wait for the truck. We could make our own way back, and be there a whole lot quicker."

She cracked open an eye to fix him with a mock-glare. "We agreed, flying shark is for emergencies only."

He shifted his hips meaningfully. "There *is* an emergency. In my pants."

"Do you *mind?*" Blaise said. She threw a pinecone at Joe's head. Seren reflexively batted it out of the air before it could make contact. "I have shifter hearing too, you know. It was bad enough having Edith and Rory whispering sexy things to each other all the time. Now with you two as well, I get it in stereo."

Rory chuckled as Edith blushed. "You just wait until you find your mate, Blaise," he said. "Then you'll understand."

"If meeting my mate turns me into a big sappy idiot, forget it." Blaise idly tossed a pinecone at him as well. "Someone has to stay cynical around here, to watch out for all you lovestruck fools. Otherwise one of these days a demon is going to leap on you while you're canoodling."

Edith's hands fluttered once, nervously. "The hellhounds and demons have been awfully quiet for the past few months. I wonder what they're up to?"

"Still haven't seen anything?" Rory asked Joe.

"Nope. I can check again if you want, though." Joe pulled out his canteen. He splashed water into his hand, casually glancing into it. "No, nothing. Still not a—huh."

A surge of adrenaline cut through her tiredness. The rest of the squad tensed too.

Joe waved them back down again. "Not demons. But everyone might want to wash their faces and try to look as photogenic as possible. Especially you, Cal."

Callum blinked at him.

The roar of an engine cut off any further questions. Instead of the boxy yellow shape of their crew transport, an unfamiliar white van came around the bend. *CBS NEWS* was written on the side.

The van pulled to a stop in front of them. A woman with a

beaming smile and an outfit that was in no way suited to the rugged terrain hopped out of the side, while a camera crew piled out the back.

"Oh, yes, perfect." The woman framed them all with her fingers, like a movie director. "Absolutely perfect. Hi, guys! Which one of you is in charge?"

"Uh, me." Rory scrambled to his feet, dusting off his Nomex pants. He took the woman's offered hand with a bemused expression. "I'm Rory MacCormick, of the Thunder Mountain Hotshots. This is my squad."

"Hotshots!" The woman's megawatt smile brightened even further. "I'm Christina Charmain, from the local news. We're running a piece on the brave men and woman battling to protect our town tonight. Can I get an interview?"

"Of course," Rory started—and then stopped, a peculiar look flashing across his face. His eyes flicked to Joe, then back to the woman. "Uh. Actually, I'm kind of busy right now. I need to take most of the squad, uh, to check for, um, uh…spot fires. But I can spare Callum, if you want to interview him."

"What?" Callum said.

Behind the Christina's back, Joe flashed Rory double thumbs-up.

"Oh my," the news anchorwoman breathed as she looked Callum up and down. "Those cheekbones. Those *arms*. Yes, he'll do very nicely. Terry, get camera one over here. Makeup!"

She bore down on Callum with a gleam in her eye like a hunting cat. Cal only had time to shoot Rory a look of wounded betrayal before the whole TV crew mobbed him, cooing compliments and bodily moving him into the best light.

"What," Seren murmured to Joe as they all left Callum to his fate, "was that all about?"

Joe shrugged. "I haven't the faintest idea."

∽

"And now, here's Christina with a very special report on the firefighters working hard to keep us all save from the wildfires raging across the county. Take it away, Christina."

Diana was elbow-deep in laundry, but the word *firefighter* snagged her attention. She glanced up at the television screen, yelped, and scrabbled for the remote control.

"Thanks, Sam!" The news anchorwoman flashed her trademark smile at the camera. *"I'm standing at the very edge of the blaze, and with me here is—"*

She found the remote at last. Hands shaking, she managed to pause the picture just as a caption flashed up at the bottom of the screen.

CALLUM TIERNACH-WEST
THUNDER MOUNTAIN HOTSHOTS

She stared at the face frozen above the words. Those narrow, emerald eyes, those movie-star cheekbones, that bright auburn hair. It was him.

It was *him*.

Behind her, Beth started to wail.

Never taking her eyes off the screen, Diana reached for her daughter. She bounced her on her shoulder, patting her back until she calmed.

"Look, baby," Diana whispered, holding Beth up so she could see the man too. "Look. That's your daddy."

∽

Discover Callum's secrets in WILDFIRE PEGASUS - coming soon!
To be notified as soon as it's released, join my mailing list.

Have you read the first Fire & Rescue Shifters series, featuring the parents of the Wildfire Crew?
If not, binge the complete series starting with Firefighter Dragon

ALSO BY ZOE CHANT

Fire & Rescue Shifters

Firefighter Dragon

Firefighter Pegasus

Firefighter Griffin

Firefighter Sea Dragon

The Master Shark's Mate

Firefighter Unicorn

Firefighter Phoenix

Fire & Rescue Shifters Collection 1

Fire & Rescue Shifters: Wildfire Crew

Wildfire Griffin

Wildfire Unicorn

Wildfire Sea Dragon

Wildfire Pegasus (coming soon!)

Wildfire Hellhound (releasing in 2020)

Wildfire [SPOILER!] (releasing in 2020)

… and many more! See the complete list at www.zoechant.com

WRITING AS HELEN KEEBLE

Author's Note: These are YA paranormal comedies, not adult romances. No sex, no swearing, lots of laughs!

Fang Girl

No Angel

"Keeble's entertaining plot contains action and suspense coupled with a witty protagonist and a great cast of secondary characters. A funny, refreshing novel." (School Library Journal)

"Quirky and fun. The authentic teen dialogue is refreshing and reminiscent of Louise Rennison's Confessions of Georgia Nicolson series." (Voice of Youth Advocates (VOYA))

"Likable voice, well-drawn characters and dead-on humor."--Kirkus Reviews

Printed in Great Britain
by Amazon